An Insurgent's Wedding

Insurgents MC Romance

CHIAH WILDER

Editing – Hot Tree Editing
Cover design – Cheeky Covers
Proofreading – Daryl Banner

An Insurgent's Wedding Description

Since the beginning, everything about Hawk and Cara's relationship has always been rough, hot, and passionate. When the VP of the Insurgents MC had first locked eyes with the feisty lawyer, he'd known he'd make her his forever. Cara fought the intense feelings she had for the rugged, tatted bad boy, but she finally gave him her heart and body.

And now, they are finally ready to tie the knot. To join their two worlds, Cara is having her classy society wedding and Hawk is throwing a big biker wedding for his brotherhood.

Nothing can destroy their joy.

Then someone from their past materializes, lurking in the shadows, and waiting to destroy the happiness the couple has fought so hard to have.

When danger comes to Pinewood Springs, Hawk and Cara's love for each other will be tested in ways no newlyweds should have to endure. Hawk will have to do whatever it takes to make sure his beloved woman is safe and by his side for life.

Will Hawk be able to be there for Cara when she needs him the most?

Weddings are stressful and marriage can be challenging, but when a woman marries an outlaw the stakes are higher and more dangerous than ever....

An Insurgent's Wedding is 67,653 words.

***Hawk's Property*, Book 1, should be read first.**

An Insurgent's Wedding is Hawk and Cara's continuing story. It is part of the Insurgents MC series and is NOT a standalone romance novel. Book 1, *Hawk's Property*, must be read in order to understand and enjoy *An Insurgent's Wedding*. This book contains violence, sexual assault (not graphic), strong language, and steamy/graphic sexual scenes. It describes the life and actions of an outlaw motorcycle club. If any of these issues offend you, please do not read the book. HEA. No cliffhangers! The book is intended for readers over the age of 18.

PROLOGUE

Federal Correctional Institution
Florence, Colorado

H E WATCHED AS she shimmied down the hall, her big tits swaying, her keys clanging with each step. When she approached his cell, she threw him a quick furtive glance and then walked past, acting like he was just another inmate. His thin lips curled up; he knew that when she came back later with four other correctional officers to do a cell block inspection he'd have her up against the wall and rubbing her breasts while she pressed into him, grinding her pussy against him like a slut. He counted on it, as she was his ticket out of the hellhole he'd been sentenced to. Their time against the concrete wall would be fast, but it would be enough to wet her pussy and have her craving his tongue on it.

Viper sat on the edge of his hard bed. His cell was a cube of concrete with a small window placed in such a way that all he could see was the sky and the red tile of the adjacent buildings. Sounds echoed down the corridors, and the ever-present din of metal against metal filled his ears.

He'd been stuck in the high-security prison ever since he'd entered his plea of guilty more than two years before. Viper often entertained himself by recreating that night's events in the way that they should have played out. He shook his head as the images of his downfall assaulted his mind. His unadulterated hatred for Hawk fueled him on; it kept him a model prisoner so he could lie low as he worked his magic on Officer Brenda Rourke.

A busty thirty-two year old, Brenda Rourke had worked as a correctional officer for the past ten years. She'd never been disciplined and had a stellar employee record, as she often told Viper. When he first spotted her six months before, she acted like he was just Inmate 10567, but the way she'd slide her eyes over him told him she was his ace in the hole in escaping. So he became the model prisoner. The fights between him and the Aryan gang members halted, he didn't cuss out the prison guards, and he did as he was told. It fucking tore him up inside each time he answered, "Yes, sir," but the anticipation of sweet freedom made his words sound sincere.

He'd even gone so far as feigning remorse for all the bad actions that had landed him in prison. That gem earned him the privilege of working in the laundry room, and it was there that he kissed and touched Brenda, her small moans disgusting him. She'd been the one to tell him that the security camera did its sweep around the room at thirty-second intervals. When it scanned past them, he had half a minute to shove his hand down her pants and touch her damp pussy. And it was always wet for him. It amazed him how horny she was for him.

After six months, she'd proclaimed her love to him in simple notes she left under his pillow after she inspected his room. He read them with humor, pretending to be touched by her proclamations of love. Her note from the previous week had read "I love you. I can't live without you. I wish you were free." Those were the words he'd been waiting to hear. She'd be instrumental in getting him out of the razor-wired fence compound that sat on a cleared patch of red-brown turf.

Viper leaned back against the cold wall, waiting for his favorite guard to come back for inspection, when all of a sudden loud shouts bounced off the walls. Pounding shoes on concrete filled the corridors as grunts and cries accompanied the thuds of bodies colliding. A stream of officers blurred past his cell as he fought to stay on his bed; he desperately wanted to be in the thick of the violence. He wanted to slam heads against the concrete, choke the life out of inmates and guards alike, and plunge his newly acquired shank deep into the belly of The Baron—the head of the Aryan gang who had a personal vendetta against all bikers.

Then suddenly, a deafening silence of voices.

Fuck! It's gonna be another goddamned lockdown. Lockdowns occurred almost weekly in the violent atmosphere of that prison. Race wars were brutal and constant, and the tension was so thick it could be cut with a knife. Lockdowns meant no more laundry room duties, no mixing with the general population, staying twenty-four seven in the cells, and no Brenda. *Fuckin' assholes!*

When she came to his cell with another colleague announcing that there was a lockdown, her blue eyes held sadness as they shined from behind the taller guard. She mouthed, "I love you," to Viper, and a faint smile twitched at his lips as she moved past his cell. He estimated that in less than two weeks he'd be free. Dustin and Shack were already setting things up so he could hide out at the Demon Riders' clubhouse for a while. The fucking badges would never think to look there.

Dustin and Shack hated Hawk as much as he did. They also hated Banger, but even though he wasn't a fan of the Insurgents MC's president, Viper's focus stayed on Hawk, the club's vice president. He and his cunt were the reason he was locked up. And every time Brenda rubbed against his limp dick, his body burned with rage at what Hawk had done to him. He unclenched his fists and breathed in and out slowly. He'd have plenty of time to cool the rage that fired his soul, but for that moment, he had to remain calm and logical. In a short while, he'd be a free man.

"DO YOU LOVE me?" Brenda gasped as his finger glided into her slippery hole.

"I fuckin' do, sweetheart," he whispered in her ear, his eyes fixed on the scanning camera. "I just wanna be with you all the time. We need more than snippets of thirty seconds, babe."

"I know," she breathed into his ear as she rode his fingers.

"I want us to live together. Get married. The whole fuckin' thing."

"I want that too." She jumped away from him and straightened her uniform. "We're on camera again." She moved away from him, and he hauled a pile of laundry into the dryer.

She stopped shy of the doorway. "I really can't stand not being able to love you the way I want to."

"I know. Me too. We're gonna have to do something about it, sweetheart."

She walked out of the room before the camera came back for another swipe.

I've just planted the seed in her empty head. He shook his head, a faint smile on his lips. It didn't take much to make some women abandon everything for a man. He guessed Brenda hadn't been all that popular with men in her lifetime. She craved his attention to the point that she'd risk her job and her freedom for him. *What a pathetic whore.* He chuckled while he loaded the washing machine with more orange jumpsuits—courtesy of the prison.

In order to make his escape successful, Viper had to enlist the help of the maintenance worker, Buddy Riester. From the background checks Dustin performed, Riester was ripe for the picking. He was broke, a gambler, and in desperate need of cash to pay off the loan sharks who were breathing down his neck. When Viper offered him half a million dollars for his assistance, the pimply faced Buddy agreed.

Over the next few weeks, time and again, Viper took Brenda into his arms as the camera moved away from them and whispered in her ear, "Sweetheart, I need you so bad."

And she'd moan and hold him closer to her. Each time he did that, he hated the scent of her perfume more. It smelled like coconut and reminded him of when he was a child and his mother had slathered him in suntan oil. Brenda always pulled away just before the camera came back around. She'd blow him a kiss and say, "Someday we'll be together. I promise." Then she'd ambled away.

The next time when they met up, she told him she needed him with her forever. He leaned in and ran his tongue over her jawline, murmuring, "I want to be with you forever too. I wanna marry you. If only I could get outta here, we'd have our lives together."

She swallowed and pulled back, her eyes wide. Viper cackled inwardly. "How could we do that? We'd be caught. It'd be worse for you... and me."

"Don't you love me, sweetheart? I know I love you more than any woman I've ever known."

"Oh yes. I love you. I adore you."

"Isn't our love worth the risk? Anyway, I'm not stupid enough to stay here. We'd head to the border. Make our way to South America where we could live together in peace. It'd be our own adventure. I dream about it all the time." He kissed her hard.

She lingered for a few seconds then jumped away as the camera made its sweep. "I love you," she said then rushed away. Viper watched her go, a big grin spreading over his face. He gave her another week before she'd be in all the way. He'd have her arrange the details he'd lay out for her to effectuate his escape. She'd have to work with Riester, but he knew she'd do anything to make her fantasy a reality. With satisfaction, he threw in another load of laundry into the washing machine.

A few days later, Brenda held him close. "I've done nothing but think about what you said. South America sounds so exotic and romantic. I want to spend the rest of my life with you. What do you want me to do?"

Viper broke away and smiled at her. "You're not going to regret this, sweetheart. I'll go over the details with you tomorrow night. We'll firm everything up, and in one week we'll be holding each other for more than a fuckin' thirty seconds."

During the week, Riester, Brenda, and he firmed up the plans, and on the planned day, he leaned against the cement walls, looked around his cell, and spat on the floor. All his patience and efforts had paid off. It was finally going to happen.

As usual, bed check was at eleven o'clock, and Viper knew the officers on duty that night were the lazy ones who skipped opening up the cells and making sure the inmate was really the form in the bed. He counted on ineptness; it always made things easier.

Brenda had arranged for Buddy to place Viper in a laundry cart right after dinner. The cart would be one among three that were headed to another facility. Riester drove the transport trucks during the nightshift. Viper lay down in the bottom of the cart, sheets piled on top of him. Buddy rolled through several doors and then out the back one, pushing the cart to the truck. He opened the doors, wheeled the cart Viper was in then went back into the prison to bring out the other two. The clang of the truck's back door sent a rush of adrenaline through Viper. As the vehicle rode through the checkpoint, he held his breath, only releasing it when the truck picked up speed and drove uninterrupted for a sustained period of time. After a while, Viper felt the truck slow down then stop. The doors opened, and Viper pulled himself out of the cart. Buddy lifted up one of the storage containers attached to the inside of the truck and Viper crawled in.

"It should only take twenty minutes max to drop off the carts. Then you can git into the trunk of my car until we git outta town," Riester said. Viper nodded.

After the three laundry carts were dropped off at the facility, Buddy parked the truck at the far end of the lot. It was dark and the perfect location for Viper to slink out of the back and slither into Riester's car that was parked next to it. Secured in the trunk, Buddy drove out of the parking lot and headed out of town. When they were twenty miles from Florence, the vehicle stopped. Viper stretched his tall frame once he jumped out of the trunk. He slipped into the passenger's seat and leaned his head back. "Don't speed. We don't need the fuckin' badges to pull us over," Viper mumbled as he lit a cigarette. He rolled down the window and let the cool air spread around him as Riester's Toyota drove on the two-lane highway, silhouettes of houses and barns rushing past them.

Later that night, Brenda met him and Buddy in a small town a hundred miles from the prison. She threw her arms around him, but he pushed her away. "We have time for that later. We gotta keep moving." He handed the rest of the money to Riester, knowing that he'd be killed before he made his way back home. There was no way Viper was leaving a witness. Dustin had arranged for a couple of the brothers to intercept Buddy and put a permanent end to his gambling addiction.

Brenda chatted incessantly as they drove deep into the night on their way to Iowa. Viper had taken some plates off a junked car a hundred and fifty miles back, so he relaxed a bit as he tuned her out and took a deep drag off his joint. It was an eleven-hour drive, and they'd already put a good seven hours between them and the prison. Viper knew they'd think he was either heading to the border or to stay with his brother or sister in nearby Kansas. They'd never think to look for him at the Demon Riders' clubhouse. He was a nomad biker, so he didn't belong to any one club.

About a couple hours from Johnston, Iowa, Viper leaned over and kissed Brenda on the cheek. "You ready to have a little fun before we get to the clubhouse?"

She smiled broadly, her blue eyes shining in her round, pasty face. "I've been dying to be with you since we met up hours ago."

"Turn down this road and pull into the cornfield. We don't want anyone spotting us." He was grateful it was a moonless night.

She did as she was told, and then turned off the engine and faced him. "I love you so much. I can't believe we're together." She giggled.

"Yeah." He pulled her roughly to him and plunged his tongue down her throat, chuckling as she gagged. He ripped open her blouse and stared at her white, full breasts. He grabbed and squeezed them, twisting her nipples until she cried out in pain. He laughed and brushed her hand away as she tried to stroke his cheek.

He pulled, pinched, and bit her as she squirmed under his touch. When her hand covered his crotch, a startled look crossed her face. "Aren't I exciting you? Don't you want me?"

A bitter smile settled on his lips as his forehead creased. "You excite me plenty. I haven't been with a woman since the night I was arrested. I got the desire, sweetheart. I'm just not able to get it up."

Her eyes were wide. "Really? What's the matter?"

"Hawk. The sonofabitch I'm gonna kill. I can still fuck you. It just won't be with my cock." Before she could answer, he was on top of her like a crazed animal, his hand over her mouth snuffing out her screams. He let his rage dictate his actions, and after some time she quit trying to push him off, quit crying against his palm. She just stopped. He released the hold he had on the belt he'd looped around her neck. Pushing her limp body aside, he straightened up and then lit a joint as he waited for the brothers to come and help him dispose of her body. He knew from the minute she checked him out that she had signed her death certificate. Outlaws never left evidence. Her car would be sold to an unscrupulous dealer for scrap metal, and Brenda Rourke would become another disappearance.

His eyes narrowed. He'd hit Hawk where he was the most vulnerable—his old lady. He'd bide his time, striking when the sonofabitch least expected it.

I'm gonna have a good time with his slut, and then Hawk's a dead man.

CHAPTER ONE

Pinewood Springs, Colorado

"YOU DIDN'T LIKE the almond filling?" Cara asked as she moved the slice of cake away from her.

"Babe, they all taste the same to me. I can't believe we've been here for forty minutes and you still haven't picked a fuckin' cake for the wedding. What the hell?"

"If you were more helpful, it'd be easier." Cara tossed her hair over her shoulder. "The chef is bringing out a couple more pieces. We have to choose. I want your input."

He laughed. "I'm not a cake guy, you know that. Chocolate, vanilla, blue velvet, or whatever else is all the same to me." He scowled as she giggled. "What's so funny?"

"It's *red* velvet cake, not *blue*. You're sweet." She blew him a kiss.

He pressed his lips together. "Whatever. You're such a little smartass." He shook his head as he scooped up a glob of frosting on his finger. Leaning over, he smeared it lightly on her nose and lips. Instinctively, she pulled back and picked up a napkin. "No way, babe. I'll clean it up. Get over here."

"You're bad," she said as she licked some of the frosting off her lips.

"Thanks." He stood up and came over to her, bending down low, his hand tilting her head back. He licked off the icing from her nose and mouth, his tongue delving between her parted lips. She hooked her arms around his neck and his hand caressed her cheek as he kissed her deeply.

Someone behind them cleared his throat. Hawk kept kissing his woman, who brought her hands to his chest and pushed him back a little. Hawk straightened up and winked at her, then sauntered back to his chair. Cara's face blushed red, and the chef, who held three more plates of cake samples, moved his eyes everywhere but on the two of them. Hawk threw his head back and laughed. The citizens' world never ceased to amuse him.

For the next twenty minutes, he passed the time by picturing Cara smeared in the white frosting she and the pastry chef were gushing about. He'd love to lick every bit of it off her luscious body. As he imagined her writhing underneath him, his jeans grew uncomfortable. *I'm gonna be pitchin' a tent if Cara doesn't hurry up and pick a damn cake.*

"Hawk. I'm asking you if the white cake with the white buttercream frosting is a good choice."

He nodded. *Just pick something, babe. All I wanna do is make love to you.* He didn't realize picking out wedding cake would be such a turn-on. He smiled as he watched the crease across her forehead deepen before she threw her shoulders back and said, "Let's go for it." She glanced at him, her eyes sparkling like a fresh glass of champagne.

"Let's get something to drink. I need a fuckin' beer after all this."

"I'm glad that's over with, and don't be so grumpy." She came over and draped her arm over his shoulder, dipping her head to kiss his jaw. "Thanks for pretending to help out." She slipped her fingers down the front of his T-shirt, her nail tugging at his nipple ring. A small grunt rose from his throat. "You like that, honey?" She ran her fingers over every groove of his tight skin. "Love the way you feel," she whispered, her breath scorching on his neck.

He looped his arm around her waist and yanked her onto his lap, his hard dick poking at her rounded ass. "Feel what you've done to me. How you gonna fix it?"

"When we get home, I'll treat you real good." She wiggled to get out of his grasp, but he held her firm.

"Fuck that. We're gonna take care of it now."

Wide-eyed, she put her hands on his chest. "Don't even think about doing it in the tasting room."

He lifted her off his lap and stood up. "Come on." He laced his fingers through hers and walked out of the dining room. Turning the corner, he stopped in front of the women's restroom.

Cara shook her head. "You've got to be joking."

"Didn't you tell me each stall is private? Come on." Before Cara could comment, he'd pushed open the bathroom door. The anteroom had a large couch, a couple plush armchairs, a full-length mirror, and a crystal chandelier. Their footsteps clacked on the marble floor.

Cara tried to pull out of his grip. "Hawk, this is insane. What if someone comes in here?"

He laughed. "That makes it more fun." He pulled her through the doorway into the bathroom where five sinks lined the wall, the white marble shining under the bright lighting. There were several wooden doors. Hawk opened one and closed it after Cara entered. The room was like a small bathroom: toilet, sink, and a small parlor chair upholstered in a fleur-de-lis design. After turning the lock, he hoisted Cara up by the waist and plopped her down on the dusty rose granite counter. He shoved up her skirt and she moaned as she leaned back against the mirror. He bent his head and his mouth covered hers hungrily as his arm on the small of her back drew her close to him, her breasts pressed against his chest.

"Oh, Hawk," she murmured.

"You're so hot," he whispered against her lips. He bit the bottom one slowly and held it between his teeth for a few seconds before moving his mouth from hers to her cheeks and then to her earlobes. She curled her arms around his neck. As he lavished kisses on her neck, his hand slowly inched toward her sex, tickling her inner thigh until she gasped loudly.

Her long nails scratched at his back. "You're driving me crazy," she said in a low voice.

"That's only fair since I've been horny for you since you took a bite from the first slice of cake. Damn, baby, you set me on fire all the time." He pushed back a bit and looked at her swollen lips, her messed-up hair, and her lace-covered pussy. She had her high-heeled shoes on the granite counter, her knees bent and her legs spread wide open. He could see a small wet spot on the crotch of her baby pink undies. His cock pulsed, itching to slam into her tightness. He moved her panties to the side and glided his finger into her juices. "Fuck, baby. I love the way you get so wet for me." He brought his finger to his mouth and licked it off. "Tasty." He winked at her.

She grasped his face between her hands and pushed it down. "Lick me. I want to feel your tongue on me."

"I thought I was the only desperate one here." He chuckled and dropped to his knees, shoving her panties aside. He spread open her engorged lips and ran his tongue up and down the length of her glistening mound. She groaned softly. The fact that she was holding back for fear of exposure turned him way on. He needed her so badly, he felt like he was going to lose it. He stood up, unzipped his jeans, and pushed his pants down. Gripping her legs, he raised them over his shoulders, kissed her deeply, and then shoved his cock into her heat.

He fucked her hard and fast until her tight walls gripped his dick as she was ready to explode. She covered her mouth with her hand, her palm absorbing her cries of pleasure as she jerked and lolled her head. He loved watching her come, delaying his climax until the tension was too much and he exploded inside her, filling her with his hot streams. He grunted and then placed her feet back on the granite counter. Burying his face in the crook of her neck, he held her close, the rush of extreme pleasure buzzing inside him.

She kissed his head, and he licked her neck. *I love her so much. I can't imagine my life without her. When we fuck, it still feels like it's the first time. She does shit to me, and I never want her to stop.* He looked up and caught her staring at him. He smiled. "Fuckin' awesome, sweetie."

"You're really something, you know?" Her eyes shined with love and satiated desire.

"You make me that way. I'm still wondering how I ever lived without you."

"I'm wondering the same thing. How did you live without me?"

He shook his head and gave her thigh a playful swat. "You keep talking smart to me, your ass is gonna get a spanking later."

She laughed, then lightly pushed him away. "We better get going. I'm afraid there may be a line to use the bathroom." He helped her off the counter and then drew her to him, kissing her again. "We'll never make it to my parents' on time," she said against his lips.

He smacked her ass, then pulled up his jeans and zipped them. "Just tell them that your man needed you to satisfy his hunger."

"Yeah, right." She took out a brush and a tube of lipstick from her purse. She straightened her blouse and smoothed down her skirt. "Let me make sure the coast is clear before you come out. I can't risk running into anyone my parents know." She brushed her hair then dabbed a tissue against her apricot-colored lips. "Ready?"

He smiled. "I love watching you put yourself back together after you've had a mind-blowing fuck session."

"Did I say it was mind-blowing? Stop putting words into my mouth." She unlocked the door.

He pressed against her back. "You tellin' me it was even better than I thought?"

She craned her neck and looked at him. "It was beyond mind-blowing. I love you." She kissed his chin.

He swept her hair to the side and kissed the back of her neck. "Love you too, babe."

She opened the door slowly and then closed it again. "There're two women by the sink. One's fixing her hair and the other is putting on some lotion," she said in a barely audible voice.

Hawk chuckled. After another few minutes, she opened the door again and walked out. "Come on. No one's in here now. Let's go." He followed her out into the anteroom and laughed his ass off when two older women came in, gasping when they saw him. Before they could react, he and Cara were striding out of the country club.

When they turned out of the parking lot, he brought her hand to his mouth and kissed it. "Do you need me to help with anything else at the club? Picking the cake turned out to be way better than I thought it would."

She shook her head. "If I have you come with me anymore, they'll ban us."

"But we'll have some fun in the meantime." He raised his eyebrows and she started to laugh. Soon they were both in hysterics. "Woman, you're the best," he said between guffaws.

"And don't ever forget it," she replied as she wiped the corners of her eyes with a tissue.

He leaned over and kissed her gently. "Don't plan to. You're mine forever."

And he couldn't be happier.

CHAPTER TWO

"HAWK'S GONNA UNWRAP you before you even have a chance to show it off to him," Addie said as Cara held up a sheer red babydoll with black bows strategically placed on the top of each cup and one in the back right above the G-string that came with it.

"He was definitely excited that this shower was a lingerie one. He was getting tired of hauling pots, glasses, and bedding from the ones my aunts had thrown for me." Cara laughed and put the racy babydoll back in the box that also contained fishnet thigh highs and a black blindfold.

"You're set for your honeymoon and then some." Baylee jumped up to grab the ribbon that was around the package. She taped it on the paper plate beside all the bows and dried flowers that had been on Cara's gifts.

"You're making a beautiful shower bouquet. I love the way you're coordinating the colors. It looks professional, girl." Cherri sat back on the couch and gazed at the paper plate bouquet that Baylee was creating.

"You know she's an interior decorator as well as an architect, right?" Addie handed her another fuchsia bow.

"Of course. That's why we asked her to do it," Belle said as she came back from the kitchen with a couple bottles of red and white wine.

Kimber picked up her beer and took a gulp, then crossed her legs. "This is the first time I've ever been to a shower. I'll admit I was dreading it 'cause I'd thought I'd be in for an afternoon of games and other schmaltzy bullshit, but this shower kicks ass. I thought there'd only be punch and finger sandwiches."

The women all laughed. "Punch in this group? No way." Belle set down the bottles of wine. "Is anyone interested in some dessert? I have cake, and Clotille baked some wonderful pralines."

"I'm fucking addicted to your pralines," Cherri said. The women sniggered when her blue eyes lit up.

Clotille smiled. "I got the recipe from Rock's sister, Isa. It was his mother's. If Rock is grumpy and scowling too much, I whip up a batch. It always puts a grin on his face."

"So that's the secret to getting rid of these guys' badass demeanor? Fucking cookies? I gotta try that. I wonder if it works if they're store-bought." Baylee put the finished bouquet on top of the pile of boxes next to the couch.

They all chuckled. "I can make you an emergency batch if you ever need it," Clotille said as she arranged the cookies on a platter.

"If you don't cook, then what the hell do you make Axe for dinner? Jax loves my cooking, and he never tires of chili and casseroles. Makes it easy for me." Cherri poured the white wine in her glass.

"Whatever Axe is in the mood for. I've got takeout menus for all sorts of cuisines. Thai, Indian, Mexican, Italian—you name it and I've got it," said Baylee.

"What if he just wants meatloaf? You do know how to make that, right?" Addie took a praline from the platter Clotille put on the table.

"Nope, but the deli section at the grocery store does. You see, there's no reason to cook nowadays. He's never complained. Anyway, the time I'd spend in the kitchen I spend with him, and he definitely likes that better." Baylee grinned.

"No wonder he's not complaining," Belle said as she sat down. "Banger is the reason behind the phrase 'The way to a man's heart is through his stomach.'"

"Jerry is happy that Cara's been teaching me how to make some dishes," Kylie said. "He was getting tired of spaghetti four times a week during the summer."

"At least you get a respite when you're at school. How's it working out living off campus?" Baylee asked.

"I love it. My roommates and I have a lot of space and our own rooms. It's especially great when Jerry comes to spend the weekends with me. I can't wait until I graduate. The commuting is getting to be too much, and when we're apart, I can't stand it."

"There's something to being apart for a little bit. Makes you crave each other even more. I'm planning on spending a few days before the wedding at my parents' house." Cara took a bite of her praline.

Addie's eyes widened. "And Hawk is cool with that? He doesn't strike me as someone who'd be okay with it."

"He doesn't know yet." Cara threw her a sly smile.

"Oh, you're bad. I'm glad I won't be anywhere near him when you tell him." The other women whispered their agreement. "He seems so pissed off all the time. I'm gonna be honest with you—your man scares the hell out of me." Addie laughed nervously.

"Me too," Cherri said.

"Yep, that goes for me as well." Baylee poured more wine in her glass.

"Uncle Hawk's a big softie." Kylie laughed. "You know I'm right, Cara."

"You are. He comes off real tough, and he is when he has to be, but he's a real sweetie."

"To you, but to everyone else, he's damn scary." Cherri wrapped her arms around her.

"Cara has him wrapped around her little finger. I've known him ever since I can remember, and I've never seen him do half the shit he does for her. You're perfect for him. He needs your fire and your softness. I still can't believe Uncle Hawk is getting married. I never thought he would."

"You and everyone else. Axe keeps telling me he never thought Hawk would get hitched," Baylee said.

"Rock is surprised too." Clotille brushed her hair from her face.

"And talk about scary. What's up with your man? He could scare the devil out of hell." Addie pretended to shiver.

Clotille laughed. "Rock can be intimidating, but he is the Sergeant-

At-Arms at the club. If you saw him with Andrew, your heart would melt. He's so gentle and loving." She blushed a little. "He's a wonderful father and lover."

"All our men are good lovers. There's something about a bad boy. Hell, there's something about a biker. I knew I was fuckin' screwed when I first saw Throttle in Hawk's shop spewing all his chauvinistic shit." Kimber laughed. "I was fucking hooked."

The women laughed and exchanged stories about funny and tender moments they'd shared with their Insurgents men. As Belle and Kylie cleared the table, the back door opened and several sets of footsteps clamored on the hardwood floor. "What the hell?" Belle said as she walked toward the kitchen. Before she reached it Banger came into view. He pulled her into his arms and kissed her. "What're you doing here? The shower's still going on. I thought you were going to play pool or something at the clubhouse," she said.

"I did. The brothers and I decided four fuckin' hours of yakking and boozing is enough. We've come to take you all out to dinner and dancing." As Banger spoke, Hawk, Chas, Jerry, Axe, Throttle, Jax, and Rock came from behind him.

Cara's heart leapt when she saw Hawk in a tight pair of jeans and his black cut, his hard muscles straining under his tightened skin. The tattoos on his toned arms beckoned her, and she wanted nothing more than to run to him, trace his tats with her fingernails, and kiss him deep and wet. His impossibly blue eyes pulled her in—they always did—and the two-day growth shading his rugged jawline made her pulse quicken. *He's so gorgeous.* He gave her his crooked smile, the one that made her nipples tingle and her legs clench together.

"Hey," he said in a deep voice as he walked to her. She stood up and he slinked his hand around her waist. The heat of his body pressed against her.

"Hey," she breathed as he cupped her chin, tilted her head back, and smothered her lips with his. Her tongue slipped through the kiss and into his mouth, coaxing his tongue to invade her own.

"Fuck, babe. You're making me all kinds of crazy." He nibbled at her lower lip, teasing and tugging it between his teeth.

Heat consumed her and the pulse in her pussy throbbed with a hungry need to feel him inside her. All of a sudden Jax's laugh cut through her desire and she pushed back a bit. Hawk, his gaze still locked on hers, stroked her cheek with the back of his hand. "You're so fuckin' sexy."

She ran the tip of her tongue over her upper lip, a surge of desire running through her when his gaze followed her every move. Focusing her eyes behind his shoulder, she saw Sherrie and Addie packing up her gifts. Since Hawk came into the room, everyone else had disappeared; it was as if they were the only people who existed on the planet. She cleared her throat and moved away from him, his hand clasping hers. "Let me help you with that," she said to Sherrie. She turned to her non-club friends. "Do you want to join us for dinner and dancing? Lisa, why don't you call David and see if he wants to go."

Lisa, a good friend of hers since law school, laughed. "You know David would love to come. He's been wanting to buy a Harley ever since he first saw Hawk's. If he can get a chance to talk motorcycles with a bunch of bikers, then he'll be all for it." She took out her cell phone. "I'll give him a call."

Cara was so happy when Lisa had finally found a good guy to settle down with. She'd had her share of jerky boyfriends, and when she'd met David at a friend's party, Cara didn't think the quiet man had a chance with her. But she was wrong. Lisa needed his calmness to take the edge off her aggressiveness. Like Cara, she was a litigator—albeit a civil one to Cara's criminal, but she was always in argument mode. David, a junior high school science teacher, was never one to raise his voice, yell, or cause a scene. So when he'd seen Hawk's customized Harley for the first time and his eyes had bugged out, Cara and Lisa cracked up. And he'd been smitten with the idea of the feel of the wind around him.

Lisa looked at Cara. "David says he'll meet us. Where are you guys going for dinner?"

Hawk turned around. "The club restaurant—Big Rocky's Barbecue."

"Of course. I've never eaten so much barbecue in my life," said Clotille.

"But you love it, don't you, *cherie*?" Rock asked, nuzzling her neck.

"Not as much as I love you." She turned around and they kissed.

Cara smiled. *Clotille has really fitted in great to the Insurgents life. And I love hanging with her, Baylee, and Addie. We've had some pretty crazy happy hours.*

Belle and Kylie came back into the dining room. "Everything's finished. I think we can head over to Rocky's," Belle said. Kylie wrapped her arms around Jerry, who smiled and kissed her.

"Let's head out," Banger said as he swatted Belle's behind. She scowled at him for a second and then chuckled, grabbing his hand and walking to the back door. The guests followed suit, and soon the quiet of the neighborhood was shattered by the screaming cams of eight Harleys. The men rode down the street with some of the women pressed behind them while the rest followed in their cars.

Dinner was a mixture of good conversation, stolen kisses, and a lot of laughing. When they left the restaurant, several of the couples decided not to go dancing. Banger and Belle wanted to curl up in front of the TV and enjoy a quiet night since Ethan and Harley were spending it at his sister's. Emily was on a school trip with her senior class. Jerry and Kylie, who lived apart from each other, wanted to spend as much time alone as possible, and Cherri and Addie had to go home since their babysitters couldn't stay past midnight.

In the end, Hawk, Cara, Clotille, Rock, Lisa, and David remained. Axe and Baylee decided to go to another bar when they heard that the group was headed to the Neon Cowboy. They weren't fans of country music, and it still surprised them how much Hawk and Cara loved it.

The Neon Cowboy looked like a set out of an old Hollywood western: wooden plank sidewalks in front of fake storefronts around the perimeter, saddles, and a sprinkle of hitching posts. The nightclub had a wraparound bar, and tables and chairs dotted the sides and front of an elevated stage. A large dance floor was in front of the stage. Several times a year, national acts would take to the stage and entertain their fans, but mostly the music was from either a DJ or local cover bands.

After ordering their beers, Rock whispered something in Clotille's ear then stood up. She followed suit, her fingers laced with his as he led her to the dance floor. "Wanna join them, babe?" Hawk said. Cara nodded and Hawk roped his arm around her waist, heading to the floor.

It always made Cara smile when she thought about how much Hawk loved to dance. He always wanted to dance at the club's parties when they'd go on Saturdays, and they usually went dancing at least two to three times a month. Sometimes they'd go with her friends, his, or both, and other times it'd just be the two of them. She loved being in his arms while he spun her around on the dance floor, humming or singing in her ear.

When Hawk had told her he loved country music, she'd been surprised. She thought he was only a hard rock and heavy metal type of guy, but it turned out they both shared a love of old country and the newer country rock music.

As they danced to the tunes of Brad Paisley, Florida Georgia Line, Sam Hunt, and Blake Shelton, Hawk held her, his hand firmly on the small of her back, leading her around the floor. When "Then" came on by Brad Paisley, Hawk's arms encircled her, hugging her close to him. They swayed together, her head on his shoulder, his chin pressed against her forehead. When she looped her hands around his neck, he lowered his hands to her butt and tugged her even closer. "I love you so much, babe," he murmured against her hair, his hot breath sending shivers through her.

"I love you too, honey." She looked up and his mouth crushed against hers. They kissed and moved around the dance floor, fused together by desire and love.

He pulled away and sang along with the lyrics in her ear then whispered, "It's true, Cara. Every fuckin' word of the song. I can't get enough of you, babe."

She buried her face in his chest and could hear his racing heartbeat.

An ache danced through her breasts as her stomach tingled, and between her thighs her pussy throbbed wildly. *I need to feel him inside me. I love him with everything I have.*

When the song was done, they were both panting and sweating, and the way he gazed at her with his smoldering eyes turned the heat in her way the hell up. They stumbled back to the table, his hand firmly clasped on her butt, and he whispered in her ear, "I'm fuckin' ready to explode, baby. Let's get the hell outta here. I've wanted to play with your tits and stick my cock in you since I saw you at the shower. I need you, babe. I'm gonna fuck you good and hard."

The rasp of his promise sent a tingle over her skin. "I need you too," she panted as she grabbed her purse. Saying their good-byes to the others, she and Hawk walked out to the parking lot. He draped his arm around her shoulders and squeezed her to him, kissing her until they reached her car and his Harley. Without a word, she jumped in her car and followed him back to his house, both of them hauling ass.

The minute he slammed the door shut with his boot, they were ripping at each other's clothes in a desperate attempt to feel each other skin-to-skin. "Let's go upstairs," he said huskily. "I wanna take my time with you." She squealed when he picked her up and laughed as he rushed up the stairs to their bedroom.

She watched him as he shrugged off his cut, his toned torso gleaming in the soft light from the floor lamp. She sucked in her breath as he kicked off his boots and unzipped his jeans, each movement making his biceps flex and his muscles ripple. When he pulled off his boxers, she moaned, the pulse in her mound throbbing. She craved him with a passion that burned hotter than fire.

He licked his lips. "Your turn."

She unbuttoned her blouse slowly then threw it on the floor. She kicked off her heels, then shimmied out of her tight jeans. Standing in front of him in her bra and panties, her body convulsed in light shakes as his hungry eyes devoured her. "Fuck," he said under his breath. He approached her and kissed her deeply as his thumbs grazed over her nipples.

He picked her up and lay her on the bed. As she looked into his lust-filled eyes, she reached for him and spread her legs. He came to her, his mouth meeting hers, and then he touched her, bit her, licked her, and finally took her hard and fast the way she loved it.

She ran her hands down his damp back and then dug her fingers into his skin as pleasure and release racked her body with a string of strong shudders. While she soared with delirious pleasure she felt him fill her up as he grunted against her ear, only to collapse next to her, cuddling her under his arm.

"You will always amaze me, babe."

"Even when I'm old and saggy?"

He chuckled and played with a strand of her hair. "Yeah... even more."

She smiled and snuggled closer to him.

He was her everything.

Hands down.

CHAPTER THREE

VIPER STUBBED OUT his cigarette with the toe of his boot as he watched the silhouette of Hawk and Cara from their bedroom. He clucked his tongue as he saw them kiss, their outlines dancing on the window's golden shade. He'd been standing in the shadows for hours waiting for them to come back, but he had no intention of making his move just yet. Viper knew he was no match for Hawk, and he wanted to savor his torment of the Insurgent. He couldn't wait to play with the bitch who caused his downfall by sticking her fucking nose where it didn't belong.

He also knew the area was brimming with badges, and he had to lie real low until the heat subsided. He'd take off in the early morning and return later in the week. *She's still so fuckin' pretty. It's too bad I gotta cut her real bad. The bitch has it coming to her, and the sonofabitch Insurgent is gonna watch me torture her. Then I'll make her watch while I slowly kill his fuckin' ass.*

Viper walked away when the lights in the top room grew dimmer. He'd parked the Harley the Demon Riders had loaned him in the bushes down the road. He'd been staying with the Skull Crushers in Alina, in southwestern Colorado. That club hated the Insurgents as much, if not more, than he did. They especially hated Hawk. He'd been the one who raided their hangout and beat the shit out of them the previous summer. They readily offered their help in destroying the vice president of the outlaw club.

He rolled his bike a ways until he switched on the ignition and took off, heading to an abandoned cabin forty minutes from Pinewood Springs. It was nestled among the aspens off several dirt roads, a perfect place for him to chill before heading back to Alina.

When he walked into the cabin, three men stood up and nodded at him. "You got the money?" the tall thin one asked.

"No 'how are you'?" Viper laughed dryly. "I got the money like we agreed. You'll get fifty percent now, then the other fifty percent when you help me kill the bitch and her old man."

"Seems fair," the shorter stocky man said.

Viper's eyes narrowed. "I don't give a fuck if it's fair or not. You do what I say. You remember that and we'll get along real well. If you forget that… let's just say you don't wanna know that outcome."

"What if the biker makes us?" the third man asked as he shoved his hands in and out of his sweatpants' pockets.

"You don't let him, dumbass. That's why I'm paying you a shitload of money. Anyway, you're trailing the bitch, not him. He'd make you or anyone out in a second. I need to know her routine, not his. Don't fuck this up." *These fuckin' idiots!*

"I'm not gonna let him find out, but the Insurgents have a pretty tough rep in town. I was just asking if we had any reinforcements."

Viper grabbed the man by his shirt and slammed him against the wall. "You're the fuckin' reinforcement. If you get made out, then the sonofabitch will bring you back to his clubhouse and they'll torture you for hours until you beg for death."

The man's eyes widened. "I don't want to get involved with this. Sure, I need the money, but things are starting to heat up and get dangerous. Count me out."

Viper clutched the man's thick neck. "You're not dropping out of anything, you pathetic sack of shit. If you even think it, I'll make what the Insurgents may do to you seem like child's play." Viper tightened his grip around the man's throat, laughing as his victim sputtered and gasped, his face turning red.

"Fuck, man. Enough," the tall thin one said.

Viper looked over his shoulder without loosening his grip. "I don't remember putting you in charge, asshole."

The man looked down. "Skip's always running his mouth off. He don't mean nothin' by it." He fidgeted in place.

Viper squeezed extra hard for good measure and then released the heavyset man, who immediately brought his hands to his neck and rubbed it while he wheezed and gasped for air. "Get the fuck over there, *Skip*." Viper shoved him toward the other two.

Skip stood by the tall man. "Let's get the fuckin' dough and get the hell outta here, Tommie."

The short stocky guy cleared his voice. "We gotta get back to Pinewood Springs if you want us to keep an eye on the bitch."

Viper's lips turned up in a cruel smile. "Next time we meet up, Pierson, you keep the fat one in check or I'll slit his throat." He bent down and pulled out a large envelope from inside his leather jacket. He locked his stare on Pierson's. "Then I'll kill you and the tall fucker."

Pierson's jaw throbbed and Viper smiled inwardly. *These fuckin' idiots have no clue what they've gotten themselves into. The minute they take the money, they're a target for the Insurgents. Dumb fucks.*

Pierson threw the envelope to Tommie. "Count it."

The man spread out the bills on a weathered wood table while Viper lit up a cigarette and lounged against the wall. The other two men stood erect, their faces covered in a thin sheen of sweat.

"It's all here." Tommie handed the envelope back to Pierson. The three men nodded to Viper and then left the small cabin.

After he couldn't hear the men's car anymore, Viper extinguished the light in the gas lamps, picked up his keys, and hopped on his motorcycle. He didn't want to take any chances that the three stooges would narc on him to the goddamned badges. As he made his way to Alina, he'd avoid the freeway, taking the small mountain roads off the beaten path. It'd add a couple more hours to his trip, but if he took the freeway, he was almost certain he'd be stopped.

The thick darkness engulfed him as he rode south.

VIPER SAT WITH his back to the bar, staring at the bored stripper swinging her sagging tits. He glanced around and saw that the majority of the Skull Crushers were snorting meth, the urge to join them taking hold of him. He held back, knowing he needed his clarity to stay one step ahead of the badges and two steps ahead of Hawk. He surmised that Cara hadn't received notification of his escape; otherwise, Hawk would've had a prospect or two watching her. Hell, he'd probably have her on lockdown, and that was one thing Viper didn't want. He knew he didn't have much time before she found out.

He ran his fingers through his hair, scowling when they stopped three inches in midair. He'd cut his long hair and dyed it blond. *I fuckin' fit in with these punky Skull Crushers. After this shit is done with Hawk, I'm gonna go to Mexico and sit on the goddamn beach all day.*

"Need some company?" a throaty female voice said.

He turned to the side and snorted. "You buying?"

"Me?" Her heavily made-up eyes widened. "I thought a gentleman bought a lady her drink."

He ran his gaze over her, lingering on her big rack. "I'm no fuckin' gentleman, and you're no lady, so you buying or not?"

"Alls I got money for is one drink. And it's gotta be a beer. I ain't rich." She called to the bartender and ordered two beers, then placed a bunch of coins she dug out of her purse on the counter.

The bartender put two bottles of beer on the bar. "Gimme mine," Viper said.

She handed him his beer. "You sure are bossy."

"And you fuckin' like it, don't you?"

She shrugged. "You don't look like you're a natural blond."

He brought the beer to his lips. "Neither do you." They drank in silence, listening as the discordant tones of black metal blasted from the speakers. When Viper took out a cigarette and lit it, the busty blonde poked him, motioning that she wanted one. He handed her his from his lips and then lit up another one. He'd like to suck her tits for a while. *I can't fuckin' wait to crush Hawk's nuts.* Each time desire flared in him, he cussed out Hawk. In prison he didn't have much use for his jewels, but it still would've been good to know that they were in working condition. The thing that sucked about not being able to get it up was that he still had the goddamned urge, just not the machinery to do anything about it.

The blonde said something in his ear, but all he heard was garbled sounds. He shook his head and pointed to the speakers. She drew closer to him, her big breasts pressed against his arm. "You wanna fuck?"

For a few seconds disgust curled around him as he looked at her heavily made-up face. *She probably caked it on 'cause she doesn't want anyone to see how fuckin' worn out she is.* He nodded and pointed to the door. He slung back his beer then walked outside, the bleached blonde following. Under the low lights, he studied her: too much makeup, great pair of tits, small waist, small hips. *Not bad.* "Where do you wanna go?"

"I live a few blocks from here. I'm at the Flamingo Trailer Park. You can take me on that fuckin' awesome Harley you got. What's your name?"

"Mathew." He walked down the sidewalk to his bike.

"Mathew?" She scrunched up her face. "You don't look like a *Mathew*."

He clenched his jaw, then relaxed it. "What's yours?"

"Kitty. *Rawr.*" She curled her fingers and reached out, mimicking a swatting cat.

He curled his lip. "You look *exactly* like a Kitty."

"Thanks." She smiled and clutched his arm as they walked to his bike.

When they reached the trailer park, a lot of people were outside drinking beer, cussing, and smoking pot. She opened the door to a single trailer and cooed to her cat, who meowed and rubbed against her leg. The cat came to Viper, but he kicked it away and it screeched loudly and bolted, hiding under a couch.

"That ain't nice. Fluffy was just tryin' to be friendly." She bent down and tried to coax her cat out from under the furniture, but it wouldn't budge.

"I'm not a pet person. You got beer?"

"Yeah. Go help yourself."

He went into the tiny kitchen and took out a couple bottles. He popped the top with an opener on the counter and drained one of the beers in two long pulls. "How long you been a biker slut?"

"That ain't nice either," she said as she dusted off her knees.

"You are, aren't you?"

"I like bikers. I like 'em like you—nice and hard. You know what I mean?" She came over and tried to kiss him, but he jerked his head back. "What's the matter? You got a woman? The men who don't like kissing always got a woman somewhere."

"I just don't like it."

She shrugged. "Have a seat. I'll be right back."

He settled on the couch with the beer bottle in hand, his eyes darting around the shithole she called home. *Why the fuck am I here? This is stupid. I'm supposed to be keeping a low profile.* He put the beer on the table, pulled himself up from the couch, and started to open the door when a warm arm circled his narrow waist.

"You ain't running out on me before we have some fun, are ya?"

He stiffened. She was beginning to annoy and repulse him. *I gotta get the fuck outta here.*

She lowered her hand and put it on his crotch, palming his limp dick as she rubbed her tits against his back. "You like that, baby?" she whispered. She kept palming him, but after several minutes, she pushed away. "What the fuck's the problem with you? You can't get it up?" She laughed a little too hard. "It figures I'd have to get the biker with the limp dick. Fuck."

Whack! Her head snapped back as he slapped her. "Don't *ever* laugh at me again, cunt. You wanna fuck? I'll fuck you." Before she could answer, he threw her on the couch and ripped open her robe, her big tits bouncing out. "You really are a slut, aren't you?" He massaged them roughly, ignoring her cries, then twisted and pulled her nipples until her black eyeliner streaked down her face. He spread her legs apart, slapping her again when she protested, then grabbed his beer bottle off the table. "I'll fuck you real good, you filthy cunt."

Her eyes were wide with fear as he felt her trembling underneath him. "No. Please don't. Please. I'm sorry. I didn't mean nothing by what I said. Please."

"I love a cunt who begs." Staring at her wet pussy, he shook his head. "You really want it, don't you? You fuckin' whore." Forcing her knees to bend, he spread her wider and then covered her mouth with one hand to muffle her cries as he had his way with her.

An hour later, Viper washed the blood off his hands in her kitchen sink and wiped them on a paper towel. Kitty lay beaten and violated on the couch. He took out another beer from the refrigerator and gulped it. He felt so much better, all his stress, hatred, and anger having been spent on Kitty's body. He threw the bottle in the trash and walked over to her. Bending down, he said in her ear, "We'll have to do this again, cunt." He tweaked her nipple hard, a low moan emitting from her throat. "Remember, I know where you live. Smart cunts live. Dumb ones die a painful death." He smacked her face and swaggered out of the trailer.

It'd been a while since he'd tortured a bitch and it felt so fucking good. But he'd have to stop having fun. He had a murder to plan, and a shitload of badges to dodge. He turned on the ignition and rode out of the trailer park toward the Skull Crushers' clubhouse.

CHAPTER FOUR

CARA FUMBLED AROUND looking for her phone as it rang. Papers and law books were scattered on her desk, and she shoved them aside when she located her phone. She groaned when she saw the name of one of the older old ladies on the screen. She stared at it, debating whether or not to take the call.

When Cara had first become Hawk's old lady, Doris was the matriarch since Banger's wife had passed away several years before. Now that Belle was his old lady, she was the one in charge, and Cara came in next since Hawk was the vice president.

In the beginning, Cara was so new to the outlaw world that she depended on the guidance of the older ladies like Doris, Marlena, and Bernie. She quickly caught on that whenever Doris called her randomly, it was always to stir the pot. She was the queen of creating drama within the club.

Ruben was Doris's husband, and they had an understanding that he was allowed to cheat at a club party once a month. Marlena's husband, Billy, was given the okay indirectly when he'd done it a few times and his old lady didn't gouge his eyes out. Both women were always trying to find out dirt on their men. They'd repeatedly asked Cara whether their men were fucking any of the club whores or hoodrats at the weekly weekend parties. Cara hated being in the middle, but she had no choice since she was the only old lady allowed to go to the weekend parties. Hawk had insisted on it the minute she accepted his patch. He'd told her that the membership was against it and he'd told them if she couldn't come with him, they'd see him once in a while. They finally relented, but Banger set the condition that if she shot off her mouth to any of the old ladies about their husbands banging any of the women, she'd be banned from coming to any more parties.

Cara had agreed, but after she'd gotten to know Doris and Marlena, she didn't feel comfortable being at the parties. She figured Hawk must have said something to Ruben and Billy, because she never saw them do anything with the club women. She suspected they did behind the closed doors of the empty rooms in the clubhouse, but she couldn't say for sure. She was relieved that the rest of the guys were faithful to their old ladies. All except Tigger.

Tigger was an entirely different story. The brother flaunted his infidelity in front of Cara, and whenever she saw his old lady, Sofia, her heart would break. Sofia never asked about Tigger. It was as though she knew and was afraid to hear it. Cara couldn't understand Tigger: Sofia was a tiny wisp of a woman, and very pretty. Sofia was shy and barely spoke to the others at family gatherings. She fulfilled her duties as an old lady—helping prepare the food, set the tables, clean up—but she did it all in silence. Cara suspected she was broken inside and she wanted desperately to befriend Sofia, but Hawk told her to keep her distance. She and Cherri were around the same age, but Cherri didn't have any better luck with breaking through to Sofia than Cara.

Sometimes Cara would see the fading yellow bruises on her skin, and when she came to family gatherings in the summertime with long-sleeved T-shirts, the old ladies would talk about what an asshole Tigger was to hit his wife. And Sofia loved him immensely. Cara could see the shine of love in her eyes each time she gazed at her husband, and she also saw the pain each time Tigger would flirt with other women when they'd have family night at Steelers, a local bar and restaurant. Sofia waited the five years Tigger had to serve in the state penitentiary. He'd been put there for beating the shit out of a guy who came on to her. Cara and many of the other old ladies couldn't understand why he served five years for Sofia and then abused her. And they couldn't understand why she didn't kick him in the balls when he cheated on her.

On the fifth ring, Cara picked up. "Hey, Doris. How are you?" She pulled out a statute from one of the code books on her desk. She had a brief due at the end of the day, and Doris could be a talker.

"I'm good. Are you busy?"

"I kinda am."

"Then I won't keep you. I just wanted to know if Hawk told you about the bachelor party the brothers are giving him."

"Bachelor party? No, he didn't mention it, but we've been real busy with the house and wedding stuff."

"He didn't mention it? Huh…. Well, the club always gives the officers their party at Dream House."

A long pause ensued. Cara rolled her eyes. *Drum roll, please. Damn, she lives for the drama.* "And…."

"And that's where they're having it. I can't believe Hawk didn't mention it to you. He's known about it for the last few days."

"Like I said, we've been busy with other stuff. And he's super swamped at the shop. I'm terribly busy at work too."

"Hawk knew it was comin' 'cause it's an Insurgents' tradition."

"Well, in the citizens' world, a lot of bachelor parties involve strippers and such. I don't think it's that big a deal."

"Not on the surface, but the one getting hitched gets to pick a stripper to give him an extra special lap dance."

Cara put her pen down. *I don't like* that. "What if he doesn't want to?"

Doris laughed, then started coughing and hacking for a few seconds. "They all want to."

"But if they don't?"

"Then a dancer chooses them."

Cara's insides twisted as Janelle's face popped into her head. The dancer was cute with long brown hair, big breasts, and legs that went on forever. Each time she'd come to the club for a special event that required strippers, she'd flirt and try to cozy up to Hawk even with Cara standing right next to him. Hawk basically ignored her, but it pissed Cara way the hell off. She knew Janelle had been chomping at the bit to rub her boobs and ass against him. Cherri, who sometimes filled in for Emma, the manager of the strip club, told her that Janelle was always talking shit about wanting to fuck Hawk. She was even saying that she could take him away from Cara because all bikers liked variety and it was just a matter of time until Hawk took her to his bed.

"You still there?" Doris asked.

"Yeah."

"I don't mean to worry you. Hawk's straight. He never flirts at the strip bar or with the whores at the club, but you know how it is when a man gets drunk. He'll be surrounded by his friends and they'll be calling him a pussy, so a lap dance doesn't seem like that big of a deal. You know what I'm saying."

"I trust Hawk. I can't be his babysitter. A lot of women check him out, and I refuse to turn into a jealous shrew. I really do have to go, Doris. I have a ton of work to do. Is there anything else you wanted to talk about?"

"No. I figured he hadn't told you, so I thought you'd like to know. The brothers are all the same when it comes to sluts. I'll be seeing you."

Cara put her phone on the desk and sighed. *Why the fuck does Doris do this shit? I'm sure Hawk would've told me before the party. Just because Ruben cheats on her, she thinks all men are that way. Damn her.* She picked up her phone and texted Sherrie to see if she was still on for their usual dinner out. Hawk went to the clubhouse on Tuesday and Thursday nights, so she usually had dinner with Sherrie on one of the two. She smiled when Sherrie's confirmation text came through. She turned her phone off, opened up one of the law books on her desk, and began tapping away on her laptop.

CARA MET SHERRIE at El Tecolote—their favorite Mexican restaurant. She'd been dying for a mango margarita ever since Doris's phone call. "How was school?" Cara picked up a chip and dipped it into the salsa.

"Crazy, but I love it. I still can't believe I got hired as the second grade teacher. I miss my little ones at the day care, but I love being a teacher." Sherrie licked the rim of her margarita.

"And how's Jackson?" Cara had hooked her best friend up with a lawyer friend of hers a few months before.

Sherrie took a big sip of her drink. "Still great. He left his toothbrush at my place the other day. That's something, isn't it?"

"Definitely." Cara smiled. "It sounds like this could go somewhere."

"I hope so. I *really* like him."

"I'm so happy for you. I can't believe I didn't think of him in the first place. Every time we bump into each other, he thanks me for introducing the two of you."

"You should go into the matchmaking business—first Banger and Belle, and now me."

"You deserve someone to treat you nicely. You've had far too many assholes."

"Most women have had too many assholes." They both laughed. "Now, are you gonna tell me what's bothering you?"

"Nothing's bothering me."

"I can tell there is. You always crease your forehead when something upsets you. You're not going through any insecurity shit because you're reliving when you found out that asshole Trevor banged a girl right before your wedding, are you? I hope not, 'cause you must know Hawk is solid."

Cara nodded. "I know. I guess I am being a teeny bit insecure. I know Hawk isn't Trevor. I guess I'm just having pre-marriage jitters." Cara then told Sherrie about her conversation with Doris.

The waiter placed a steaming plate of enchiladas in front of Cara and tamales in front of Sherrie. "This looks awesome. I'm so damn hungry," Sherrie said as she picked up her fork and dove in. "Isn't Doris the one who's always trying to cause trouble between the men and their wives and girlfriends? She's done this shit to you before. Remember that time she called and said some sexy, stacked woman was hanging onto Hawk's arm at his shop? Doris just happened to be there, and you were, like, in court?"

Cara laughed. "I forgot about that. Yeah, it was crazy. She was going on and on about it, and I was like 'What the hell do you want me to do about it? I'm getting ready to pick a fucking jury.' She can be so annoying at times."

"For sure. So now that you know about it, are you gonna tell Hawk not to go?"

Cara took a bite of her cheese enchilada. "No. I trust Hawk, but I do know that I don't want him getting a lap dance. I don't think he'd choose anyone, but I know Janelle is waiting for an opportunity to get her claws in my man."

"Bitch. Just tell him no lap dances."

"I should, but I'm hoping I don't have to. I want him to say it on his own. Silly, huh?"

Sherrie shook her head as she scarfed her tamale and then dipped a chip in the green chili on her plate. Suddenly her eyes lit up. "I know. Oh fuck, this is going to be good. Jen, Lisa, Megan, Tricia, Sarah, and I were planning your bachelorette party. Baylee and Addie want to be involved in it too." She shoved the chip in her mouth.

"That's nice of you guys. It'll be fun to eat pizza and get drunk while telling stories about our men."

"Fuck that. We'll have the party at Jim Diamond's. We'll go to dinner first, then head over there afterwards."

"The strip bar off Forest Street? What the fuck?"

"The bar has male strippers on Saturday nights from ten to two. This is perfect!"

Cara shook her head, chuckling. "Hawk will flip out."

Sherrie's eyes twinkled. "That's the point, isn't it? The guys can ogle the women while we feast on some nice firm asses and pecs. It's not fair that they get to have all the fun."

"You're so bad. And how the hell do you know the schedule at Jim Diamond's?"

Sherrie lifted her eyebrows and smiled widely. Soon they were cracking up until tears rolled down their cheeks. The rest of the conversation revolved around the wedding and reminiscing about their friendship.

After paying the bill, they walked out to their cars that were parked by the curb. "Let's have the party at Jim Diamond's. I think it's time we shake the men up for a change," Cara said.

Sherrie laughed. "I've always liked a good fireworks display."

"Then you won't be disappointed. I promise you that."

"I'll start working on it. I've always wanted to see one of these shows. This will be so much fun."

"You're crazy, but that's why I love you." Cara gave Sherrie a quick hug before she opened her car door. "We'll talk soon."

As Cara pulled out into the street, a tall shadow appeared in her rearview mirror. The hair rose on the nape of her neck and arms; it was as if something dark and dank had reached out from her past and manifested itself. She shuddered and stared at the mirror, but it seemed as though the shape had disappeared into the long shadows of the branches as they swayed in the autumn breeze. Rubbing her eyes, she looked behind her shoulder, but there were only the headlights from passing cars. Chiding herself for being spooked over a few outlines in the night, she drove off into the darkness toward home.

CHAPTER FIVE

WHEN HAWK ENTERED the bar he was surprised to see how many brothers were there for a Tuesday night. Spotting Throttle and Rock, he went up to the bar and picked up the beer the prospect put down. "What the fuck's going on tonight?"

"That's what we were wondering." Rock slugged back his shot of whiskey.

"Rock was saying that his Harley's got a clunking noise that just started up. It sounds to me like it may be the transmission." Throttle shifted on the barstool.

"Could be. Bring it to the shop and I'll take a look at it," Hawk said.

"Kimber could tell you in a heartbeat what the fuck's going on with it," Throttle said.

Rock chuckled. "So you've changed your mind 'bout her not getting near your bike?"

"I changed it a long time ago. She's a kickass mechanic. Am I right, Hawk?"

Hawk nodded. "She's one of the best in my shop. She's also fuckin' busy all the time, so she can't work on yours. Like I said, I'll take a look at it. Bring it by in the morning."

"Hey, dudes." Bones's loud voice snaked around them. "Do you wanna play a game of pool before the initiation?"

Hawk look at Bones sideways. "Who's the club initiating?"

"A chick named Della. She wants to be a club whore. Brandi recommended her. She's been a hoodrat for over a year."

"Why didn't anyone tell me? I need to do a background check before someone's brought into the club. We don't need any stooges from rival clubs or an FBI bitch." Hawk knitted his brows.

Bones shook his head. "There's no way she's a badge. She's fucked most of the brothers. She gives an awesome blowjob. Anyway, Wheelie did a full background check since you've been preoccupied with your classy country club wedding."

"I heard you're wearing a tux. Fuck, never thought I'd see the day. Maybe you should be drinking champagne or some expensive-as-shit cognac instead of beer." Throttle waved the prospect over. "You got any champagne for our brother here? His tastes don't tolerate beer anymore."

"Fuck off," Hawk growled.

"I don't think there is any champagne," the prospect said, apprehension etched on his face.

"Don't worry about it. The brothers are just full of shit." Hawk took another gulp of beer.

"You sure you wanna stay in the club with us? You may be too high-class." Rock laughed, and Bones and Throttle joined in.

"You fuckers better back off or my fists are gonna rearrange your faces. The country club shit is for Cara. I'm planning our biker wedding. Enough. You still wanna play pool?"

Bones nodded and the four of them meandered to the pool tables.

As they played, Hawk felt someone staring at him. He looked up and a pretty brunette with gold highlights captured his gaze. She slid her finger over her full lips, a sheen of lust misting her green eyes. Hawk broke away. "Who the fuck is the chick with the green eyes?"

"Della. She's the one who's gonna get initiated into the club. She looks like Cara, don't you think?"

Hawk shook his head. "Nah."

"She kinda does," Rock said as he leaned against the pool table. "She's got eyes for you."

"I'm only interested in my old lady. Rack up the balls. When's this shit starting with her?"

"In about an hour. We should be able to get through a game. You gonna join in on the fun?" Bones asked.

"No." Hawk chalked the tip of his cue as he looked at Throttle and Rock. "What about you guys?"

"Fuck no," Throttle said as Rock shook his head.

"Damn, your old ladies got you in dick lockdown." Bones laughed. "That's why I don't want one of *them*."

"Don't say that, dude. Every time one of us thinks we don't need a fuckin' woman in our lives, we get reeled in." Rock chuckled.

"That's for sure, but I wouldn't want it any other way," Throttle said as he took out four joints and passed them around.

"We playing or jabbering like a bunch of pussies?" Hawk lit up his joint, then leaned down and hit the cue ball, scattering the solid and striped balls.

After the game was over, Hawk pocketed his money along with Throttle and they headed back to the bar. Wheelie came over and hit his fist against Hawk's. "How's it going?" he asked.

"Good. Bones told me you ran a check on this chick who's donning the club's property patch. Nothing funny in her background?"

"Nah."

As Hawk and Wheelie spoke, a warm hand touched his forearm. He looked down and saw Della standing next to him, a shy smile playing on her lips. "Hi. My name's Della. I've been wanting to meet you for a long time." Hawk stared complacently at her. "You're the VP. A lot of the other girls talk about you. I heard you were quite the ladies' man. You're totally handsome."

"Is there something you wanna talk to me about?"

"Not really. I just wanted to let you know who I am."

"Okay." He turned back to the bar and motioned Buzz for another shot. The prospect delivered it.

"I'm looking forward to having you give me a try during the initiation."

He shook his head. "I'm not part of it."

Della's face fell. "I though all the guys had to do it."

"It's a brother's choice."

She leaned in close, her tits pressed against his arm. "I wanna feel your mouth on my tits and your dick inside me. I hear you like big tits. Do you like mine?"

He chuckled. "You'll make a good club whore. I've got an old lady. Move on to another brother." He put the beer bottle to his lips.

"There're several brothers who have old ladies, but it doesn't worry them any."

"I don't give a shit what the other brothers do. I'm happy with my woman. I'm not looking for another one. We're done talking now." His phone pinged.

Cara: *I just got home. The enchiladas were great.*

Hawk: *Good. U tipsy?*

Cara: *Why? Do u want to have ur way with me?*

Hawk: *Always.*

Cara: *That can be arranged. What time will u b home? I miss u 2 much 2nite.*

Hawk: *Soon.*

Cara: *K. See u soon.*

Hawk: *I love u.*

Cara: *Me 2.* ♥♥

He smiled and slipped his phone in his pocket. A loud whistle blew and most of the men shuffled over to the pool table that had been covered with a tarp. He saw Chicory and Wheelie lift Della and place her on the table. She locked eyes with Hawk as she yanked off her top. The group around her started whistling and hooting as she slowly pushed her shorts down. Hawk drained his beer, pushed away from the bar, and walked out into the chilly night air. He noticed Throttle's and Rock's Harleys were gone.

He swung his leg over his bike and switched on the motor, anxious to get home to his woman.

CHAPTER SIX

C ARA PICKED UP the file that had been sent to her from the Alternate Defense Attorney panel. She rarely received any cases from them since most clients went through the public defender and the alternate public defender. Whenever there was a three-or-more-defendant case the attorneys listed on the panel would pick up one.

She thumbed through it, noticing that the defendant who had the most charges had lawyered up with a prestigious Denver law firm who had a satellite office in Pinewood Springs. *The guy's family must have some money. Hellerstein Brady Hastings and Sherman isn't cheap.* The case was an armed robbery with serious injury. It appeared that her defendant was the getaway driver, but she wouldn't know the extent of his involvement until she received discovery from the district attorney's office and interviewed her client. If he told her the truth—the majority didn't—then she could start working toward severing his case from the others since his part in the crimes didn't appear to be as serious.

Her landline phone buzzed and she picked up. "What's up, Asher?" she asked her legal assistant.

"An attorney is here. He said he's on the armed robbery case, the one I put on your desk."

"I was just reviewing it. I don't remember setting up an appointment. Is he from the public defender's office?"

"No, he's from the private law firm. He doesn't have an appointment. His name is Trevor Hollick."

Her breath caught as her stomach dropped. "Trevor Hollick? Are you sure that's his name?"

"Yeah, I'm looking at what I wrote down. Why?"

"I knew a Trevor Hollick, but it can't be the same person. It'd be too weird if it were. Give me ten minutes and then send him in." Cara hung up the receiver and stared in front of her. *Can it be Trevor? I heard he was teaching law school in Denver. It can't be him.*

She closed her eyes as memories flooded her mind. She'd met Trevor when she was in her first year at law school and he was in his third year, and they'd begun dating. After he'd graduated he'd secured an adjunct professor position teaching legal writing. She'd fallen in love with him and had been thrilled when he'd asked her to marry him after her graduation. On a warm spring afternoon, she'd gone over to his apartment to drop off some groceries she'd bought for the dinner party they were having at his place the following night. When she'd opened the door, something hadn't felt right. The subtle scent of candied apples had been in the air. Her heart had raced. She'd placed the bags of food down on the kitchen counter and went to his bedroom. Through the paper-thin door she'd heard the groans and moans of lovemaking and her stomach soured. When she'd opened the door, she'd seen Trevor's ass flexing as he banged a woman who was on her knees. He was pulling her hair and telling her to "Fuck me like a slut."

Cara yelled out, calling him a fucking asshole. His shocked look would've been hysterically funny if her heart hadn't been shattering. She'd run out and never gone back. She'd then learned that he'd fucked most of the first-year law students in his class. She'd called off the wedding and moved back to Pinewood Springs to open up a practice. For four years she'd thrown herself into her practice, effectively building a brick wall around her heart. Then Hawk had come into her life, crashing and tearing down the wall brick by brick until he'd captured it. He was the best thing that had ever happened to her, and the way she loved him didn't even compare to the way she'd loved Trevor. Hawk was more than she ever could've hoped for.

The intercom buzzer made her jump. "Okay, Asher, I'm ready for you to send Mr. Hollick in." *I hope it's not him. I never want to see him again, let alone work on a case with him.*

A tall man in a dark blue suit with short brown hair and blue eyes entered. *Fuck! It's him.* Her heart sank.

"Cara. How are you?" He walked toward her but she remained seated. He stopped, then strode to the front of her desk and sat in one of the leather chairs. "It's been a long time." He smiled.

He looks older, a few lines around his eyes, but he's still handsome in a generic way. Not like my Hawk with his rugged lines, gorgeous blue eyes, and jet-black hair. When Hawk came into a room, he commanded it. Desire inched its way over her as she thought about him. *I wish he were here so we could have some fun on my desk.* She smiled and focused back on the man who'd broken her heart six years before.

"So it's you. How did you end up with a criminal defense case in Pinewood Springs? You're obviously not teaching anymore."

"I haven't taught for over five years. I'm an associate with the law firm, and I was asked to handle this case. The woman who normally deals with criminal cases for the satellite office had to have emergency surgery. Our client's parents are paying big bucks, so I was sent to take care of it. I was thrilled when I saw you were representing one of the defendants."

"I noticed the heavy in this case was represented by private counsel."

He ran his eyes over her and she cringed. All she wanted was for him to get out of her office. "How's your practice going?" He looked around the room. "You have a nice office."

"It's going great. As a matter of fact, I've gotten too busy, so I'm referring a lot of cases out. I'm starting to lean more toward guardian *ad litem* cases."

"Isn't that where the court appoints you to take care of someone?"

"It's the state who appoints you. I'm working on cases that deal with abused children who have to be withdrawn from their homes. I represent their best interests. I'm also working with truant juveniles. The cases can be emotionally draining, but I like them. I feel like I'm helping to make it a bit easier for some of the kids I represent."

"You haven't changed, always championing for the underdog. You know, that's one of the things I loved about you. I'm glad to see that you're still true to your beliefs."

"Yeah, well…."

He leaned forward in his chair. "You look real good, but you always were pretty."

"Thanks," she mumbled as she opened her file. "The DA's office hasn't made discovery available yet, but from seeing the charges filed against your guy versus mine, I'm pretty sure I'll be filing a motion to sever. There's no way I want my client tied together with yours."

"I figured as much. Can we go out for a drink after work to talk more about it?"

"Can't."

"Can't or don't want to?"

"I don't want to."

"You can't still be pissed over what happened six years ago. I tried to call you and get in touch with you. You never let me explain."

"There was nothing to explain. It was what it was."

"I don't want you to think that I didn't love you. The girls didn't mean anything to me."

Cara shrugged. "It doesn't matter anymore—none of it. I'm actually in the final stages of planning my wedding."

"You're getting married? When?"

"In about a month."

"Is he a lawyer?"

She smiled broadly. "No. He's a fantastic guy and I'm very happy. What about you? Are you married?"

"No. You've made it hard to find a replacement." He licked his lips and fixed his gaze on her.

What a fucking asshole. "I'm sure you'll find the right person one day. I hate to throw you out, but I have to meet a client."

"Maybe we could get a drink sometime. I'll be here until the case is finished. I'll probably go back to Denver on the weekends, but I'm free during the week. Is your fiancé the jealous type?"

She laughed. "Drinks after work is definitely *not* going to happen. And yeah, my man doesn't want me having drinks with other men."

"Even an old friend?"

You're not my friend. At one time I thought you were, but you proved you were a cheating jerk. I don't want to be your friend. I just want you to do your job on the case and leave me the hell alone. She nodded. "I really have to go. We can meet up with the other attorneys and talk about the case."

"Over lunch?"

"Sure. I know everyone in the public and alternate public defender's offices, so I'll call over and see who got the assignments." She pushed away from the desk and started putting her laptop in its case.

Trevor rose to his feet. "You know, over the years I wanted to call you many times, but I figured you wouldn't want to talk to me."

She looked up and brushed her hair from her face. "You figured right." She stood up. "I can walk out with you." She walked past him and he followed after her.

AFTER MEETING WITH her client, Cara was dying to tell Sherrie that her ex was on a case with her. She still couldn't believe that he was in Pinewood Springs. Ever since she and Hawk had gotten together, she hadn't thought about him. She never thought she'd ever see him again. *What the hell are the chances that he'd be on a case with me? Too damn weird. And he's still such a bullshitter. He just looks like he's a player. He's the most insincere man I've ever known. No, wait. Luke was an insincere jerk too. Fuck, I really didn't know how to pick them. I'm so happy Hawk's in my life.*

She swung a right into Johnson's Fresh Market to pick up a couple steaks, potatoes, and vegetables for grilling. Warmth spread through her as she pictured Hawk at the grill, flipping the steaks and veggies. He loved to grill so much that he never shut it down, even during the freezing weeks of winter. She dialed Sherrie, who told her she only had ten minutes to talk because it was parent-teacher night and she had to prepare her classroom. Cara quickly told her about Trevor.

Sherrie gasped. "Fuck. What are the chances of that? Hawk's gonna lose it when he finds out."

"I know. It's silly, really. I have no intention of hanging out with the ass, and once my client is severed from the case there's no real reason for me to ever speak with him again."

"So does that mean you're not going to tell Hawk?"

She blew out slowly. "I guess it does. I know he'll freak even if I tell him not to. If the judge doesn't let me sever my client and I have to work with Trevor, then I'll tell Hawk. I don't see a reason to cause any drama. I've got enough shit to worry about with the wedding and my practice. Doesn't it make sense not to tell him?"

"I can just see you blaming this shit on me if Hawk finds out. You'll tell him that Sherrie thought it made sense not to tell him." Sherrie chuckled. "I can see your point totally. Hawk is so protective of you, and not just in a physical way but in an emotional one too. He wouldn't want to have you near the man who broke your heart. I probably wouldn't tell him unless you have to."

"I know Hawk trusts me. The problem is that he doesn't trust any man around me. I mean, he even sometimes goes a little caveman-like with some of his brothers if they look at me a bit too long."

"I know. I've seen the death glare he gives guys when we all go out dancing or to restaurants. The chance of him finding out about Trevor is slim, especially since you won't be working with him too much longer."

"Exactly. I'm so glad you picked up. I needed to talk this out with you."

"Anytime. I have to get going. I'm nervous about my first parent-teacher conference."

"You'll do great. You work so hard for your students, and they all love you. I'll let you go. Let me know how it goes." After Sherrie hung up, Cara put her phone in her purse, then opened the car door and headed inside to do her grocery shopping.

When she came out of the store, she pushed the cart to Hawk's SUV and opened the back. As she loaded the groceries, a sudden shiver ran up her spine and a pervasive sense of darkness and gloom wrapped around her. *Someone is watching me.* She took a deep breath to force an internal calm, but her heart wouldn't stop racing. It was like a shadow was trying to grab hold of her and drag her into a nightmare. *Nothing's going to happen. There're a ton of people in the parking lot. Nothing is wrong.* She closed the back of the car and pushed the cart into the stall. When she turned around to go back to the SUV, she casually looked around. Nothing. Everything seemed like an ordinary day in the grocery store parking lot, but something was amiss. She couldn't pinpoint it; she could only *feel* it. Wrapping her arms around her, she glanced around one more time, then slipped into the driver's seat and headed to Hawk's house.

As she drove, she kept checking her rearview mirror to see if anyone was following her, but no one was. Once inside the house, calmness replaced her jitteriness. *Maybe I'm feeling out of sorts because of the wedding. And Trevor.* Seeing him again dragged the painful memories of infidelity to the forefront of her mind. And she hated thinking about Janelle prancing about naked, shoving her boobs in Hawk's face every chance she'd get at his bachelor party. *Hawk isn't Trevor. He loves you and would never hurt you. He's true to you.* She knew that, but her mind kept tumbling out images of Janelle rubbing against him during her lap dance.

Stop it!

She busied herself with preparing the marinade for the steaks and cleaning and slicing the red and orange peppers. When she'd finished, she poured a glass of merlot and went into the family room. After starting a fire in the fireplace, she sat on the couch and sipped her wine. As she stared into the fire, listening to the crackle of the burning logs, images of Hawk's firm, sexy body rubbing against her flitted in her mind. They'd made love in front of the fire the week before, and as she replayed the passion of their lovemaking, she clenched her legs, her sex softly pulsing. She glanced at the time and smiled. *He'll be home soon. I can't wait. I'm so horny for him.*

When she heard the garage door open, she leapt from the couch and waited by the back door. The rumble of his bike stopped and she knew he was walking toward the door to come in. When the doorknob turned, she tingled all over and bounced on her toes. Hawk walked in, looking damn good in his jeans and leather jacket. He smiled at her and opened his mouth to say something but she threw herself into him, pressing her lips against his as her arms curled around him. His body leaned into hers and she pushed past his lips, dipping her tongue into his warm mouth. He tasted like cinnamon and smoke, and the scent of motor oil, gas, and fallen leaves wound around her as she held him.

"That's a fuckin' hot way to greet your man, baby," he rasped against her neck. "Let me take a quick shower and change. I've got grease all over me."

She pulled his face toward hers and kissed him deeply. "I'm so horny for you."

He chuckled. "I picked up on that." He pinched her ass. "Babe, I'm gonna make you dirty."

She licked his lips and locked her gaze on his. "You've already made me dirty." She ran her hand through his hair and breathed against his ear, "And I love it."

"Fuck," he growled. His lips went to hers and she eagerly met them, their kiss a soul-deep press of open mouths and tangled tongues.

A rush of heat spread through her as her heart rate increased. Hawk's breathing deepened and each time he growled into her mouth, the need for him hit her deep and hard in her throbbing sex. Shamelessly, she rubbed against his leg like a cat in heat as she twisted and pulled his hair in her fist. He pulled away for a moment to tug off his jacket and then held her flush to him, squeezing her ass cheeks. "You're so fuckin' sexy, sweetie," he murmured against her throat as he peppered it with feathery kisses.

Trailing his tongue downward, he licked the top swells of her tits before he bit her nipples still covered by her T-shirt. She arched her back toward his mouth in a desperate attempt to relieve the aching need she had deep inside. "Fuck," he rasped. He grabbed the hem of her shirt and yanked it over her head, shoving her bra upward over her breasts before devouring them with his lips, tongue, and teeth.

He spun her around and roughly placed her hands flat against the wall while he spread out her legs with his. He shoved up her skirt and tucked it into its waistband, then ripped off her panties. "Bend over. I wanna see your pretty ass in the air."

She bent over, her breasts swaying, her butt and pussy displayed for his enjoyment. She knew her sex was sopping wet, and just thinking about him looking at it glistening with all her juices made her hot. His fingers seared her flesh as he aroused and teased her all over. Soft moans escaped through her parted lips, and electric heat moved through her as her need for him intensified.

"Do you want me to fuck you?" he whispered as he reached around her and massaged her tits, pinching and pulling on her hard nipples.

"Yes, please," she whimpered, her body on fire and in desperate need of him inside her.

He nibbled her neck, then ran his finger up and down her wet mound. "You're so fucking wet for me, baby. I love that." His fingers trailed to her rounded ass cheeks and he dug in, kneading them as he placed little kisses all over her back. "Love your ass," he said against her flesh, the vibration of his voice pebbling her skin. Then he smacked her ass hard. She jumped and yelped, her behind wiggling. "You like that, don't you?"

She moaned and wriggled, trying to clench her legs together to bring relief to her pulsing pussy. "I love the way you touch me. I'm on fire, honey."

"I can't get enough of you, sweetie. You've been in my blood since I first saw you at Rusty's." He slid his finger back and forth, her swollen lips quivering. "Damn, you're wet," he murmured against her skin. She heard him unzip his jeans before he grabbed her long hair, pulling it back hard as he plunged his cock deep inside her.

"Oh God!" she cried as he pulled out and plunged back in harder than before. She pushed back into him, taking as much of him inside of her as she could.

"I love that you like it rough and hard. Fuck, babe, the way you're moving is setting me off." He grunted as he pummeled in and out of her, his finger flicking her sweet button.

When the building tension reached its peak, she exploded as her orgasm tore through her body in wave after wave of relief. "It feels so good, Hawk. Oh, Hawk," she cried hoarsely as her legs began to shake and the energy seeped out of her from every pore. Hawk's cock was still thrusting in her when she felt his tight balls against her ass and his guttural moan as he filled her up with his hot seed.

He wrapped his arms around her waist to hold her up, his head nuzzled between her neck and shoulder. They both stood there panting—she a shivering mess of euphoria, he a grunting, spent man. He lifted up and pulled her with him, her back pressed against his chest. "Woman, you know how to please your man," he whispered against her ear, taking her earlobe in his mouth and biting it softly.

"And you know how to satisfy me. Real good." She craned her neck and kissed him on the chin.

He chuckled and kissed her hair before he pushed back a bit, swatting her ass. "I gotta take a shower. You wanna join me?" He winked at her.

"I don't think I could survive it." She winked back as she pulled her T-shirt over her head. "I'll make the salad. The steaks and veggies are ready for you to grill once you come back."

Zipping up his pants, he leaned in and brushed her lips with his. "I'll be down in fifteen minutes." He picked up his leather jacket and walked out of the kitchen and up the stairs.

She watched him go, her love for him filling every part of her.

Later that evening, after all the dishes had been put away, she lay in his arms as they watched an action film on TV. Her arms were curled around his thighs, her head in his lap as he combed his fingers through her hair. Every once in a while, he'd lean forward to take a gulp from his beer and then resume stroking her hair, his hypnotic touch lulling her to sleep.

CHAPTER SEVEN

HAWK WAITED IN front of Cara's office, his fingers thrumming on the steering wheel. Their appointment with Baylee was in fifteen minutes and he knew they'd never make it on time. Baylee was waiting for them at their new house to do a final inspection with them. After five long months, their house was finally finished and they could start moving in. *I'll be so fuckin' glad to stop playing musical houses.* For the past two years, the couple shared their time between Hawk's and Cara's places, but in the last year, Cara had spent the majority of her time at Hawk's. It'd be good to be in one house they could call *theirs.* He took out his phone and was ready to call her when he saw her rush through the large glass doors and come to the SUV.

"Sorry I'm late," she said as she leaned over and kissed him on the cheek. "I called Baylee and told her that I was running behind. It's been crazy for the last hour. How was the shop? Insane as always?" She fastened her seat belt and settled back.

"It's always this way when the weather is good. Everyone wants to ride, but when the cold and snow start it slows way down. It's like that every damn year."

"It's good to have the respite, right? Are you gonna be okay with Dwayne handling the shop when we're in Italy?"

Hawk had told Cara to plan their honeymoon. He said he didn't mind where they went as long as it was with her and far away, so she picked Italy. He'd called ahead and found out he could rent a Harley so they could ride around some of the scenic spots while they were on their trip.

"Dwayne's good to go. Banger and Jax will drop by to make sure everything's good."

She smiled and placed her hand on the back of his neck, lightly massaging it. "I can't wait to see our house. This is so exciting."

"Yeah. I can't wait to fuck you in our new house."

"Oh, Hawk. You would say that." She rolled her eyes and shook her head, a small smile playing on her lips.

He turned onto a large circular driveway and parked in front of a big stone house resembling a large French country house. "I still can't believe how fuckin' big this place is."

"That was your doing. I was fine with a smaller home, but you're the one who wanted six bedrooms in addition to the master and ten bathrooms. I still don't know what we're going to do with all the damn space." She pulled down the sun visor and touched up her lipstick.

Hawk leaned over and rubbed her stomach. "I'm planning to fill them up with our kids, babe."

She snapped the visor shut and looked at him with wide eyes. "Six kids? You've got to be joking."

"We'll see." He winked at her and got out of the car.

Baylee came out on the porch and waved at them. "You're going to love the finishing touches you guys added to the house. I went through the whole place and everything seems up to par."

They walked past her and entered an enormous marbled foyer. "This is gorgeous," Cara said. "You were right in suggesting the lighter color, Baylee. Very pretty."

They made their way through the rooms on the first floor, the two women discussing decorating ideas. Hawk squeezed Cara's hand. "I'm gonna check out the pool and backyard, babe." He left the women and went out the French doors that led to a large patio. He breathed in deeply, happy that they were able to buy a lot that didn't have any neighbors to the back of them, only pine and aspen trees.

As he enjoyed the landscape he saw something move out of the corner of his eye. He glanced to the right, expecting to see a deer. Instead, a heavyset man stood behind one of the pine trees, his gaze fixed on the house. Hawk darted off the patio and ran in the direction of the man. He immediately fled, and Hawk cussed as he fumbled with the latch on the back gate. Finally opening it, he tore after the rotund man, but as he reached the edge of the road, he saw him speeding away in a dark blue Jeep. The setting sun was directly in his eyes as he strained to read the license plate number. *Fuck!* He picked up a rock and flung it at the disappearing vehicle as he cursed the sun's glare. His blood pumped and he sucked in air as anger coursed through him.

Hawk turned around and walked quickly back to the house. His instincts told him that this wasn't a random guy sneaking peeks hoping to see a woman. *This fucker was watching our house on purpose. Something's not fuckin' right here.* He clenched his jaw. *This shit is most definitely related to the club. I'll bring it up to Banger. I don't need any shit from the Demon Riders.* He decided to keep a sharp eye on Cara until he could sort this mess out. He wouldn't tell her since there was no reason to worry her until he knew for sure what the hell was going on.

"There you are," Cara said as he walked in. "We were wondering where you went, although it's easy to get lost around here. It's so big." She slipped her hand in his and he squeezed it. "Everything looks good to me. What do you say?"

"Uh… yeah. It looks fine."

Baylee smiled. "Did you like the way the pool area came out? It's going to be great to be able to swim year-round with the ceiling opening up in the summer. The tiles are placed the way you wanted, Hawk."

"Yeah. It looks great. The house is good."

Baylee chuckled. "It should be since you corrected a million things in the last three months."

Cara laughed. She leaned in to him and said in a low voice, "Are you okay? You seem distracted."

He kissed her gently on the lips. "I'm good. The house looks great. Baylee, do you and Axe wanna join us for dinner? We're gonna grab some at Burgers & Beer Joint."

"That sounds great. Let me text Axe and see what he's up to." A few seconds later, Baylee's phone buzzed, and she looked down at it. "He says it's a go. I'll lock up here and meet you at the restaurant."

"We'll wait for you to finish, and then we can all leave together." There was no way in hell he was leaving her alone after that incident with the prowler.

Baylee nodded, giving him a funny look. After she'd secured everything, they left, Hawk making sure Baylee's car was in front of his. On the way to dinner, Cara chatted about the house and how they should decorate it while Hawk kept his focus on the rearview mirror. No one was following them. When they arrived at the restaurant, he didn't notice anyone watching them, and he greeted Axe with a fist bump as they walked inside the eatery.

The place was packed, but since the Insurgents owned it, they rarely had to wait for a table; the waitstaff always made room to accommodate the brothers. After ordering two beers and two glasses wine—white for Baylee and red for Cara—the group of friends placed their orders and settled back for a wonderful evening. Cara and Baylee talked about shoes, purses, and the best boutiques in Denver and Aspen while the guys talked about the new Harleys that had just come out.

While they were eating, a tall man in navy blue dress pants and a red pullover sweater with short brown hair and blue eyes stopped at the table and stared at Cara. Hawk stiffened when he saw the man's gaze lock with Cara's; her face paled and she seemed nervous.

"Hi, Cara. I wondered if I'd run into you one of these nights. The town is small so I figured I would. How've you been?"

"Good," she mumbled as she grabbed her wine glass and took a gulp.

Hawk straightened in his chair. *What the fuck? Why's Cara acting so nervous? Does she know this asshole?* "Who the hell are you and why're you talking to my woman?"

The brown-haired man's gaze left Cara's and skimmed over Hawk's face, then went back to Cara. "Is *he* your fiancé?"

Before Cara could answer, Hawk leaned forward in his chair. "Yeah, I am. Now who the fuck are you?"

Cara grabbed his hand and squeezed it lightly. "It's cool, honey. We're handling a case together," she said in a low voice.

Hawk glared at him. "You're a lawyer?"

The man's face tightened. "Yes." His eyes scanned the faces of the small group, and then he cleared his voice and stuck out his hand to Hawk. "I'm Trevor. Cara and I know each from our law school days." He smiled warmly at her and Hawk began to stand up to rip off his face, but Cara firmly grasped his wrist.

Hawk looked at Cara, one eyebrow cocked up. She laughed dryly. "It's such a small world. I was assigned to represent a man in a four-defendant case. I was shocked to find out one of the defendant's had retained counsel, and even more surprised when I learned it was Trevor who was that attorney. Who would have thought it?"

Trevor chuckled along with Baylee and Cara, but Axe and Hawk stared at the man stone-faced. Trevor pulled down the cuff on his shirt. "Well, I better be going. Nice meeting you," he said to Hawk. "I'll see you tomorrow at lunch, Cara." He smiled at her again, then walked to a table at the back of the restaurant.

Cara motioned the waitress and ordered another glass of red wine. She sipped it, but Hawk kept staring at her. She looked up and met his gaze. "What?" she said as she wiped the corners of her mouth with her napkin.

"Is that the fuckhead who broke your heart?"

"Um… yeah." She leaned closer to him. "I don't want to talk about this in front of Axe and Baylee," she whispered in his ear.

"Okay. That's cool."

The rest of the meal, she seemed uncomfortable, and he noticed fuckface kept stealing glances at her. He was just about ready to storm over to the asshole's table, yank him by his shirt collar, and drag him outside when Cara called over the waitress. "Can we please have the check?"

"You in a hurry to go?" Hawk asked.

"I have some work I have to do for an early morning hearing."

"And you've had three glasses of wine? Doesn't that break one of your fuckin' rules about no drinks if you have to work?"

Cara's face tightened. "I'm not infallible."

"You got that right."

Baylee and Axe exchanged looks, but Hawk didn't give a damn what they thought. Cara grabbed her purse and stood up. "I need some fresh air. I'll wait for you by the car." She whirled around and walked toward the front doors.

Baylee jumped up. "Wait up, Cara. I'll go with you."

When the women left the restaurant, Axe let out a long breath. "What the fuck's going on?"

Hawk, his eyes glued on Trevor, said, "If that fucker gets up and follows her out, he's dead."

"Who the fuck is he?"

"Someone from Cara's past."

"Okay. Why're you so pissed?"

"I wanna know why she didn't tell me he was in town."

Axe nodded. "Gotcha. Yeah, I'd be pissed if an ex showed up and Baylee didn't tell me. Makes you start thinking about all kinds of shit."

Hawk jutted his chin out and grunted, then took out his wallet and threw down his credit card. Axe placed his share in cash on the small black tray holding the bill. After they settled up, they walked outside, the cool autumn air wrapping around them. The scent of hickory and tart apples wafted in the breeze. He spotted Cara, bathed in gold from the amber streetlight, resting against the car, laughing with Baylee. He opened the doors with his remote and Cara jumped, then looked at him. He avoided her gaze and hit his fist against Axe's.

Baylee walked toward Axe. "I'll call you tomorrow. I have a wonderful interior designer I think you'll love," she said to Cara. Axe pulled her to him and kissed her as Hawk turned away and opened the car door.

"Get in," he said to Cara. She slipped into the passenger seat and looked out the window as they rode in silence for a couple minutes. "When did you find out fuckface was on the case with you?"

Silence.

"Fuckin' answer me." Hawk's nostrils flared.

"I'm not going to talk to you when you're acting like a jerk."

"Me? I'm not hiding shit from you."

"Neither am I."

"When did you find out he was on the case?"

She sighed and rubbed her forehead. "This is exactly why I didn't want to tell you. I knew you'd overreact and make a big deal out of something that means absolutely nothing."

"If it didn't mean shit, then why didn't you tell me? The only reason I'm reacting is 'cause you kept it from me, and I wanna know why."

"Because I didn't think it was worth mentioning. It doesn't mean anything. I'm filing a Motion to Sever after the bail review hearing, and I'm pretty sure the judge will grant it since my guy isn't the heavy in the robbery. So I won't have to deal with Trevor at all. Like I said, no big deal."

"Bullshit. I saw the way he looked at you. He still has something for you. I was ready to beat the shit outta him if you hadn't stood up and left the restaurant."

"Did you happen to see the way *I* looked at *him*? If you had, you would've seen that I don't give a shit about him. Why would I? He broke my heart, and it took me a helluva long time to get over it, but I did. I ended up falling in love with you, and now we're getting married. Do you seriously think that I'm even remotely interested in Trevor? This whole argument is ridiculous."

"Look, baby, you made me think something the minute you didn't share he was in town. You know that fuckin' sucks, and you'd be all over me if I did that. You made this into more than it should be."

Cara slammed her fist on the dashboard. "Okay. I should've told you. I didn't. I'm sorry. Now are we done with this?"

He just shook his head, pissed at her for keeping Trevor a secret. He didn't doubt her loyalty and love for him, but it was like she wanted to savor the fact that her ex was back in her life if only for a short time. "If fuckface wouldn't have been there tonight, you never would've told me, would you?" She shrugged. "Fuck, Cara. You would've been having lunch, meetings, and whatever other shit lawyers do, and I wouldn't have known about any of it. Do you think that's cool?"

"I think you're overreacting," she gritted.

Hawk glanced at her, but she didn't meet his eyes. Instead, she stared straight ahead. "You're not going out to lunch with him tomorrow."

"Are you ordering me or suggesting?"

"Ordering." When he said it, he knew he'd crossed the line, but he was too damn proud and pissed to take it back. His knuckles were white from gripping the steering wheel.

They rode the rest of the way to his house in silence. Each time he glanced at her, she stared ahead, unwavering. When they pulled into the garage, she gripped the door handle. "I'm not a child. I'm an adult, and I will *not* be told what I can and cannot do." She stepped out of the SUV.

"So you're going to lunch with him?"

"It's a business lunch with two other attorneys. I wouldn't go out alone with him. I don't want to, and I wouldn't disrespect you like that."

"But you plan to have lunch with him tomorrow?"

"And the two other attorneys? Yes, Hawk. I do."

Those four small words pricked his skin like hot needles. He shifted the car in Reverse. Cara swung around, her face slack. "Where're you going?"

"To the club. I wanna hang with my brothers."

"I thought we'd watch a movie."

"You have to work, remember? Or was that bullshit too? I'm outta here."

"What time will you be back?"

"Late." He sped down the driveway, hung a U-turn, and watched the garage door go down as he drove away.

CHAPTER EIGHT

WHEN HE GOT to the club, several brothers were engaged with the club girls, and the hard rock music that normally blasted was silent. A group of men sat around the TV watching the football game. If it'd been a Broncos game, the room would've been packed and the club girls would've had to amuse themselves for the duration of it.

Hawk plopped down on a barstool and nodded to Banger who'd just entered the great room from the hallway. He looked tired as he walked over to Hawk. "What're you doing here on a Wednesday night?"

"Having a drink. Why the fuck are you here so late? Is Belle at a school event?"

"No. She's holding dinner for me. I had so much shit to do that I lost track of the time." He threw back the shot of Jack the prospect had placed in front of him. "You look pissed. You and Cara have a fight?"

"Yeah, something like that." Hawk downed his beer in one long pull. "I don't wanna talk about it."

Banger nodded. "You interested in the game the guys are watching?"

"Not really. I was gonna play a game of pool and then head out. I just need to chill for a bit."

"Yep. I'd play you, but Belle's patience will wear too thin if I don't get home soon. Another time."

Hawk tilted his head as Banger ambled out of the clubhouse. He motioned for another beer, taking out a joint from a pocket in his vest and lighting it.

"You got one for me?" a soft voice said next to him.

He turned and saw the woman who had been initiated into the club the previous night. He handed her a joint and watched her jump up on the stool next to his. She wore a cut that read "Property of Insurgents MC." "I see you got through the initiation all right."

She chuckled. "Yeah. It was pretty intense, but I did a good job. All the guys cheered and clapped. I felt like I won a beauty pageant or something when they handed me my vest. It was totally awesome." She put her beer bottle to her lips. "I was sorry you didn't stay."

"Yeah… well…. What's your name?"

"Della. I love your tattoos." Her fingertips grazed over his hawk tattoo on his forearm, its piercing eyes staring fiercely.

He jerked away. "Don't be touching me."

"I'm sorry. You don't like it?" She pushed out her bottom lip in a faux pout while she arched her back, making her large breasts jut out more. Her skimpy top was cut low, and he could almost see her nipples.

"No, I don't. Why don't you be a good girl and hit on another brother? I just came here to chill."

"I can be quiet if you want me to. I just want to sit next to you."

"You heard him. Get the fuck away," a hard female voice said.

Hawk smiled. Kristy was always watching out for him, especially when it came to the club whores. Kristy had been a club girl for a year before Hawk had joined up with the Insurgents thirteen years before. She'd been drawn to him right from the beginning, and she'd always hang around him and try to engage him in conversation that didn't deal with motorcycles, fights, booze, or women. Since he was a prospect, all the club whores were off-limits, but once he patched in, he'd chosen Kristy as the woman he wanted to fuck. Over the years, she'd become his favorite club girl, but it didn't mean she was exclusively his. He fucked plenty of the other club girls and hoodrats, but she pleasured him much more than any of the others.

"I'm not going anywhere. I said I'd be quiet, and Hawk's good with that," Della said.

"Actually, I'm not. Go on. I wanna talk to Kristy."

Della smiled at Hawk and then jumped down, giving the other woman a dirty look. Hawk chuckled. Pre-Cara, he would've gotten a kick outta watching these two busty ladies fight it out in front of him, would've even egged them on, but not anymore. Cara had stolen his heart and soul, and he couldn't imagine wanting any other woman but her. She was his everything, and it still blew him away how she'd come into his life when he'd never been expecting it.

"How've you been, Hawk?" Kristy said softly.

"Good. What're you drinking?"

"Whiskey."

"Prospect. Two shots of Jack."

The prospect set the shots in front of them. Kristy picked up her glass and clinked it against his. "Best of luck on your upcoming wedding." She threw it back.

"Did you ever sign up for the classes at Pinewood Community College?"

She shook her head.

"Why not? You know the club will pay for the tuition. Fuck, the offer is out there for all the club girls. This past summer, you were so excited about signing up for a couple psychology classes. What happened?"

"I dunno. I guess I'm intimidated about being the oldest one in the classes."

"That's bullshit and you know it. There're a lot of older people who go to school. Hell, I went when I got out of the Marines. I wasn't exactly eighteen."

"I know. Can I have another one, Buzz?" She placed her hand over Hawk's. "I'll get there. I just need some more time."

He caught her blue gaze. "You don't wanna be a club whore forever, do you? You wanna end up like Mary? She's been here for thirty years. You're going on fourteen years. You're still young, only thirty-three. You should be looking for a nice guy, have a couple kids. You're smart, Kristy." He slid his hand away from hers.

"Yeah, real smart." She drank her whiskey. "You know I'm in love with you, right? Of course you do. Everyone in the goddamned club knows it, and they think I'm fucking pathetic."

"How much have you had to drink?" Hawk frowned when Buzz put another shot of whiskey in front of Kristy.

"Enough to tell you how I've felt about you all these years. You were my strength more times than I can count. You always built me up, cheered me on. How fucking disappointed you must be with me. I couldn't even register for college. I fucking chickened out. I'm such a loser."

Hawk blew out his breath in a huff. "You're not a loser. You and I go back a long time. You're a good woman. You need a good man."

"I thought I had one." She stared at him, her eyes brimming. "I wanted so badly to be your old lady. I figured as the years went on that you were destined to be like Sparky and Rob, confirmed bachelors. You and Throttle seemed to be vying for the position. But then you brought Cara to the club and I saw the look in your eyes, and it crushed me. I knew I never had a chance."

Hawk fidgeted on his stool, uncomfortable with the direction the conversation had taken. "I don't know what to say."

"Did you ever love me? For even a night when we fucked?"

"You know you were my favorite club girl. You still are."

"Am I?" Her eyes lit up like Chinese lanterns on a dark night. "If you ever cheated on Cara, would I be your first choice?"

"I'm not gonna cheat on her."

"But if you did?"

"Yeah, it'd be you. Don't drink anymore. I want you to sign up for those classes in January. I'm gonna ride your ass about it. You got more to life than spreading your legs for a bunch of men all the time."

She laughed wryly. "You don't think I have any self-respect?" He lifted his eyebrows. "Well, you're right. I don't. I would've done anything for you, Hawk. I still would. I love you so much. How could you fall for a citizen who wasn't even in the lifestyle? What was it about me that you couldn't love?"

"The connection just wasn't there. I can't explain it. I never thought

I'd fall in love. I didn't even think I was fuckin' *capable* of loving anyone. Then Cara happened. I don't know. If someone like Cara loves me, you definitely will find a good man to love you."

She blinked her unfocused eyes and nodded. "You're right. Okay, enough said. Forget we had this conversation. I think I'm gonna go to bed." She stood up and swayed, collapsing next to him. He put his arm around her. "I'm good. Thanks. You just keep doing what you were before my drunken ass came over to you. I feel like such a damn fool."

"You shouldn't. There's no way you can manage the stairs alone. I'll help you to your room." Hawk and a staggering Kristy clamored up the stairs until he opened her door in the attic, making sure she'd made it to her bed to pass out safely. He walked down to the third floor and went to his old room; as an officer of the club, he still had one. Sometimes he and Cara would crash overnight if they'd had too much to drink at one of the weekend parties. He took out his keys and opened the door.

Closing the door behind him, he walked to the window and looked out into the night. Twinkling stars littered the expanse of a jet-black sky, and the harvest moon glowed like a golden halo. Hawk stood by the window for a long time watching the occasional headlight flash by on the two-lane road in the distance. *Cara was right. I fuckin' overreacted about that fuckhead. Just thinking of him being close to her drove me crazy. She loved him before me, and as irrational as it sounds, it pisses me way the hell off.*

After a couple hours, he walked out of his room. The chilly night air pricked at his face as he slid into the driver's seat of his SUV. Normally he would've taken his Harley, but he'd been so pissed when they got home from dinner that all he wanted to do was get away. Right then, his reaction seemed silly. He tilted his head at the two brothers who were manning the gate as he drove out of the parking lot.

When he came home, the house was dark. He disengaged the alarm and entered. After guzzling a bottle of water, he walked upstairs and went into the bedroom. Cara was cocooned in the blanket, her long hair spilling around her. He stripped down to his boxers and then slipped between the sheets. The scent of Cara's perfume—brown sugar vanilla—floated around him. He could tell by her breathing that she wasn't asleep. He scooted close to her and wound his arm around her waist, drawing her to him. He kissed the top of her head. "I acted like a fuckin' asshole tonight."

"You did," she said in a nasally voice.

"Sometimes I love you too much."

"I'm sorry I didn't mention Trevor. You were right when you said I'd be mad if you had done the same thing." She placed her hands on top of his. She curled into the curve of his body, and her cute butt rubbed against his waking dick.

He cupped her chin in his hand and pushed her head back, kissing the tip of her nose, then her eyes, before finally kissing her soft mouth. Her small moans roused his passion even more, and he explored the soft lines of her waist and hips with gentle hands. "You're so sweet," he murmured against her lips.

She kissed him again, then broke away. "Would you be okay if we just cuddle tonight? I love being in your arms when I drift off to sleep."

He smiled. "Do you have to be in court early in the morning?"

"At eight o'clock," she groaned.

He glanced at the digital clock on the nightstand; it read one thirty. "Come closer, babe. He tugged her to him, holding her flush against his body. She tucked one of his hands under her chin like a child would a favorite stuffed toy or blanket. "I love you so much, sweetie." He smothered his words in her hair, loving how her hair smelled like fresh-baked cookies.

She kissed his hand, then tucked it back under her chin. "I love you too, honey."

He lay listening to her breathe until he fell asleep.

CHAPTER NINE

CARA SMILED BROADLY when she received the judge's order severing her client from the others in the armed robbery case. She was off the case with Trevor and her client had a real shot of getting a good deal; she viewed it as a win-win. She grabbed her phone to call Hawk.

"Guess what? The judge granted my motion to sever in that robbery case."

"The one fuckface is on with you?"

She giggled. "Yeah. Anyway, I'm a free agent with my client, which means my client can get a much better deal with the district attorney's office, and I won't have hardly any contact with Trevor. His client is the heavy, so I know he'll try and muddy the waters by implicating mine."

"So fuckface doesn't have to talk to you?"

"Not really. We're now on two separate cases."

"Good. And if he bugs you, you tell me and I'll set him straight."

"I'm sure you will."

"What should we do to celebrate?"

"Is the celebration for me or for you?"

"Me. Knowing fuckface isn't gonna be around you makes me less likely to end up in prison."

"I have to get the damn ring on my finger before you go away," she joked.

He chuckled. "You got an hour or two free now? I'd love to come over and have some fun with you on your desk."

Cara breathed in as a tingle ran through her. "Sounds like fun, but I have to be in court in thirty minutes."

"Fuck. Just thinking about it has gotten me all hard. What the hell am I gonna do?"

"Go back to work on that pain-in-the-ass bike you've been complaining about for the last few days. I'll take care of you later."

"Damn straight you will."

She laughed as she put her phone on her desk, then picked up her file for court. She skimmed it again, making sure she hadn't missed anything for her hearing. The next couple hours were going to be grueling as she listened to a ton of evidence in the abuse of the three-year-old girl she represented. She began to pack her briefcase when her phone rang.

"Hi, Cara. I'm presuming you received the court's order on severing your client," Trevor said.

"Yeah, I did. I'm just ready to leave for a court hearing."

"Even though you're not on the case, I'm still going to see you, right? You know, seeing you again made me realize that I was a fool to blow what we had."

"Damnit!" she cursed under her breath as her finger caught in her desk drawer. "Trevor, there's no reason to get together now. I have my own case. So good luck with yours."

"Did you hear what I just said?"

"Yes, and it doesn't make any difference. I wish you the best." Her finger was throbbing, and drops of blood dripped from it onto her desk.

"I can't believe you let that bully you call a fiancé tell you who to talk to and hang out with. I thought you were a stronger woman."

She wrapped a tissue around her bleeding finger. "Hawk's not a bully, and he's not telling me what to do. You and I were thrown together because of this case and now that the case has been severed, there's no reason for us to have any more contact. I don't want to be your friend. The truth is I don't like you. You're a jerk."

"You really are a bitch. After all these years, you're still mad because I fucked around on you. Did you ever ask yourself why I had to go to other women?"

"Of course I did. Many times, and the answer was always because you were an asshole."

"Did it ever occur to you that you weren't enough to satisfy me?"

"No, and by asking me that, you're proving me right. You've always been an asshole, and I'm glad I didn't make the mistake of marrying you."

"You think you're going to be able to satisfy your fiancé? I bet he's fucking a few women on the side. If I remember correctly, you weren't the best lay."

"Lose my number. You really are pathetically insecure. I'm still at a loss over what I ever saw in you." She clicked off the phone, anger burning through her. *What a despicable jerk! If he calls me again, I will tell Hawk. He can deal with the asshole.* She picked up her briefcase and walked out of the office, ready to do battle.

AS CARA LOCKED her office door, weariness swept over her. The hearing had been trying and heartbreaking, but she was elated the judge had severed the mother's parental rights to the toddler and agreed with Cara to place the child with her paternal aunt. It made her feel good to know that, with therapy and love, the small girl had a chance to grow into a loved and secure young woman.

Cara wrapped her scarf tighter around her neck as the bitter air touched her skin. She looked up at the cloudy sky, not able to see even a twinkle of a star. The air smelled and felt like snow, and she shivered as she walked on the sidewalk toward the streetlight. As she waited for the light to turn, Trevor's words echoed in her ears. She winced as she recalled them, chiding herself for being insecure and giving any credence to what he'd said. But the truth was that sometimes she was very insecure in her ability to keep Hawk interested in her long-term. He'd been with so many women, and sometimes she was afraid that he'd get bored with their lovemaking. That he'd want some variety. How would it be in five, ten, or fifteen years? *Stop it. Hawk loves you and has told you that you're enough for him.... But am I really? Trevor used to tell me that too, and look what he did to me. But he was a fucking asshole. Hawk isn't.*

She crossed the street and entered the parking lot. All she needed was to get home and change into her comfy pajamas, then snuggle into Hawk's warm embrace. *I love him so much.* He was the man of her dreams, but he was also her support, friend, and awesome lover. She couldn't even begin to imagine her life without him. She couldn't wait to give him a child—*their* child.

With her keyless remote in her hands, she walked toward the back of the lot, lost in her thoughts until she heard the crunch of footsteps behind her. She paused and so did the footsteps. She swallowed hard; it wasn't just footsteps behind her—the stench of cheap cologne, stale beer, and desperation crept ever closer. She picked up her pace. Out of nowhere, a gust of cold wind blew fiercely and strands of her hair covered her face. It was as if she were looking through Venetian blind slats. Her car was just a few feet in front of her and she bolted, pressing the remote and feeling a bit of comfort when the headlights and interior lights switched on. She clawed at her car door and opened it, tossing her purse and briefcase inside. As she was ready to slide into the driver's seat, something slammed against the back of her calf.

Hard.

Then it dropped by her feet with a thud.

She whirled around and looked down.

The wind swallowed her scream.

On the ground, next to her feet, lay the dying body of a rat, blood oozing from its mouth. Its dull eyes stared at her.

She jumped into the car and switched on the ignition, trying to stop her chattering teeth. She threw her car in gear and hauled out of the lot as several people moved out of her way. As she drove it felt like the rat was still slamming into her calf, and she reached down and rubbed it even though she knew the sensation was all in her head. *How disgusting! Did someone actually throw the rat at me, or was it poisoned and came over to die?*

Her brain told her it was a deliberate act, but her emotions didn't want to believe it. It was too horrible. *Who would do such a thing?* Maybe it was a family member of one of her clients. Sometimes they weren't too pleased if their loved one went to prison. *Last week Jimmy's brother was really upset when Jimmy got three years in prison. Maybe he did it to scare me.* She shuddered and pushed down harder on the accelerator. She had to get home.

When she came into the house, the sweet, smoky aroma of cherry wood chips curled around her as she glanced at the deck and spotted Hawk standing over the fire, holding a pair of stainless steel tongs. She went to the cupboard and took out a large wine glass, then poured a deep red Merlot in it. By the time she drained the glass, her nerves had calmed a bit. Needing a shower desperately, she poked her head out the French doors. "I'm home," she said to Hawk.

He jerked his head up and smiled wide at her. "Come give me a kiss."

"I'll be back in a few. I need to get in the shower." She turned away knowing that she'd just made Hawk very suspicious, but she needed to scrub away the blood on her left calf. She couldn't even begin to talk about the incident until she took a long hot shower. She dashed up the stairs and went into the bedroom.

When she came into the family room, her skin pink and glowing, Hawk was setting two plates down on the kitchen table. His eyes traveled over her body encased in flannel pajama pants and a short, long-sleeved T-shirt. "You look soft and tempting."

She smiled and padded over to him.

Gathering her into his arms, he held her snugly. "Did you have a rough day?" He gently rubbed his nose against her hair.

Not wanting to ruin their dinner, she squeezed him tight and just nodded. They held each other for a few minutes, and then Hawk pulled away. "I forgot about the fuckin' peppers on the grill." He rushed outside.

When he came back in with the burned peppers she laughed. "I didn't want them anyway. I'll make us a salad."

He chuckled and placed the ruined vegetables in a bag, then went to the garage to throw them away.

After dinner they sat together on the couch to watch an action drama, Cara sipping a glass of wine as he nursed a bottle of beer. Cara bent over and placed her wine on the coffee table. She stroked his thigh, loving how the material of his sweatpants was soft under her fingers. "I had a strange episode when I was in the parking lot after work."

He dipped his head and kissed the top of hers. "What do you mean?"

She took a deep breath and told him what happened to her.

His muscles tensed. "Did you see anyone?"

"No, but I swear someone was behind me. I heard footsteps coming close to me, and then the pervasive smell of cheap cologne and beer hit me. I picked up my pace, but when the rat hit my calf, I was so horrified and freaked I just jumped in the car. I didn't really look around. I just wanted to get the hell out of there." She shivered and he held her close to him. "I've had a feeling someone's been watching me a few times in the last couple weeks. It kinda creeps me out."

"Have you seen anyone?"

"Yes. No. I'm not sure. But when Sherrie and I had dinner at El Tecolote a couple weeks ago, in my rearview mirror, I could have sworn I saw a tall man looking at me. He was obscured in the shadows of the streetlights and trees, and it was so damn dark that night, but I'm pretty sure he was real."

"This isn't good, babe. I definitely saw a guy behind the evergreens when we were at our house with Baylee a few days ago. When I spotted him, he took off and I chased the fucker, but he had too much of a head start. He jumped into a Jeep parked on the road and zoomed off. I couldn't get the license plate. I don't like it. My instincts are telling me something's going down. You need to lay low until I figure this shit out. I'm gonna get Sinner to watch you."

"The new prospect?"

"Yeah. He's been doing a good job, and the way he reacted and jumped into a fight at the rally a few weeks ago makes me think he's a good choice. I'll talk to Banger about it in the morning. Fuck, it's always something."

She craned her neck and kissed his chin. "I'm sure it's nothing." He ran his finger over her jawline and smiled, but she knew he didn't believe it. Hell, she didn't either. *Why can't people just let us live in peace?* "Do you have problems with any of the other clubs?"

"You know I can't discuss club business, but I'll tell you that outlaws always have troubles with each other. It's the way our world is. Don't worry about it. I'll take care of it." He moved her hair away from her face and brushed his lips against her cheeks. Then he held her tight for the rest of the evening.

She felt so warm and safe in his arms that she wished she could freeze that moment forever.

They didn't talk about it anymore, but when they got ready for bed, she saw him open his dresser drawer and take out his Glock, setting it on the nightstand next to him. He drew her close and stroked her hair until he fell asleep.

Cara stayed up for a long time listening to the wind groan outside as it weaved between the tree trunks, making the brightly colored leaves tumble and then rustle across the driveway. She burrowed deeper into Hawk's embrace, feeling protected in her makeshift cocoon. Even though her pulse raced with apprehension of something being amiss, her heart melted as her love for him spread over her. *As long as we're together, nothing can hurt us.* The words became her mantra, and she fell asleep with them on her lips.

CHAPTER TEN

THE FOLLOWING MORNING Hawk walked into the clubhouse and straight to Banger's office, tapping on the open door as he entered. Banger looked up and smiled at him. "Hey, what's up? Thought you'd be at the shop."

Hawk sank down in one of the chairs. "I'll be heading there soon, but I wanted to talk to you about something."

"Wanna close the door?"

Hawk shook his head. "Nah. Some shit's going down with me and my old lady. My gut tells me it's club related, but it seems that Cara and I are the only ones being targeted. Fuck. Something's not right here. I can take care of myself, but I'm scared for Cara. I can't let her be without someone watching her all the time. I wanna put Sinner on her when I'm not around. He's a good kid, proved himself at that fight that broke out a few weeks ago. Even though he's only twenty, he's got a good head on his shoulders."

Banger scratched his beard. "What's been going on?" Hawk filled him in on the events that had taken place over the past two weeks, and Banger nodded. "You're right that something's not right. I haven't noticed anything, and none of the brothers have said anything about shit going on with them. I can ask around, but it does seem like someone's focusing on you and your woman. Maybe you're the target and your woman is the way to get to you. You got any shit with anyone outside the club?"

Hawk shook his head. "No, and I've got no doubts this shit is meant for me. But I can't figure out who it is. I thought about Dustin and Shack, but they hate your ass more than mine, so it doesn't make sense that this shit is aimed just at me. They'd be messing with all the Insurgents. Same with the Demon Riders. Even the fuckin' Skull Crushers knew the whole club would kick their asses, not me alone." Hawk spread out his hands on his denim-clad thighs. "I just can't make sense of it."

"Me neither. Have you heard any shit from the grapevine?"

"Nope. The whole thing's fuckin' strange."

"Yeah. I'll put Sinner on duty to watch your old lady when you're not around. In the meantime, I'll dig around and reach out to some people to see if anything is more off than usual in the outlaw world."

"Thanks, dude. I'll give Cara a call, and then I'll talk to Sinner."

"You up for a beer before you head back to the shop?"

"Fuck yeah. I'll meet you in the great room."

As Hawk walked out of the office, he dialed Cara's number. She seemed relieved when he told her Sinner was going to be watching out for her when he wasn't around. After he ended their call, he sought out the prospect, told him his duties, and sent him packing. Then Hawk went into the great room and ordered two beers. As if on cue, the president came into the room and sidled up to him. Hawk handed him a beer.

"You talk to Sinner?"

"Yeah. Now I can fuckin' breathe easier when I'm not with her. The timing of all this fuckin' sucks. The wedding's in less than three weeks."

"Shit, it's always that way. Speaking of weddings, Belle told me she got a call from Cara's friend Sherrie. The chick told Belle that she and a few other gals are planning your woman's bachelorette party. She said that—"

"Bachelorette party? What the fuck?" Hawk set his beer down.

"Those were my exact words to Belle. It seems that a lot of citizen women have parties similar to the guys before they get hitched. Anyway, Belle said the party's the same night as the one the brothers are giving you at Dream House."

Hawk shrugged. "Okay. Was Sherrie asking Belle to use your house?

I know her apartment's too small for all of Cara's girlfriends and the old ladies."

Banger shook his head, his brows creasing. "Nope. She told Belle the party was gonna be at Jim Diamond's. She was calling to invite Belle."

Hawk jerked his head back. "That's the strip club. You sure your old lady heard right?"

"Yep. It seems that the bar has a male strip show on Saturday nights starting at ten."

"What the fuck? There's no goddamned way I'm letting my woman watch a bunch of naked men wiggling their pussy asses. Fuck no!"

"I heard the fuckers give lap dances to the women, especially brides-to-be."

"Sherrie's gone fuckin' crazy with this one. I'm sure Belle told her no, right?"

"Nope. She said she couldn't wait to see the show. She also told me not to even open my mouth if I was gonna tell her not to go."

"But you told her not to, didn't you? Fuck, you can forbid it."

"And be in the deep freeze for the goddamn winter?" Banger chuckled. "I don't think so. Anyway, she can go and look at those young fuckers all she wants. It'll only make her appreciate me more when she gets home."

"I can't believe Cara knows about this. I bet it's a surprise."

"Her friend didn't tell Belle it was a surprise. Anyway, all the old ladies have agreed to go. You know they're doing this for spite 'cause we'll be at Dream House. Now when we watch the strippers jiggle on stage, all we'll be thinking about is our women ogling naked men. Fuck. You gotta admit it's clever, and I know they're enjoying sticking it to us."

Hawk narrowed his eyes. "I'll talk to Cara. I know it's Sherrie who came up with this fucked-up idea. The women should have a party at my house. I'll buy the booze. I'll straighten this out."

"Sure you will." Banger motioned for another beer.

Chas and Jax came in, making a beeline for Hawk. "What the fuck's going on, dude? Addie told me she's going to a male strip club for Cara's bachelorette party? What the hell?"

"Cherri told me the same thing. I don't want my woman looking at naked men," Jax said as he straddled the barstool.

Hawk scrubbed his face. "Banger just told me. I didn't know anything about it. Cara didn't mention it. I think it's a surprise, but I'll talk to her. I was telling Banger that the women can come to my house for their party."

Jax's face lit up. "Yeah, that's a great idea. Cherri can make chili. She makes the best chili I've ever tasted."

"You're right about that. I told Belle to get her recipe." Banger took a pull on his beer.

"Addie loves to cook. She can make one of her great appetizers. The women can all bring something, you know, do the potluck thing they love so much. They can eat, drink, and gossip. It sounds like a fuckin' great party to me," Chas said.

"Damn right it does," Jax chimed in.

"I'll get Cara on it." Hawk took out his phone and sent a text.

Hawk: *Hey, babe. How's it going?*

Cara: *Good. U still with Banger?*

Hawk: *Ya. Leaving soon. He said Sherrie's giving u a party???*

Cara: *Ya. I know.*

Hawk: *Thought maybe it was a surprise.*

Cara: *No.*

Hawk: *Banger said something crazy. The party is at Jim Diamond's???*

A long pause. No response.

Hawk: *U still with me?*

Cara: *Sorry. Court called. Super busy. Gotta go.*

Hawk narrowed his eyes.

Hawk: *Is party at Jim Diamond's?*

Cara: *It is. Gotta go. ♥u! xoxoxx*

It was like a wall of bricks fell on him. He stared at the screen, re-reading her text. *What the fuck does she think she's doing? There's no fuckin' way I'm gonna allow this.*

"So Cara agreed to have the party at your place?" Jax asked.

"We're gonna talk about it tonight. She had to go to court."

"She's a real busy lady," Banger said, a twinkle in his eyes.

"Yeah, she fuckin' is. I said I'll take care of it." Hawk pushed his chair back and stood up. "I gotta get to the shop. Later." He walked away, feeling the stares of his brothers on his back. He had to convince Cara to have the party any place but the strip bar. *I oughta wring Sherrie's neck, the fuckin' troublemaker.* He switched on the ignition and his bike roared to life. He waved to Wheelie at the guard post, then hit the road leading to Pinewood Springs.

BRILLIANT STREAKS OF indigo, saffron, and persimmon streaked the sky and saturated the clouds as the sun descended in the horizon. Hawk pulled his Harley into the garage, now awash with the golden reflection from the sky. He hit the button to close the door and went into the house. The aroma of onions and garlic swirled around him as he stepped into the kitchen. He raised the lid of a pot on the burner, the rich scent of basil and tomato infiltrating his nostrils. Another large pot full of water was beginning to boil on the back burner. His stomach growled. He grabbed the French baguette on the counter next to the stove, tore off a piece, and then dipped it into the sauce, his stomach dancing with the first taste.

"Does it taste good?" Cara came up behind him and slinked her arms around his waist.

"Damn good. I'm fuckin' starving." He put the lid back on the saucepot and whirled around, circling his arms around her. "How was your day, babe?" He bent down and kissed her lightly on the lips.

"Busy and tiring. I'm glad I don't have to do any work tonight. We can snuggle and watch a movie after dinner. It's my turn to pick the movie."

He groaned. "Another sappy love story?"

She punched his arm. "No. And the love stories I watch aren't all sappy. Anyway, I thought we'd watch a legal thriller."

He smiled. "That works for me. I'm just gonna shower and change."

"Perfect. When you come back down, dinner will be ready."

After eating, they cleaned the kitchen and then settled onto the couch in the family room. Hawk had thrown a couple logs into the fireplace, and the room was toasty and glowing. Cara placed her glass of red wine on the coffee table.

"Are you ready to watch the movie?" she asked as she picked up the remote.

"In a second, babe. First I wanna talk to you about this crazy-ass party Sherrie's arranged. She called Belle inviting her to it. Banger told me, and I'm gonna admit I was fuckin' surprised when he said your party's gonna be at Jim Diamond's. You know nothing much surprises me, but this fuckin' did. Why don't you call Sherrie and tell her you want the party here? I can buy the booze, some of the ladies can bring food, or I can get Big Rocky's to cater, and you can all have a great time. The guys and I were talking about it this morning, and we think you'd all have such a fun party."

Cara picked up her wine glass, took a sip, and then looked at him. "So you guys basically planned my bachelorette party?"

Hawk chuckled. "Yeah, I guess we did. I know you like having people over, so this would be perfect, you know?"

She nodded. "Since you're planning my party, it's only fair I plan yours. You and the brothers can go to Jax's or Banger's house and have some drinks, eat barbecue or chili—I'm sure Cherri would make it—and play poker and shoot some pool. I know you love playing pool and poker, so this would be perfect, you know?"

Hawk jutted out his jaw, his muscles tightening. "Dream House is a tradition for the brothers since before I was born."

"I see. Well, Sherrie is making Jim Diamond's a tradition for our group. When she gets married, Lisa, Jen, and I promised we'd reciprocate." She smiled sweetly and took another sip of wine. "It looks like our friends already planned our parties, but I'd love to have the party you suggested after we get back from our honeymoon." She picked up the remote. "Ready?"

"Fuck no. I don't want you going to the strip club to watch naked men."

"I don't think they're naked. I'm pretty sure they strip down to a G-string. I can ask Sherrie if you want clarification on that detail."

Hawk shook his head. "You don't have to be a smartass about it. The point is I don't want you to go."

"If I told you I didn't want you to go to Dream House and have Janelle or someone else give you a lap dance, would you stay home?"

He ran his hand through his long hair. "Didn't you fuckin' hear what I said? Dream House is a tradition, and the lap dance is too."

"So you're going to have one of the dancers rub her boobs and ass all over you?"

How the fuck does she twist everything around and shift the conversation? "We weren't talking about that."

"*You* weren't. You were too busy telling me that you didn't want me to see almost-naked men move their stuff on stage. And I'm telling you I feel the same about you watching totally naked women."

He leaned over and held her hand. "Babe," he said softly. "It's different for me."

"Why?"

"'Cause I'm a man. We're wired diff—"

She pulled her hand away. "I just *knew* you were going to say that crap. I was hoping you wouldn't, but you did. God! What a fucking ridiculous reason."

"It's true. Men are visual, and women aren't into that kind of shit."

"Some women must be because every Saturday night a bunch of men gyrate to a sold-out female crowd. Kinda blows your theory, huh?"

The pulse in Hawk's jaw twitched. "A good old lady doesn't do that shit. I forbid you to go."

Wine spurted out of her mouth. She grabbed a napkin and wiped her lips and T-shirt. "Forbid? What the fuck? I don't remember agreeing that you can tell me what the hell I can and can't do. We're not back in the Middle Ages. And every single old lady is going to be at Jim Diamond's, so I guess the club doesn't have any *good* old ladies." She jumped up from the couch and stormed into the kitchen.

She's so fuckin' stubborn. This isn't going the way I planned. Fuck! "Get back over here. We're not done talking."

She came back into the family room. "Are you going to have a lap dance?"

"If I don't, will you have the party here?"

"Wrong fucking answer!" She marched out of the room.

Damnit! I wasn't planning on anyone giving me a lap dance. She made me so pissed I'm saying things I don't mean. Fuck! "You're a piece of work, babe. You know damn good and well the only reason you're going to watch a bunch of pussies strip is to punish and spite me because I'm going to Dream House. You're not fooling me at all."

"I'm going upstairs to read. Think whatever you want." The door slamming shut echoed through the house.

What the fuck am I gonna tell my brothers? They're gonna give me a hard time about not being able to control my woman. He gulped down his beer. *If they start shit with me, I'll just remind them that they can't control their women either since all of them are going too. Fuck!*

A few hours later, he climbed the stairs and went into the bedroom. The lights were off and he saw the outline of Cara's body covered in a fleecy blanket. He sighed and kicked off his boots before stripping down to his boxers. He slid in next to her. She didn't turn around. He dipped his head and kissed her on the temple, whispering, "I never intended to get a lap dance."

She craned her neck. "Thanks for telling me that."

He ran his fingers down her arm. "We good again?"

"Yes, but my bachelorette party is still going to be at Jim Diamond's."

He bit the inside of his cheek. "And I'm still going to Dream House."

She turned her head away from him and pulled the blanket closer around her. "Then I guess we're good. Good night."

He wanted to wrap her in his arms and tell her that this whole thing was stupid. That all that was important was what *they* wanted, not the brothers or her friends. He wanted to tell her that they'd have their own party, go to Aspen for the night and fuck their goddamned brains out.

"Good night," he said.

Then he turned on his side, his back to hers.

He drew the covers over his shoulder, knowing that it wouldn't do any good in relieving the icy chill that was running through his veins. Cara's decision to go to Jim Diamond's shook his outlaw sensibilities. In his world, women acquiesced to the men, and her refusal to do that shook him to the core, making him feel something he hadn't felt for a very long time—powerless.

Fuck.

CHAPTER ELEVEN

VIPER THREW SKIP against the wall, his face inches from the scared man. "What the fuck didn't you understand about not letting Hawk spot you? You're a goddamned moron!" He plowed his fist into the man's chubby cheeks.

"He didn't know who I was."

"That's not the fuckin' point. He's got a goddamn member watching her. You asshole!" Viper sunk his fist into Skip's stomach, and he groaned.

"Okay, I fucked up. I've been real careful since that time. Maybe the Insurgent put the guy on his woman because she got notification of your escape." Hope laced his voice.

"She'd have at least two or three fuckers watching her if that was the case. The cunt's been slumming at Hawk's house for the last two weeks. The notice is probably waiting for her at her house. You fuckin' screwed up my plans." Viper kneed Skip hard in the balls and then let go of him, turning his back as the man slid down to the floor.

"This asshole's fuckup may work in your favor." Dustin rose from a chair in the sparsely furnished room. "The fuckin' badges are everywhere. You gotta get the hell outta Colorado. The minute the bitch finds out you're out, fuckin' Banger and Hawk will spring into action. The Insurgents will be on high alert. Fuck, dude, you can't be dodging badges and Insurgents at the same time."

"I know what the fuck I can and can't do. I don't need you telling me shit." Viper eyed Skip, who was curled up on the floor, and kicked him hard in the stomach. "You piece of shit! I oughta kill you."

Dustin pulled Viper away. "Calm the fuck down! You can't lose your head at a time like this. You had this fuck rent this house, and you can come back to it. For now, you need to come back to Iowa and lay low at our clubhouse. Let things chill, blow over, and then strike when no one suspects it."

Viper grunted and leaned against the wall. The house he'd been staying at for the past few days was on the outskirts of Pinewood Springs, conveniently shrouded by evergreens and pine trees. The rental had a few pieces of furniture: double bed, a tatty couch, two straight-backed chairs, a coffee table, and one lamp. Besides the seclusion, Viper had been drawn to the house for its basement. It was dark, musty-smelling, and soundproof. He surmised the previous tenants had used it for some wicked sexual fun, and he appreciated all the effort they went through to make the walls absorb all noise. The hooks on the walls and the ones suspended from a large beam in the ceiling also made him smile. He'd put all that to good use when he had Hawk's cunt gagged and trussed. Just thinking about the bitch at his disposal made him acutely aware of his inability to jack off. He'd make sure Hawk paid for what he did in a slow and agonizing way.

Skip's moans as he pushed up from the floor drew Viper's attention back to him. He'd have to let the fucker live until everything was settled. The house was rented under his name, so Viper didn't want to draw any unnecessary attention. *Once I gut the bitch and destroy the fuckin' Insurgent I'll gladly slit this pussy's throat.*

"I'll make sure no one spots me again," Skip said as he rubbed his hand over his swelling face.

"You fuckin' better 'cause you've just used up your last chance. Now get the fuck outta here."

Skip hurriedly limped to the door and closed it behind him. Dustin laughed and shook his head. "Where the fuck did you find *that* one?"

"He came with the other two. He's a goddamn moron. There's no way Hawk's letting this go. I guess Iowa will be my home for now. We should move out tonight. Once Tommie and Pierson give the signal, I'll be back. I've waited a long time for this, so a delay is no fuckin' big deal."

"We can't wait for you to kick that arrogant sonofabitch's ass. Shack's been dreaming 'bout you using the VP's hot slut ever since he spotted her at the motorcycle expo in Denver last summer."

"Yeah. That nosy cunt caused me all sorts of trouble. It's time she paid for it."

Dustin nodded. "We'll move out when the night crawls in."

Viper took out a cigarette and lit it. "It's a perfect night for it. There isn't a moon."

Dustin sank into the couch. "I'm gonna try and get in a few winks. It's gonna be a long-ass ride dodging the freeway 'til we get outta Colorado. You should get in a nap."

"I'm good." Viper went over to the curtained window and peeked out of it, staring at the trees while he ran through all the things he was going to do to the cunt when he had her in his control. The tip of his cigarette glowed as he took another puff, the cloud of smoke swirling around him. Since he'd been in prison he'd become adept at waiting.

He'd wait until nightfall.

He'd bide his time until he had the bitch in his clutches.

And he'd relish the anticipation of watching the fucking Insurgent's face when he sliced his old lady open.

The reward for waiting's gonna be fuckin' sweet. He snorted disdainfully, then stubbed out his cigarette as a harsh smirk formed on his face.

CHAPTER TWELVE

HAWK SAT ON the easy chair in the bedroom watching Cara take the rollers out of her hair. When she bent over and finger-combed her long tresses, the slow burn that had been smoldering since she first went upstairs to get ready for her bachelorette party burst into a fierce blaze.

"Why the fuck are you spending so much time getting ready for this bullshit?"

Cara threw her head back and glanced at him, her eyes wide. "I always spend time fixing up before I go out. You know that." She smiled. "You've complained enough about it."

"You're taking more time than usual," he growled as he crossed his arms over his chest.

"No, I'm not." She walked over to him and caressed his cheek with the backs of her fingers. "You look real handsome tonight." She bent over and kissed him. "And you smell sexy as hell."

He didn't flinch, just grunted as he stared straight ahead. "What time is this shit supposed to end?"

She moved away and walked back to her vanity table. "I don't know. We're going to Prime Steakhouse for dinner first. What time will you be home?"

"Fuckin late. Real late. I plan to get good and drunk and have a fuckin' ball." He stood up and swaggered past her. He combed his ebony hair and secured it in a low ponytail, then looped his belt around his tight black jeans. He threw a glance at Cara whose eyes were glistening. For a split second he felt a pang of guilt for being suck a goddamn dick, but then he pictured a muscular dude thrusting his hips at her while his cock bulged behind some flimsy G-string and a wave of anger washed over him.

Cara turned away and picked up her shoes. Hawk narrowed his eyes as he watched her put on her "fuck me" heels. *You're fuckin' pulling out all the stops, aren't you, baby? Well, two can play that game.* "If you need a ride home, call me and I can come pick you up. I don't plan on getting wasted."

She brushed past him, the scent of her sugared vanilla perfume swirling around him and clinging to his dick. "I'll do that." He lounged against the door frame, blocking it so she couldn't pass.

"Hawk, I have to get going. I promised my cousin Maria I'd pick her up at seven and I'm already running behind."

"Push me outta the way."

"Why are you acting like this? I already told you that this is nothing. You trust me, right?" He nodded but held his stance. "If I were having the party here, you wouldn't be acting like this even though you would *still* be going to Dream House. This is so hypocritical."

"I'm not telling you not to go. I'm just telling you that I'm gonna be home real late, you have to push me outta the way to get past me, and I'm gonna have a fuckin' good time tonight at the party my brothers are throwing me."

She sighed and squeezed her way around him. "I'm glad you'll have fun because I plan to have one helluva bachelorette party." She marched down the stairs as he followed her. When they were in the foyer, she turned to him. "On second thought, I won't be in any shape to pick you up. I'm going to raise hell tonight. You'll probably have to take me to get my car tomorrow from Jim Diamond's parking lot." She smirked at him and paused in front of the hallway mirror to fix her hair.

The fury he'd been holding inside uncoiled. "That's fine with me. While you're ogling fuckin' pussies on stage, I'll be doing the same while I think about which dancer I want to give me a lap dance. Maybe I'll pick Janelle. She's been hot for me for over a year."

When Cara's pain-stricken face met his gaze, he knew he'd gone too far. "Do whatever the fuck you want. I'm not your damn babysitter."

Her voice broke at the end. She grabbed her silver mesh evening bag and rushed out of the house.

Fuck! "Babe...." Hawk went after her, but she'd jumped into her car and nearly crashed into the large bush on the edge of the driveway. "Cara. Hold up a minute. I didn't mean what I said." Her windows were rolled up as she sped away. A sick feeling grabbed hold of him. *Why the fuck did I say that shit to her? Why the hell did she have to look so damn sexy tonight?* He watched as she turned the corner at the end of the street, Sinner following behind her on his Harley. He closed the door and made his way to the garage where he started his Harley and drove to Dream House.

When he arrived at the strip club, over seventy Harleys crowded the parking lot. The Insurgents had shut the club down to the public due to Hawk's bachelor party, and several Insurgents from around the state came to party with the vice president.

He pushed open the doors and entered a large room filled with black leather and denim. Topless waitresses balanced large trays on their hips as they squeezed through the labyrinth of men. The only women in the club were the dancers and waitresses, and they were very much outnumbered. After a few hours, the men would go back to the clubhouse so they could have fun with the club girls and hoodrats who were anxiously awaiting their return. The strippers were off-limits for any fucking; the Insurgents were very strict about it. The men could touch and squeeze, but nothing more. The dancers weren't even allowed to give blowjobs in the private rooms where the lap dances took place.

Hawk bumped fists with a ton of brothers as he made his way to the bar. He needed a double shot of Jack. Now. He had to lose himself in the moment and stop thinking about Cara and Jim Diamond's. *Fuck.*

"Our women watching a bunch of naked sissies fuckin' blows, dude." Throttle stood next to him and ordered a Coors.

"Tell me about it. I blame all of this on Sherrie."

"Point her out next time she's around. I'm gonna tell her to stop stirring the fuckin' pot. Kimber had a smug look on her face all fuckin' afternoon." He picked up his beer and chugged it. "When she gets home later, I'll show her how a real man shakes his ass."

Hawk stared at him, then laughed. The image of Throttle shaking around like one of the jerks at Jim Diamond's was ludicrous. Throttle must have made that connection with the same mental image, because he started laughing as well. Soon the two of them were snorting and, thanks to the booze, the idea of their women at the male strip show wasn't as infuriating as it had been earlier.

As Hawk talked to one of the brothers from the northern Colorado chapter, he felt a tug on his T-shirt, and he turned around. He smiled. "Hey, Janelle."

The petite dancer smiled warmly and pressed against him, her big breasts spilling out of her small top. "Hiya. Congratulations on your upcoming wedding. I'm sure you're making a lot of women sad."

He chuckled. "You dancing tonight?"

"Just for you, babe. I'm hoping later on I'll be the one you choose for your lap dance." She ran her tongue over her lips.

"We'll see."

"I gotta go change into my outfit for my set. You're gonna watch me, right? I'm only asking because most of the times when you come with the brothers for parties you rarely watch the dancers."

He shrugged and brought his beer to his mouth. She patted his arm and took off, disappearing among the throngs of people. Bones and Rags came up to him. "Who're you picking for your lap dance, bro?" Bones asked as his eyes scanned the stage. "The one up there is new, but she sure has got the following already with some of the brothers and a lot of the citizens."

Hawk glanced at the stage and saw a tall blonde woman wrapping herself around the pole as she bent backward. Her breasts jiggled as she moved her waist, smiling at the crowd as they applauded.

"Isn't she fuckin' hot?" Rags stared at the dancer. "I wish we could get rid of the 'no fucking' rule for special parties. I'd like a piece of her. I'm a sucker for blondes."

"And big tits," Bones added.

Hawk chuckled. "Most of us are a sucker for big tits." At that moment, Cara flashed through his mind and a hole of want and ache opened up. Then the crowd exploded as the blonde bowed, scooped up the bills that littered the stage, and rushed off. The loud beats of Kix's song, "Girl Money," pounded out of the speakers and Janelle strutted out on stage in a skimpy bridal outfit. The men went wild and pointed at Hawk. He smiled, but his mind was on his sexy bride-to-be. He glanced at the clock on the wall and figured Cara should be finished with dinner and heading over to Jim Diamond's at that moment. Perspiration beaded along his hairline and under his arms as he bounced his knee up and down, darting his gaze from his phone to the clock and back.

"She fucking wants to rub her big tits all over you, dude." Hoss came over and pulled up a chair next to Hawk.

Distracted by images of a ripped man thrusting his hips in front of his woman, Hawk looked at Hoss. "What?"

Hoss pointed to the stage. "Janelle, dude. She's staring right at you and she's stripped down to her thong. Fuck. What's up with you?"

Hawk glanced at the stage and saw Janelle smile broadly as she cupped her breasts and rolled her fingers over her nipples. Hawk looked down at his phone again. He pulled up Cara's number and sent her a message.

Hawk: *Hey. Just checking to make sure u have enough gas in the car.*

He scrubbed his face with his hand. *How fuckin' pathetic and lame is that text? She's gonna see right through it. This woman drives me fuckin' crazy.*

Cara: *I filled it up b4 I left.*

He had to give her credit for not scoffing at his pathetic excuse to contact her.

Hawk: How was dinner?

Cara: Good. Did u eat?

The noise around him was deafening, and he looked up in time to see Janelle smearing something that looked like whipped cream over her tits and pussy. She jumped off the stage and sashayed over to him, her breasts swinging with each step. Her eyes shone with desire as she licked her lips.

"Fuck, she's hot tonight. I love the way Crystal dances, but Janelle's giving it to you good." Hoss laughed and chugged his beer, his eyes fixed on the dancer as she approached their table. Hawk looked down at his phone.

Hawk: Ya. U at the club?

Cara: Yep. U?

"Hey, sexy. Why don't you lick me off?" Janelle stood in front of him wearing nothing but a short veil and whipped cream. The brothers yelled, egging Hawk on to taste the hot stripper.

Hawk smiled and then put up his finger, mouthing, "Hang on a sec." He looked at his phone again.

Hawk: Ya.

Cara: U having a good time?

Janelle curled her hands around his tight bicep and breathed into his ear, "After you lick me off, I'll give you the best lap dance you've ever had."

He nodded, then tapped his fingers on his phone.

Hawk: Not really. U?

"Are you choosing the horny bitch?" a loud voice boomed out from the back corner. Janelle scooped up some whipped cream on her finger and placed it against his lips. "Taste it, and then you can try me. You'll

91

see that I'm even sweeter."

Cara: *Not so much.*

Hawk wiped the cream off his lips and stood up. He stepped back and put his hands up. The guys yelled for the DJ to cut the music. A loud hum surrounded him as the brothers talked amongst themselves. He cleared his throat. "This party is fuckin' cool. I can't believe I'm getting my ass hitched in a couple weeks."

"We can't believe anyone wants your moody ass," Wheelie yelled. The brothers guffawed and voiced their agreement.

"I can't fuckin' believe Cara's gonna be mine forever. Damn." He threw back the shots the brothers had placed on his table. *Enough of this touchy shit. I'm acting just like a fuckin' chick.*

"Now that you've just proven you're pussy whipped, get your cock back and lick Janelle clean." Bones pushed the young stripper toward him.

Hawk held up his hands. "I'm gonna pick who I want." Janelle's face fell. "I'm picking Crystal to do a lap dance for my brother Hoss."

Hoss jumped up. "What the fuck? I'm not gettin' hitched, or at least I don't think I am." The brothers hooted and whistled as Crystal came over to Hawk. Janelle's eyes brimmed with tears. He tugged her close to him and whispered in her ear, "Don't take it personally. I got my old lady on my mind tonight. Go over to Bones. He's been eyeing you all night, and I'm sure he'd love to clean you up."

She smiled and gave him a quick kiss on his cheek. "I hope your woman knows how lucky she is to have you."

He winked at her, then laughed as she walked over to Bones. "Let's have some music as Janelle and Crystal give our two brothers a helluva good time." All eyes were on the two women as they swayed and ground their firm bodies against the men. Hawk went to the bar and grabbed a bottle of water. He took out his phone again.

Hawk: *Sorry, babe. Is Sherrie acting like a woman on steroids?*

Cara: *Actually no, but a lot of women here are. Oh. Gotta go!*

He narrowed his eyes.

Hawk: *What the fuck does that mean?*

No response. He leaned against the bar looking at the clock as the seconds ticked away, trying to hold off the volcano that was threatening to erupt inside him.

What the hell is she doing?

CHAPTER THIRTEEN

THE SMALL TABLE lights blended with the blue and yellow lighting from the stage. A tall, muscular man bumped and ground on stage, his dress shirt, tie, vest, and pants in a pile behind him. His eyes were fixed on Cara as he ran his hands over his body, winking at her. Several groups of women screamed and cheered as the dancer—the DJ announced him as Ricochet—pushed down on his G-string.

Cara, seated on the blue velvet couch, smiled weakly before taking another sip of her watered-down vodka and tonic. She glanced at her phone and groaned when she saw that the group of them had only been at the strip bar for thirty minutes. Her heart soared when she received Hawk's text, and then she laughed because it was so obvious that he'd made up something silly to reach out to her. She texted back, and for the next several minutes she entertained herself by "talking" to him.

Then the women yelled louder than they had since she'd arrived. She looked up just as Ricochet jumped off the stage and strutted toward her with a strong air of confidence and bravado. She swallowed hard and squirmed uncomfortably in her chair as she told Hawk she had to go. She put her phone on the table and shook her head quickly, trying to convey that she wasn't interested. Fat chance. He kept coming to her. Behind his imposing shoulders, she saw the old ladies and some of her other friends laughing and clapping their hands. When he reached her, he held out his hand, but she shook her head again. He leaned over and picked up the rhinestone tiara she'd been handed when she'd first come into the club. She'd been told to wear it, so she'd stuck it on her head and then had promptly taken it off when they'd arrived at their table.

Ricochet laughed and placed the tiara back on her head, even though she kept shaking it and tried to swat his hands away. He tugged her to her feet, urging her to move with him. Cara blushed, and an image of Hawk walking in and finding her next to a nearly naked man as he gyrated to J. Holiday's "Bed" almost made her pass out. Doris and Marlena came over and pushed her into the dancer. His sculpted arms wrapped around her; he smelled like soap.

"Come dance with me, sweetheart," he breathed into her ear.

Twisting in his arms, she sought to break away. The glittering tiara fell to the wood-grained laminate floor. "Let go of me!"

"Is this your game? You wanna play hard to get?" He began rubbing his body against hers.

"Work it!" Marlena yelled as Doris laughed and smacked his butt, then dug her fingers into his ass cheek.

"It's not a game. I really don't want this."

Ricochet pulled back, a stunned look on his face. He brushed the hair from his forehead, then dipped his head near her ear. "I'm sorry. I thought this is what you wanted. It's my standard with brides-to-be."

Cara smoothed down her dress. "I'm not into this, you know?"

He nodded and then swung around, giving his attention to Doris and Marlena as they groped him, laughing each time he thrust his hips. After a few minutes, Cara took out a couple twenty-dollar bills and handed them to him as he brushed past her on his way to join the other dancers. He nodded his thanks and jumped back on the stage.

She went back to the couch and plopped down, wondering what Hawk was doing at Dream House. *If Janelle gives him a lap dance, I'll be crushed. I just know I will. I wish I hadn't been such a bitch earlier.* Just the thought of any woman touching her man drove her crazy. She'd never been the jealous type, but with Hawk she was downright feral. Women were always coming on to him, and she loved the way he'd pay extra attention to her when they were. It wasn't that she didn't trust Hawk; it was more like she didn't trust the other women—of whom there were many. *Maybe I should've had the party at Hawk's house.*

"This wasn't such a good idea, was it?" Sherrie slipped in next to her, a margarita in her hand.

"Not really. It sounded a lot more fun when we were planning it." Cara pushed her drink away.

"I know. Well, at least Doris and Marlena are having fun." Sherrie and Cara watched as the two women swung their hips and wrapped their arms around a couple of the ripped dancers on stage. The two friends burst out laughing.

"Hey, I think Jen and I are going to leave," Lisa said as she leaned down and hugged Cara. "David was cool with me coming here, but even though he didn't say anything, I know he'll be pissed if I get home late."

"I'm glad you guys came out. I wish I was more into the show. Dinner was a blast," Cara said.

"You've got Hawk on your mind," Lisa replied.

Cara nodded. "Just like you've got David on yours and Sherrie has Jackson on hers." The women chuckled and then headed out. Soon Addie, Cherri, Baylee, Clotille, and Belle followed them. Doris, Marlena, and Bernie were having a ball, and Cara loved watching them let loose. Sherrie came back to the table with another margarita and a champagne cocktail for Cara.

She clinked her glass against Cara's. "Best friends forever. I'm so happy for you."

"I still can't believe Hawk's going to be my husband." She took a deep drink. "It's your turn next."

Sherrie beamed. "I'm working on it."

As the women watched a couple men gyrate and hump the pole, Cara's eye caught the flash on her phone. She looked down and saw Hawk was texting her.

Hawk: *Whatcha doing?*

Cara: *Not much. U?*

Hawk: *Wishing u were here.*

Cara: *Me 2.*

Hawk: *Sinner needs 2 talk 2 u. Go outside.*

Cara: *About what???*

Hawk: *Security.*

Cara: *Tell him I'll be there in a sec.*

Hawk: *K. See u later.*

Cara slid her phone into her small purse and finished her drink. "Hawk just texted me and told me the prospect wants to talk to me about something. I've got to go out and see what he wants. I'll be right back."

"I'm ready to go, so I'll walk out with you," Sherrie said.

Cara grabbed her wrap. "After I talk to Sinner I'm going to go home too. Doris, Marlena, and Bernie look like they're having a blast, so I don't think they'll even miss us." She and Sherrie walked out the front door together, Sherrie waving to her before she went to her car. Looking for Sinner, Cara's eyes fell on Hawk who leaned against his Harley, his legs crossed at his ankles. His tight T-shirt showed off his well-formed pecs and abs. A small smile pulled at his lips, and his brilliant blue eyes shone with desire and love. Tickles of desire spread through her, making her nipples stiffen.

"Hey," he said as he cocked his head. She wrapped her arms around her chest, her hardened nipples throbbing under the pressure. "You surprised to see me?"

She nodded. "But very happy." She walked over to him and flung her arms around his neck. "I thought about you all night."

"Did you? That's good 'cause I couldn't get you out of my mind. I had to see you, and when I walked in, I saw you sitting on the couch looking so damn miserable. I fuckin' loved it."

"I didn't see you come inside. Why didn't you come over?"

"I didn't wanna take away from the fun Doris, Marlena, and Bernie were having. Besides, I wanted to see you under the moonlight, not the cheesy lights in there."

She nuzzled his neck and breathed him in, loving the way he curled his arms around her and pressed her close. "I wish I wouldn't have gone.

Sherrie and I agreed this was a bust. Did you have fun?"

"It was good talkin' to the brothers, but I'd say my night was a bust too."

"Did you have your lap dance?" she mumbled into his skin.

"I chose Crystal." She held her breath and felt his chest vibrate against hers. "For Hoss."

She glanced up. "Crystal didn't dance for you? You didn't have a lap dance?"

He dipped his head and touched his lips to hers. "Not yet."

When she opened her mouth to ask him what he meant, his tongue slipped in and her insides short-circuited. Desire, arousal, and love tangled with one another as his mouth took hers roughly and possessively. He pulled back and placed his finger between his teeth, then ran it over her jawline and lips before pushing it into her mouth. She twirled her tongue around it and then sucked. "Fuck," he muttered under his breath. He withdrew his finger and, with one hand firmly clasped on her butt cheek, yanked her to him. Moving her hair to the side, he sank his mouth into the curve of her neck and shoulder and bit and kissed her skin. She moaned and tilted her head farther to the side, her fingers burying into his arms. The more he sucked her tender flesh, the weaker her knees got until she collapsed against him and he scooped her up in his arms.

"Let's go home, babe."

She nodded and buried her head against his chest, loving his familiar scent of leather, wind, and earth right after a rainstorm. She inhaled deeply, feeling warm, safe, and loved in his strong arms.

He kissed her forehead, and then his lips moved against it. "You okay to drive?"

No. I never want to leave your arms. I want to stay like this forever. She nodded and he carried her to her car in the parking lot. Opening her door, he placed her carefully on the leather seat like she was the most precious treasure in the world. She pulled his face to hers and kissed him hard and wet. His short breaths ignited a fire in her, and she wanted nothing more than for them to crawl in the backseat and rip each other's clothes off before they fucked like crazy.

He drew up and took her chin in his hand, tipping her head back so her eyes fixed on his. The heat in his eyes sent a pulse of desire between her legs. "I choose you to give me a lap dance, babe."

A devilish smile spread over her lips. "Then what are we waiting for? We better get going." She playfully shoved him away, closed the car door, and switched on the ignition. As she drove back to his place, she grinned each time she glanced in her rearview mirror and saw the single headlight of his Harley behind her. She couldn't wait to rub her body all over her man.

As soon as she entered the mud room, Hawk's hands greedily explored her body. Hungry shivers zinged through her body as he slid his hand under the hem of her dress. When his fingers grazed her pulsing sex, she moaned and pushed into them, craving their touch on her sweet spot. As they moved past her crotch, she missed them immediately, longing for his fingers to get lost between her swollen folds. She whimpered and kneaded her aching sex against his denim-clad leg. His chuckle came from deep in his chest. Then his hand cupped her breast and squeezed it, his thumb stroking her pointed nipple teasingly. It felt so good she wished he'd never stop. But he did, pulling away and leading her by the hand into the family room.

"Why'd you stop?" she asked in a strained voice.

"I want you nice and wet for my lap dance." He winked and kissed her cheek, then threw off his jacket and placed his cut carefully on the side table. Kicking off his biker boots, he stripped down to his boxers before settling on the couch.

"You love seeing me needy and desperate, don't you?"

He nodded, a grin spreading over his chiseled face. "You have no idea how fuckin' hot you look when you're horny, babe. I never get tired of seeing it."

She narrowed her eyes and put a hand on her hip. "Okay, so the rules are no touching the dancer. I can touch you and feel you, but your arms have to remain at your sides, just like in a real strip bar. Got it?"

"No way, babe. How the fuck am I gonna be able to control *that*?"

She shrugged. "You'd be expected to control yourself at Dream House, so just pretend you're there."

"Yeah, but I'm with *you*. With you rubbing all over me it's gonna be fuckin' hard, sweetie."

She licked her finger and ran it down his chest. "I love seeing you all hot and bothered."

He shook his head. "All right. Deal. But after we're done, you're mine."

"What song do you want?"

"I want 'Pour Some Sugar on Me.' Also, keep your heels and thigh-highs on. Have I told you that I love thigh-highs?"

She looked over her shoulder as she fumbled with the stereo. "Like only a million times. I have two drawers full of them." She giggled and pulled out one of Def Leppard's CDs. She slipped her dress over her head and switched on the song, then turned her back to him, loving the quivers as they trembled over her skin when she heard him suck in his breath. She wore sheer black thigh-highs with a lace band, a lacey black bra, and a thong that showed off her rounded globes perfectly.

The music filled the room as she tossed her long tresses in front of her face and then whipped her head back, making them cascade down her back. She bent forward slightly, looking back at Hawk coquettishly while she stroked and lightly slapped her ass. Hawk smiled as he crossed his hands behind his head, leaning into them. She bent lower until her ass pointed right at him as she grabbed her ankle and slowly ran her hand up the inside of her leg and thigh, all the while looking at him over her shoulder. She smacked her butt several times. His eyes smoldered with lust as they took all of her movements in.

Over the course of the song, she flung her bra at him, massaged her breasts, ground her ass against his bulging crotch, and rubbed herself over his thigh as they locked gazes, his chest heaving. When she placed her knees into the space in front of his crotch, straightened up, leaned into him, and slid slowly all the way down his body until she was kneeling on the floor in front of him, he grasped her shoulders and pulled her up. Startled, she yelped as he put her on his lap and hungrily sucked on her aching nipples, his hands running over her ass cheeks and up her back.

The song ended and the only sounds in the room were his sucking and her low moans as she arched her back, shoving more of her tits into his demanding mouth. "Fuck, babe. I can't get enough of your tits." His lips tickled her soft flesh. She pulled off his hair tie and raked her fingers through his long black hair, loving how it was soft as cotton.

When she bit his neck, he groaned and pushed her off his lap and onto her knees on the couch. "I gotta have you, babe. Now." He held her head down on the cushion and spread her legs open with his knee. Her ass was high in the air, the coolness teasing her wet sex. "Damn, you're wet. I fuckin' love that." He slid his fingers into her juices and she wriggled her behind as jolts of white-hot pleasure arced through her. "Oh baby." His low, hungry moan drove her arousal higher, and she couldn't wait to have him buried inside her.

"I love you so much, honey. I need to feel you inside me."

"I'm so fuckin' in love with you. I'm enjoying your body first, and then I'll give you what you want." He lay down on the sofa, his head between her knees, and guided her down so her pussy sat right above his mouth. His warm tongue on her wet clit made her wiggle from want. "You like that?" he said against her swollen folds.

"I love it."

As he sucked her wet clit, his tongue flicking against her hardened bud, she arched her back, pushing her hungry pussy into his mouth. She cupped her breasts, massaging them and pinching her throbbing points as the tension coiled tighter at her core.

After what seemed like forever, he slid out from under her and gently turned her around to face him. With his hand behind her head, he drew her face to his for a long, passionate kiss, and she tasted her juices on his tongue.

He tilted his head back and their gazes locked. "Do you want me to fuck you?" he whispered as he ran his finger up and down her wet mound.

"Yes. Please," she whimpered, her body on fire and in desperate need of him inside her.

He kissed her again and then eased her down on the couch. She reached out for him and he dipped his head down and covered her mouth with his before trailing his tongue down her throat, past her breastbone, and across her ribs. When his tongue swirled inside her belly button, goose bumps peppered her skin, and she felt like she was on fire from the inside out.

Hawk's tongue continued its journey down to her inner thighs, teasing her with soft taps and strokes. He stood up and stripped off his boxers before quickly returning to searing her flesh. His hard dick poked her legs and she reached down and grabbed it, running her thumb over the smooth head as she smeared his pre-cum over it. He grunted and then glided his tongue over to her needy sex, licking it as he inserted a finger into her heated slit. She bucked underneath him.

"You're so fuckin' wet for me," he said against her skin.

"I've been wet for you since I came out of the club and saw you leaning all sexy-like against your Harley. Now will you please fuck me?"

He laughed and inserted another finger inside her; she squirmed and clenched her wet walls around his digits. As he pulled his fingers in and out, she rode them, desperate to come. His wicked tongue kept stroking her impossibly hard nub, and she tried in vain to close her legs so she could fuck his fingers better.

As if he sensed her utter neediness and frustration, he took out his fingers, spread her legs more, and then guided his cock inside her. She moaned and he lay still, his smoldering eyes locking onto hers as he slowly withdrew and then entered her harder and deeper. He increased the pace as he thrust in and out of her, his mouth covering hers. Cara clung to him, her own body matching his pace and rhythm.

"That feels real good, babe," he said against her lips.

"I love it. Go harder. Give me all you have."

Then his hand was in her hair, pulling and yanking so tight that tears slipped out of the corners of her eyes as she reveled in the delicious pain. He leaned down again and kissed her deeply before pulling back, pushing her knees up near her ears, and pummeling her pussy. Hard. Fast. His breath was coming in heavy, ragged gasps.

"Grab my ass," she panted, and he did. Hard. As he squeezed her cheeks, a fire raged through her. She glanced up and met his gaze; it was filled with love, passion, and desire, and she lost it. A cloud of euphoric release engulfed her, and as she yelled out, his mouth covered hers, muffling her moans of pleasure. As her climax began to descend, she felt him stiffen before his feral grunts rippled through her from her lips down to her toes. She held him tightly as he sank down on her, panting near her ear. She stretched out her legs and curled a long ebony strand around her fingers.

"Am I hurting you, babe?" he asked in a gravelly voice.

"No. I like the warmth of your body covering mine."

He kissed the side of her face. "That was fuckin' incredible."

"It was. You always know exactly what I crave."

"It's because we're one with each other—heart, body, and soul. You know you're my soulmate, right? I used to hear people say that a lot when I was out in the citizens' world, but I never knew what they were talking about. I just saw it as a crock of shit. But I know now. Fuck, baby. When I first saw you at Rusty's, I knew in my gut that something was different about you. I felt a connection to you I've never felt with anyone, not even my brothers."

"I felt it too, but it scared the shit out of me." Cara laughed.

Hawk sat up and pulled her close to him. "I didn't know what the fuck it was, and it pissed me way the hell off." He stroked her head. "But I know now. You're the only one for me. We connect on every level, and we do it deeply. It still fuckin' blows my mind."

"I feel the same way. Even when we argue and you piss me off, I still have a deep love and connection to you. It never occurs to me that we won't be together forever."

"You piss me off too. And you're right. I know that it's just part of life, but I know I could never live without you. I need you in my life. One of the things I love about you is you give me a challenge."

"That's good to know." She laughed. "You're not exactly easygoing, but I feel that our differences and challenges just strengthen us."

He kissed the top of her head. "You said it, babe. The fuckin' best thing is that just holding your hand or smelling your perfume throws me into a whirlwind. Fuck, I love you so much."

"Me too. You're my soulmate as well," she said, her voice breaking.

"What the fuck's wrong?" He put his hand under her chin and tilted her head back, his gaze scrutinizing hers. "You crying?"

She dipped her head down. "No, I'm just happy. I can't believe you just said everything that you did. You usually don't talk about your feelings. It just touched me, that's all."

"Just because I don't always voice my thoughts doesn't mean I don't have them."

"It was nice to hear." She craned her neck and kissed him on his chin. "What do you say about me making popcorn and us watching a movie?"

"Sounds good. By the time the movie's over I'll be ready to take you up to bed and make love to you, slow and gentle."

"Mmm… I like that. Let me wash off my makeup and change and I'll be back down. You pick the movie. After all, it's your bachelor party." She jumped up from the couch.

As she walked past him, he swatted her ass. "And a fuckin' awesome one it turned out to be."

She chortled and sprinted up the stairs. *And I thought this night was a bust. I was so fucking wrong about that.* She grinned and went into the bedroom to change.

CHAPTER FOURTEEN

THE SCENT OF rain hung heavy in the morning air as Cara watched the blue sky being overtaken by the grayness climbing over the mountain tops. In the distance the low growl of thunder rumbled. She opened her garage door and pulled her car in, noting that she really had to get someone over to haul off all the junk in there before the closing of her home the following month. Cara and Hawk used to spend weeknights at her place and weekends at his, but over the past six months she'd stayed more at Hawk's and less at her place. She tried to come by once a week to pick up her mail and check on the house, but she'd been so busy with the wedding plans, their new house, and work that it'd been almost three weeks since she'd last been there.

She switched on the kitchen light, went over to the refrigerator, and took out a bottle of water. Unscrewing the top, she took a long drink and then went into the hallway. Envelopes and magazines sprawled over her hardwood foyer, and she stooped down to pick up three weeks of mail. She went into the living room, sank down on a cushy chair, and began to sort through her mail.

A white, legal-sized envelope caught her attention since it bore the seal of the Department of Justice. She ripped open the envelope and saw it was from the Victim Notification System. It was a department that interacted with victims of violent crimes, informing them if an inmate had been released or escaped. She scanned it, her hand flying to her chest as a sudden coldness hit at her core. *What the fuck! Is this right?* She read the phrase "Rob Pinter, aka Viper, has escaped…" over and over, all the other words blurring around it. Her stomach lurched and the letter fell from her hands, fluttering down at her feet. She darted her eyes around the house. *Viper's out there. What if he's in my house? Oh God. What am I gonna do?* She gulped in air in an attempt to calm her racing heart. *Be logical. The alarm was on. How could he be in the house if the alarm was on?* She threw open the front door and motioned to Sinner to come over. At first the prospect held back, indecision etched on his face.

"Sinner, Hawk's fine if you talk to me. I have a problem. I need you to come to the porch. Please."

After a few seconds, the lanky young man walked up the sidewalk and stood by the porch. "What's the problem?"

"I need for you to come inside with me and make sure all the windows are locked." His eyebrows shot up, but he didn't ask her why; rather, he did as she asked and walked quietly through the house, checking locks and closets. When he was finished, he tilted his head at her and went outside, sitting on the front step.

Cara grabbed her phone and dialed Bob Boles, the United States Attorney who prosecuted Viper's case. On the fourth ring he picked up. "Why the hell wasn't I notified sooner that Viper had escaped? I signed up for notification by phone and mail, and no one from the DOJ called me? That's bullshit. What the hell are they doing to catch this psycho?"

"Whoa, Cara. I swear I was going to call you this afternoon. I'm actually headed to a hearing. I just found out myself. Someone in the notification department fucked up. I'm sorry."

"Do they have any idea where he is?"

"They thought he'd head to his brother's in Kansas or his sister's down in Texas, but there's no sign of him."

"Do they know if he's in Pinewood Springs?" she whispered as the image of the tall shadow she'd seen the night she and Sherrie had eaten out flitted across her mind. She shivered.

"They've been watching for him there too. No show. I suspect he's laying low until the heat dies down. Someone's hiding him. The Feds have even staked out the Deadly Demons in New Mexico, but no sign of him."

She chewed her nail as she bounced her knee up and down. "They've got to find him. He's only been out a couple weeks, and more than ninety-five percent of escapees get caught within the first month. They have to get him. This is awful. My wedding is in two weeks."

"Please calm down. Hawk will know how to protect you. Be extra careful. We all know what he's capable of. I'm really sorry, but I gotta go, I'll call you later."

When she clicked off her phone, her body started to shake, and she tried in vain to keep her teeth from chattering. She grabbed her mail and tossed it in her tote, then went to the front door. She saw the prospect staring out at the street. "Sinner, I'm locking up now. I'll be in my car in a few minutes." The man nodded and stood up, ambling toward his Harley. Cara checked all the locks on the doors and windows again, then engaged the alarm and climbed into her car. She drove out of the garage and turned her vehicle in the direction of Hawk's shop.

As she drove, the incident with the rat in the parking lot assaulted her mind. *I know he had a hand in that. How did he escape?* Her hands shook and she gripped the steering wheel tighter. This was her worst nightmare coming back to haunt her all over again. She sighed loudly, glancing at the rearview mirror. Having Sinner following her gave her a bit of peace, but she knew Viper was cunning. She also knew he was going to come and get her.

She dashed into Hawk's motorcycle repair shop, and Patrick glanced up from his phone and smiled when he recognized her. "You here for Hawk?"

"Yes. Is he in his office?"

"No. He's in the bays." He started to get up when the metal door swung open and Kimber came in. Her face was misted in sweat.

When she saw Cara, she smiled and said, "Hey. I never see you here. Have you recovered from Saturday night?" She laughed.

"Yeah, I'm good. Can you do me a favor and tell Hawk I'm here? I have to talk to him about something."

Cara turned away when Kimber scanned her face. "Everything okay? You look kinda sick and nervous."

"I'm good. Can you please tell Hawk?"

"Sure. Hang on a sec. Good seeing you." She went back through the metal doors.

Cara felt bad that she wasn't too friendly with Kimber, but she couldn't bring herself to chitchat when Viper was on the loose.

Hawk walked through the door, wiping his hands on a rag. He wrinkled his brow as he approached her.

"Are you okay, babe?" he asked her.

She shook her head. "Let's go into your office. I have something to tell you." She walked ahead of him until they went into his office.

He leaned against his desk. "What's wrong? You look like you're scared to death."

"I am," she said in a low voice. "I got a letter informing me that Viper escaped over two weeks ago. I called the prosecutor and he was just—"

"What the fuck? That motherfucker is out? Why the hell didn't they call you? Those goddamned badges."

"The DOJ screwed up. I was supposed to be notified by mail and phone if he was ever released or escaped. I just can't believe it."

Hawk's jaw clenched so tight that she could see the muscles twitching. He reached out for her and drew her into his arms. "It'll be okay. I gotta talk with the brothers about this. For now, I'll get another prospect to watch you. You know you'll probably have to stay at the club."

"How can I? I have a trial this week and a damn wedding coming up. How can this be happening? I worked so hard through months of therapy to get past the horror of that night. That one dark night changed me forever, but I was finally able to get past it. Now the demon has resurfaced. How am I going to get through this?" She buried her head in his chest so he wouldn't see the tears spilling from her eyes.

"I'll get you through it. I'll find the sonofabitch and kill him. I should've done it that night." He kissed her head and squeezed her tight. "Don't cry, babe. I had your back the last time, and I have it now. The fucker is as good as dead."

His words stroked her while his arms cocooned her, making her feel safe. She pushed down the fear and got lost in his scent, his strength, and his love. *Hawk will make sure everything's fine. The Insurgents will find Viper. Everything will be okay. I have Hawk.* She snuggled closer to him and snuck a peek at him. His expression was tight, his lips were flat, and a stormy darkness raged in his eyes as he stared out the window. She trembled and hugged him firmly, desperately trying to ward off the feelings of impending doom.

"VIPER'S ESCAPED FROM prison, and I know he's zeroing in on me and my woman. The fucker has some assholes trailing her, or at least he did. Having Sinner tail Cara has discouraged it, but there's no fuckin' way the bastard is gonna abandon his plans." Hawk's nostrils flared as he addressed his brothers in an emergency church.

"He's gotta be getting help from somewhere. No way he'd be able to hide out this long without it." Rock crossed his arms over his chest.

"The fucker's not getting it from the Deadly Demons. Reaper's still pissed at him and his gang for cheating them out of hundreds of thousands of dollars. I agree with Rock though. The loser's got someone helpin' him out. He couldn't have escaped on his own."

"And where would he get the money to do it? You know he had to have bribed someone to get out of the joint. Maybe it's another club." Bones leaned back in his chair.

"That's what I think. And the club would have to hate the Insurgents' asses in order to help Viper out. They'd be taking a big risk, and giving money to some scum who'll never repay them? The motivation for aiding the asshole has to be pure hatred." Hawk scanned the faces of his brothers, pride swelling within him when he saw their anger and determination. They were ready to jump in and come to the aid of his old lady without any discussion.

"That gives us some possibilities," Banger said.

"The first ones who come to mind are Dustin and Shack. Fuck, the whole Iowa Demon Riders chapter has wanted to mess with us since the Denver expo. Dustin and Shack have been chomping at the bit to bust Hawk's and Banger's balls." Chas scrubbed his face with his fist.

"Don't forget the goddamn Skull Crushers. They've hated us since we sent three of their brothers to a better place and kicked their ass. You should get ahold of Steel in Alina and see if he's noticed some tall fuck hanging with the skinheads." Jax took a gulp of his beer.

Hawk nodded. "I'll call Steel after church. I wouldn't be surprised if the fucker was getting help from both clubs, but my guess is the Demon Riders are in this all the way. I can smell their shit from here."

"I'm with Hawk and Chas on this. Dustin and Shack won't ever forget gettin' their asses thrown outta the club. Question is what the fuck are we gonna do about it?" Banger leaned against the wall.

"I'm gonna ask the club to provide security for my wedding in a couple weeks. It'd be just like these assholes to crash it. I can't risk it," Hawk said. When all the brothers voiced their solidarity, he swallowed the lump forming in his throat. "And I'm gonna need another prospect to watch Cara when I'm not there. She's got a trial starting tomorrow, but I'm gonna insist that she stay at the club until the wedding."

"I'll tell Pike to help Sinner out. We can't afford to have more than that. Fuck, we've gotta be on high alert. Who knows what this fucker is gonna do?" said Banger.

"I know fuckass is vying for Cara, and he's doing it to get to me. I should've killed the motherfucker when I had him that night. I could shoot my own ass for not doing that." Hawk kicked the leg of the table.

"Dude, we all have shit we wished we would've done differently. We're gonna get this fucker, along with Dustin and Shack. I can't wait to bust some heads." The membership voiced their agreement with Rock, and soon everyone was talking about someone's ass they should've beaten or killed. The frenetic energy around the room made Hawk and Banger laugh.

After church was adjourned, Hawk thanked his brothers for their support, downed a couple shots, and left the clubhouse. He wanted to be with Cara. He knew she was upset, and he figured she'd go ballistic when she found out that her pretty little ass was moving into the clubhouse the following day. And to top it all off, he'd have to break it to her that their wedding was gonna involve more than the few bikers who were going to be in the wedding party. He grimaced. *She's gonna fuckin' lose it. I should've killed your skinny ass, Viper.*

He tilted his head at Sinner and Pike when he pulled into the driveway. The two prospects switched on their bikes and rode away. When he entered the family room, he saw Cara's head resting against the back cushion of the couch. He padded over to her, dipped his head down, and kissed her on her lips. "Hey, babe. You feeling better?"

She wrapped her arms around his neck, tugging his face closer to hers. "Not really, but now that you're here, I do. I still can't believe he's out there... somewhere." She shivered. "I'm still pissed like hell that the DOJ didn't call me. That's bullshit." She kissed him, then murmured against his lips, "Come sit by me." She let go of his neck and patted the spot beside her.

Hawk came around the couch, shrugged off his jacket, and plopped down next to her. He put his arm around her shoulder and drew her close to him. "It's gonna be okay. We'll get the fucker. To think that you were in that danger and I didn't know he was loose makes me all kinds of crazy." He kissed the side of her head.

She nestled into him. "I'm glad that you insisted on steel shutters that we can roll down and steel roll-down doors for our new house. I thought you were just being paranoid, especially after you insisted that all windows be bulletproof."

"You can never be too sure in my world." He lifted her hand and kissed it tenderly. "Anyway, I gotta be sure my family is safe."

She craned her neck up and smiled at him. "You're good about doing that."

He placed his hand on her belly, drawing circles on it. "I can't wait to see our baby growing inside you. You're gonna be the hottest pregnant woman in Pinewood Springs." She laughed and kissed his chin.

"You know you can stop using the pill. We're gonna get hitched in a couple of Saturdays."

"So you want to start having a family right away? You don't want to be newlyweds for a while?"

"Fuck no, babe. We've been playing newlyweds for almost two years. You know that when I asked you to wear my patch, for me, it was like we got married. I don't wanna look like our kids' grandpa when they're born." He twirled a few strands of her hair around his finger.

"You'd look like a sexy grandpa, and I'd have to beat off all the old ladies who'd want to get in your pants." She laughed and he swatted her playfully on her arm. "I'm totally fine with starting a family right away. I'll stop my birth control."

"I can't wait to see our baby. I can't wait to rub and kiss your big belly. Fuck, just thinking about it makes me hot."

She giggled and wrapped her arm around his waist, then tucked her legs under her butt. They sat there holding each other for a long time before Hawk cleared his throat. "Babe, I gotta talk to you about some things."

"What things?" She pulled away from him and brought her knees to her chest, wrapping her arms around them. "Tell me."

"We gotta stay at the clubhouse. It's the only way I know you're one hundred percent safe. I know you've got a trial starting tomorrow, but we'll spend our nights at the club and I'll take you to and from work. Sinner and Pike will keep watch while I'm at the shop." He placed his finger on her lips to silence her protests. "It's the best way. I don't want anything to happen to you, and the club is fuckin' secure. It's gotta be that way for now."

She breathed out. "For how long?"

"I don't know. We're gonna be gone for almost three weeks on our honeymoon, so hopefully either the fuckin' badges or the Insurgents will have taken the asshole down."

"And if they haven't?" she asked in a low voice.

"We'll deal with that when we get back."

"Okay. I just want a nice wedding where we can put all the violence and nightmares aside for one day."

"Yeah, well… about that. The brothers are gonna be there for security at the church and reception."

She stiffened. "What? Oh crap. My mother's going to die."

"She may not be the only one if we don't have security. There's no way I'm trusting anyone but the brothers to handle this. They'll make sure they're discreet." He caught her gaze. "I'm sorry." He tugged her arm and drew her close to him. "It has to be done."

"I know. I was just hoping this was all a dream. I'll tell my parents."

As he held her, a cold clamminess looped around his muscles and veins. His stomach was rock-hard. He'd faced a lot of shit in his life, and he'd always swallowed the fear and did what he had to do. He'd always figured death was a part of life and knew it sometimes came sooner than later. But now that Cara was in his life, he was experiencing the fear of losing someone he loved for the first time ever. *I love her so much that I can't imagine my life without her. She's my woman, my friend, and the future mother of our kids. Fuck! I gotta keep her safe.*

As if she heard his thoughts, Cara tilted her head back and locked her eyes on his. "I love you so much. We'll get through this. I trust you with my forever."

He squeezed her and gently pushed her head on his shoulder. In that moment he knew she'd always be his heart and his life, and no one or nothing could ever change that.

CHAPTER FIFTEEN

THE PAST WEEK had been a whirlwind of emotions and activity. Cara had to juggle her trial and last-minute wedding details while building the courage to tell her mother about the biker security team that would be at the church and reception. She sighed as she got out of her car and walked up to her childhood home. She unlocked the door and went inside.

"Mom, I'm here." She kicked off her heels in the foyer and went to the sunroom. The room had always been her favorite one in the house, and she spent many hours reading in there when she was a child and teen. She loved the large windows and the way the sunlight filtered in.

"You look exhausted, dear." Her mother sat down on the cushy love seat across from her.

Cara smiled. Her mother always looked so put together, no matter if she was just staying home or attending a charity ball. She marveled at her skill in doing that. "I am. This trial is grueling."

"Why you would've taken on a trial right before your wedding is beyond me. Would you like some iced tea?"

Cara held up a bottle of water. "No, thanks, I'm good. I didn't choose to do the trial. The court picks the dates. My client has speedy trial rights. Anyway, I just finished delivering my closing argument. It's in the jury's hands now."

"I hope you'll lessen some of your load once you get married. Hawk has enough money to support you, and you'll be busy with charity events. I have a couple boards I think you should be on."

She smiled while she clenched her teeth. Her mom always thought of her as *playing* lawyer. She brought the bottled water to her lips and took a sip. "Viper's escaped from prison."

"Viper? Is that a friend of Hawk's?"

She laughed. "Hardly. You remember the one who attacked me that night in the shed?"

Her mother's face paled. "*Him?*" Her fingers flew to her parted lips.

"Yeah. I received the letter a week ago. I didn't want to freak you and Dad out. Anyway, Hawk and I don't trust this scumbag not to do anything at our wedding, so Hawk's having some of the guys from the Insurgents club do security duty."

"What does that mean?"

"They'll be present at the church and reception. They'll be as discreet as possible. I'm afraid it's a necessary inconvenience, Mom. It'd be awful if something bad happened. We both know what that animal is capable of."

Her mother sat mutely, watching her. The creases around the top of her nose wrinkled as she looked everywhere but at her daughter.

"I know this is upsetting, Mom, but isn't it better than the wedding being ruined? I don't want anyone to get hurt, and I know you don't either."

Cathy Minelli wrung her hands, then folded them in her lap. "If this isn't reason enough to call off your wedding and meet a man who doesn't have evil men after his fiancée, then I don't know what is. Do you *really* want to live a life where you're always looking over your shoulder for the next lowlife to attack you? Is this the way your father and I raised you?"

Her insides twisted. "I didn't cross paths with Viper because of Hawk or his club. It was because of Eric and his association with him, you know that." Whenever she said her cousin's name a mixture of love and hate weaved through her. "Hawk is keeping me safe, Mom. His whole club is, and he's perfect for me. I couldn't have asked for a better man to spend the rest of my life with."

"I still can't imagine you with a *biker*. I simply don't understand it."

Cara pressed her lips together. "I just wanted to let you know so you wouldn't wonder who all the men were. Shouldn't we get the supplies for the *confetti*? Maria will be here soon." She rose to her feet, happy to have diverted the conversation in another direction. She was looking forward to her cousin coming over to prepare the *bomboniere* for the wedding. Adhering to Italian tradition, colorful sugar-coated candies—*confetti*—were placed in white tulle bags called *bomboniere* and then secured with white ribbons which had their names and date of the wedding on them. Ever since she was a little girl, Cara loved sucking off the sugar coating before biting into the almond.

With an exaggerated sigh, her mother stood up and followed Cara to the kitchen. When they were setting out the candies, bags, and ribbons, her mother yelped. Cara swung around. "What happened?" Concern flooded her face.

"There are two men lurking outside. What if one of them is that Viper man? They look mean and nasty."

Cara's face paled and she rushed over to the window, then giggled. Relief washed over her as she spotted Sinner and Pike coming back from patrolling the house. "No worries, Mom. They're the two prospects from the club who are keeping an eye on me when Hawk's not around."

The color slowly came back in her mother's face. "Oh, Cara. How can you put up with all this?"

Saved by the doorbell, Cara padded to the front door and greeted her cousin with a hug. "You came just in time. I told my mom about Viper and having to have bikers guard my wedding. And she just saw the two prospects."

Maria chuckled. "Oh shit."

"Are you ready to tie three hundred bags of *confetti*?"

"As long as you keep the wine flowing, I can tie a thousand of them." She hooked her arm in Cara's and they walked into the kitchen.

BY THE TIME Cara slid into her car, waving to her mom and dad, she didn't want to see another sugar-coated almond candy ever again. She

massaged her right shoulder lightly and then started the car. Her parents had insisted she stay with them, but she didn't want to drag them into the mess with Viper. The minute her dad had come home from the office that evening, her mom had run to him and told him everything. Of course he was concerned, but Cara assured him that Hawk was the best bodyguard she could ever have. He agreed, but worry clouded his eyes and she cursed Viper for causing her parents pain. She hoped he'd be back in prison by the time she and Hawk returned from their honeymoon.

Before she exited the car, Hawk was standing by it looking sexy as hell. She could never get enough of his muscular body and handsome face. Sometimes she'd catch her breath when he'd enter a room, his blue eyes framed by dark lashes pulling her in each time. Other times, her heart would pound and tingles would shimmy up her spine when she'd take in his tight biceps, the piercing eyes of the hawk tattoo on his forearm, and his long, ebony hair. *How I love running my fingers through your hair and then over your flexing biceps.* Just looking at him watching her as she came out of the car made her panties dampen.

She flung her arms around him, inhaling his familiar scent. "I've missed you." She kissed his collarbone.

He tangled his fist in her hair and pulled her head back, then captured her mouth in a hard and messy kiss. "Me too," he said against her reddened lips. "Did you have a good visit with your parents?"

"Yeah. Maria came by and we made hundreds of bags filled with candies. My shoulder and neck are so sore."

He placed his hand on her shoulder and kneaded it. "Fuck, babe. You're tense as hell. Let's go up to our room and I'll rub out the kinks. I thought we could get a pizza."

"Do they deliver at the clubhouse?"

He chuckled. "Nah. I'll have Buzz pick it up for us. I'm pretty beat. Too damn much work at the shop. I'm glad I have Dwayne and Kimber to rely on when we're on our trip."

She snuggled against his chest and he circled his arms around her

waist. "I can't wait to get away from here for a while. It'll be wonderful not to think about Viper, bodyguards, clients who don't listen, and all the other crap that goes on. It's just going to be you and me, hanging out at the beach watching the Mediterranean ripple under the sun. It can't come soon enough for me."

"I'm with you, babe. Three weeks of you all to myself is gonna fuckin' rock." He brushed her hair aside and kissed her neck. "Did your trial end?"

"That feels good, honey." She cocked her head closer to her shoulder to give him better access to the sensitive spots that he knew so well. "The case went to the jury at four o'clock. All I can hope for is that they convict him of a lesser charge."

"Not too confident about your persuasive arguments?" His tongue licked up and down her neck.

She moaned. "Uh… it's not that. It's that the evidence was so strong. I told him to take the plea, but he wanted his day in court. Oh, honey… that feels so good." He nipped at her soft skin, and when he took her earlobe between his teeth, her insides melted. "Let's go inside."

"You don't like the crisp air and the fuckin' awesome hickory scent that's coming from the grill in the yard?" His hands were on her breasts, kneading them as his thumbs brushed back and forth over her stiff nipples. Hawk kissed her wet and soft all over her shoulder.

She groaned and clenched her legs together. "What is it with you guys and barbecue? I love it… but every night?"

"It's fuckin' good and easy to make. I'd like to slather you in barbecue sauce and lick every bit of it off you." He pressed her closer to him, his hard dick pushing against her lower back. "Would you like that?"

She wriggled her butt into him. "Sounds like it would be sweet and sticky."

"Just the way I like it." His wandering fingers glided down her stomach to the waistband of her jeans. He popped open the button and pulled the zipper down, then slid his hand over her purple-striped cotton panties. "You're wet, babe." His chuckle hit her beaded nipples and went

straight to her aching sex. He scratched the outside of her panties over and over and she arched her back and pressed her head deeper into his chest. The pulse of his erection pushed her arousal, and he kept flicking his finger back and forth over her wet panties.

"Oh, Hawk, that feels so good." She was glad that they were in the shadows of the big pine trees that lined the far corner of the parking lot. Most of the brothers were in the great room or in the yard, so her pleasure was private. When he slipped his finger into her slick folds, her clit throbbed under his touch, begging for more. She bucked toward his hand, grinding against it until his finger found her sweet spot, and he flicked it in steady strokes.

"Oh, Hawk. Fuck!" she panted as the tension built. When he pinched her nub, her orgasm tore through her in wave after wave of relief. Her legs were jelly; had Hawk's arms not been around her she would've slid to the ground.

"You're so beautiful," he whispered in her ear. The scent of whiskey and the warmth of his breath on her neck weaved around her. On wobbly legs, she whirled around and collapsed against him, feathering his neck and face with kisses. He scooped her up and walked toward the clubhouse.

The smokiness burned her eyes when they went inside. Loud music bounced off the walls, and Cara saw a few of the brothers clapping and egging Lola and Rosie on as they danced half-naked on the bar. She burrowed her head into the crook of Hawk's neck, her arms snug around him. In the hallway, he asked for Buzz. The rumble of his deep voice vibrated against her and she found comfort from it.

"Whatdaya need?" Buzz asked.

She felt him shift her to the side as he took his wallet out of his back pocket. "Here's forty bucks. Go to Gennaro's and get us an extra-large pepperoni, mushroom, and sausage pizza. You want salad, babe?" His hot breath tickled her face. She nodded. "An antipasto salad with creamy Italian dressing. Keep the change."

"Sure. You want me to bring it up to your room?"

"Yeah." Turning, he climbed the stairs until they reached his room on the third floor. He opened the door and kicked it shut, then gently placed Cara on his bed. He leaned over and kissed her. "You fuckin' rock my world. You're my sweet wildcat." He winked at her. "I'm gonna take a shower. We'll eat and have a few beers, and then I'm gonna fuck and make sweet love to you for the rest of the night."

A large smile broke over her mouth. "Sounds like the perfect night."

When he closed the bathroom door, she got up and changed into her flannel pajama bottoms and a short, long-sleeved pajama top. *I can't get enough of him. He's my everything.* At that moment, Viper's cruel, dark eyes flashed through her mind, and she shuddered. *I wish this wasn't happening. I hope they catch him soon.* Icy fear replaced the warmth she'd felt in Hawk's arms just minutes before. *Where the hell is that asshole? Not knowing is the worst.*

She turned on the TV and grabbed a Sherpa blanket off the foot of the bed, wrapping it tightly around her as she leaned against the headboard. *They'll find him before he hurts us. They have to.*

She stared blankly at the flickering screen, anxious for Hawk to come back to her so she could snuggle in his arms and pretend bad people like Viper didn't exist, even if it were only for one night.

"SO THE CUNT'S been moved to the clubhouse. Guess she found out about me." Viper laughed dryly. Picturing the bitch scared out of her mind gave him a rush of pleasure. He loved it when women were scared of him, the terror in their eyes the biggest turn-on for him. Hawk's whore needed to be used hard. It was because of her that he was in prison. The snoopy cunt had everything he was going to give her coming to her. He'd dreamed of this moment for so long. The best part was she didn't know when he was going to come for her. Hawk didn't either, and that made the cat and mouse game even more enjoyable. He'd hated Hawk for years, but when he saw the look in his eyes the night he busted into the shed and he saw the bitch on her knees with his dick in her mouth, he knew he'd found Hawk's weakness. And when a man had a weakness for a woman, it rendered him irrational and an easy target.

"Her man's added another prospect to watch her," Tommie said.

"I figured he'd do that. I bet security's gonna be tight at the wedding. All the Insurgent fuckers will be out in full force."

"Yep. Doesn't seem too smart to strike at that time, does it?"

"Shut the fuck up. I don't need any input from a loser like you." Viper hated working with amateurs, but he didn't have a choice under the circumstances. Once he killed the slut and the goddamned VP, he'd be able to get far away. He would not return to prison. If he had to kill every fucking cop, he'd do it. There was no way he was going back.

"I wasn't telling you what to do." Tommie's voice cracked with tension. "It's just that Pierson and Skip were wondering when they were gonna get the rest of the money. We all have debts we need to settle. I got some fuckass breathing down my neck."

"That's your fuckin' problem, isn't it? You'll get paid the rest of the money when the job is done. Don't fuckin' bring it up to me again, or I'll have to end our association." Viper put a cigarette between his thin lips and lit it. He had no intention of ever paying the three stooges. Once he'd exacted his revenge, the men were dead. He would never leave any fucking witnesses.

"It's just that the guys were asking. When are you gonna strike?"

Viper blew out, a cloud of smoke swirling around him. "You don't catch on too fast, do you, dumbfuck? You don't need to know the details. Just do what the fuck I tell you to and we'll be cool. Questions are not something you need to be askin'. We'll talk soon." Viper clicked off his phone. *Where the fuck did Dustin find these motherfuckin' morons?* He lifted his legs and plopped them on the table in front of him. He was antsy as hell, wanting to get all this shit over so he could move on. The Demon Riders' clubhouse was okay, but he wanted to get the hell out of the country so he didn't always have to look over his shoulder. He knew patience was his trump card, and before he went to prison, he would have been climbing the walls and busting some heads until he'd be able to strike the bitch and Hawk. Sitting his ass in prison for the past two years taught him how to plan, prepare, wait, and then strike. So he'd wait. A false sense of security would be his weapon, and the takedown would be that much sweeter.

He leaned his head against the wall and blew smoke rings in the air.

I'm coming for you, bitch. I'm gonna finish what your fuckin' old man stopped me from doing. Only this time, you and me will have all the time in the world to really get to know each other. He wet his lips as images of what he planned to do to the cunt consumed his mind.

It was the perfect way to spend a rainy afternoon.

Chapter Sixteen

"I DON'T HAVE a fuckin' clue how to get this shit around my waist. And these damn studs are a pain in the ass. Are you having any luck with yours?" Hawk tugged and pulled at his tuxedo shirt.

"I'm just as fuckin' clueless as you, dude. What the fuck was your old lady thinking making us wear this shit? Give me denim and leather any damn day." Throttle threw down his cummerbund.

Banger chuckled. "You sure as fuck are marrying a princess. You're in for a helluva ride, brother. I bet we'll need a diagram at dinner to figure out which fork outta the hundred that we'll have is the right one to use. Fuck this shit."

Jax and Bear grumbled their agreement.

Hawk scowled at Banger. "Will you stop with the fuckin' comments and get Belle over here to help us figure this out? The limo's gonna be here soon and none of us are fuckin' ready."

"Blame Cara for that. She's the one who picked out these nerd suits," Jax said.

Banger picked up his phone and called his wife. While he was talking to her, Jax and Bear complained about the patent leather dress shoes they had on. "Why the fuck do they make shoes so damn uncomfortable?" Bear sat down and placed his feet on the coffee table.

"Belle's on her way. I'm gonna have a beer. All this dressing has made me thirsty. It's a goddamn workout."

"Agreed. Grab one for each of us," Throttle said.

"I don't want one. I just wish I could figure this out. Fuck. I just came up with a software for bike repair shops, and I can't even get these studs and cufflinks on right. What the fuck?" Hawk threw down the box on the couch and paced.

"Tomorrow's wedding's gonna be much simpler. Bikes, jeans, barbecue feast, shots of Jack, and hard rock music. *That's* what a wedding's supposed to be." Jax reached out for his beer when Banger came back into the room.

"I hear ya, but this is important to Cara. She and her mom have been planning this day since she was a kid. If it was up to me, the biker wedding would do it, but I know Cara wants this."

"A princess, like I said. Fuck, you're gonna have to be on your toes for the next fifty years, dude." Banger laughed and popped open his can of beer.

Hawk nodded. "She's fuckin' worth it." He watched his brothers guzzling their beer and stretching out on the chairs. "Oh hell, I'm gonna grab a beer. Anyone want another one?" All three brothers grunted, and Hawk ambled to the kitchen. When he came back into the living room, Belle's sparkling blue eyes greeted him. "Hey, Belle. Glad you're here."

A big smile filled her face. "You guys having trouble dressing?"

Banger circled his arm around her and kissed her hard. "I'd rather have you undressing me," he said, and the men sniggered when Belle blushed two shades of red.

After twenty minutes, the groom and the four groomsmen were dressed and ready when the limousine driver rang the doorbell. Banger was Hawk's best man and Jax, Bear, and Throttle would stand by their brother and friend during the marriage ceremony, alongside Cara's cousin, Tony.

By the time they arrived at Saint Dominick's, several people were there who he didn't recognize. He presumed they were Cara's relatives; he knew many had come up from Denver. She had such a big family on her dad's side that he'd given up a long time ago trying to remember everyone's name and how they fit into the family tree.

Cara's dad came over to Hawk and shook his hand. "I'll show you where you can wait until the action begins."

As the men followed, Throttle said in a low voice, "I hope there's a bottle of Jack in the room. I could use a shot. What about you, brother?" He placed his hand on Hawk's shoulder.

"Fuck yeah," he muttered under his breath.

The brothers were in luck—an unopened Jack Daniels on the counter greeted them. A smile skated across Hawk's lips. *My woman's perfect.* He opened the bottle and poured shots. Each one took a glass and Throttle held his up. "Thank God for princesses who know how to treat their men." They threw theirs back and poured another.

THE CANDLELIGHT CAST a warm glow as the delicate scent of roses ribboned around the full church. Cara's arm was looped around her dad's and she blinked repeatedly trying to keep her tears from falling. *I haven't even walked down the aisle and I'm ready to break down sobbing. Get it together, Cara.* She stood in the vestibule of the church with her bridesmaids in front of her. Sherrie, her maid of honor, turned around and winked at her. Cara smiled, but her lips quivered slightly. Her other bridesmaids, Maria, Kylie, Addie, and Lisa, looked over their shoulders occasionally at her, their eyes glimmering.

"You look beautiful, honey. I'm very proud of you."

"Oh Dad, don't start saying those things or I'm going to lose it for sure."

Vince Minelli patted his daughter's hand. "I love you. I hope Hawk knows what a precious gift I'm giving him today."

Cara leaned over and kissed her dad on the cheek. "I love you too. Thanks for being such a good dad. Oh crap, I'm starting to cry." She took the tissue her dad offered her.

"Aren't you glad I insisted you wear waterproof makeup?" Sherrie winked at her, then turned to face the altar.

Johann Pachelbel's "Canon in D" flowed from the violins. Kylie took the first step and began the march down the aisle to the altar. Cara breathed in deeply. "It's showtime," she said softly to her dad as he squeezed her arm.

The bridesmaids, dressed in frosted violet chiffon dresses with spaghetti straps, walked down the aisle and took their places at the altar. Then the string quartet filled the church with the first few notes of Wagner's "Here Comes the Bride," and all eyes were on Cara as she and her father walked slowly down the aisle. She wore an elegant ivory white allover lace gown with long lace sleeves, a V-neckline, a low sheer back with small pearl buttons running down from the neckline to the lower back, and a sweep train. A sheer, barely there lace veil flowed down from the middle of her head.

As each bridesmaid approached the altar, she saw Hawk standing tall and so elegant in his tuxedo. A bolt of desire surged through her. *He looks so sexy and yummy. Damn, he's gorgeous.* From the way his eyes traveled over her—slowly and hungrily—she knew he was enjoying taking her in as much as she was him. When her father presented her to him, she brushed a few tears from the corner of her eyes and held Hawk's hand. They both faced the priest. As he began to talk, Hawk leaned in to her. "You look fuckin' beautiful, babe."

Warmth spread through her as she glanced at him from half-lidded eyes. Love and tenderness with a streak of lust reflected in his gaze. She squeezed his hand. "You're gorgeous in your tux." The priest paused and gave each of them a stern look before continuing. They both snickered and then focused their attention back on the priest.

After an hour-long ceremony and a hot kiss that she was sure shocked some of her family and guests, Hawk wrapped his arm around her when three trumpets played the first notes of Mendelssohn's "Wedding March." They walked down the aisle—her beaming, him smirking—as husband and wife.

When they finally made it to the reception after endless photo shoots, applause spread across the room. Chairs scraped on the laminate floor as guests rose to their feet for a standing ovation while Cara and Hawk made their way to the bridal table. Before they sat down, Hawk leaned in for a kiss, and his Insurgents' brothers cheered and whooped. Cara's mother looked horrified even though her tight smile never left her face. Hawk threw his arm up in the air, his hand fisted, and his brothers followed suit. Everyone around the room looked at the exchange in varying degrees of amusement, merriment, and confusion. The married couple sat and chairs scraped again as the guests took their seats. The room buzzed with excited chatter.

Cara and Hawk kept sneaking peeks at each other during the seemingly endless toasts that friends and family bestowed on the couple. Cara's insides were so full of love and happiness that she thought she'd explode before the first dance with her father. She laughed several times in inappropriate places during conversations she was having because Hawk's hand, under the table, kept trying to find a way to get under her dress, but never seemed to be able to master it. *He's persistent.* But then how could she forget the way he'd pursued her in the beginning. She shook her head and whispered in his ear, "Honey, you're going to rip the lace in my dress. Just chill until after the reception."

"I can't believe how fuckin' difficult these wedding clothes are." He caught her lips and kissed her hard. "How long do we have to stick around?"

"We can leave after we cut the cake. Aren't you having a good time?"

"Yeah, but I wanna get you to the hotel so I can peel off your dress."

She smacked his hand. "Is that all that's on your mind?"

"With you? Fuck yeah. You're my wildcat who knows how to make my blood boil. I wanna see what you're wearing underneath all those clothes. I bet it's something sexy."

"Maybe. You're going to have to find out. *Later.*"

The rest of the night they played host to the guests at the reception. And after Hawk swallowed the first bite of cake, he had Cara in his arms, said good-bye to everyone, and nestled in the back of the limousine. As the limo drove to the Palace Hotel, Hawk attempted to pull up Cara's dress, but the train kept getting in the way.

"Fuck, babe, can you help me here?" She just shook her head because she was laughing so hard, and just when he found a way, the limo pulled up to the hotel. "Damn," he muttered. She laughed harder, positive the numerous glasses of champagne that she'd drunk were prompting her.

Once they checked into the bridal suite, Hawk didn't even wait for her to kick off her shoes before he was kissing her and trying to undo the twenty-plus buttons on the back of her gown. "Fuck! What is it with these damn buttons? We had to get Belle to come over to help us with all the goddamn studs in the shirts, and now you have like a million small buttons that I can't even begin to undo. Fuck, it's like you're wearing a damn chastity belt."

Cara howled and when she pushed him away and went to pour some champagne, he pulled her back to him. "Babe, remember we got the biker version of today tomorrow morning. You're already blasted off your ass. Help me figure out how to take your dress off."

"You have to unbutton it." She giggled. "Sherrie helped me put it on, and you have to help me take it off. I can't do it by myself."

"Fuck. You better be wearing some sexy shit under this." His voice was gruff, but she knew he was teasing by his dancing eyes.

After what seemed like an eternity, Hawk had Cara stripped down to her ivory sheer bra and matching panties, her lacey garter belt, and shimmering gold stockings. His heated gaze roved over her, and he whistled softly. "Totally worth it. Fuck, babe... you're gorgeous." He curved his arm around her waist, tugging her to him until they were firmly chest-to-chest. The heat of his body pressed against her. They kissed deeply, and then he walked her backward to the bridal bed. He lay her down and ripped off his shirt, studs pinging against the headboard and nightstand. She reached out and brought her husband close to her.

Their night was just beginning.

"DID YOU SEE the look on the desk clerk's face when he saw my biker wedding dress?" Cara laughed. She'd ordered the white leather corset with black ties and white chiffon skirt with jagged edges from an online store that specialized in biker wedding attire. Four-inch white biker boots and a short veil completed the outfit. Over her corset she wore her leather cut with the proud words "Property of Hawk" embroidered in white on the back.

Hawk's gaze journeyed over her. "You look fuckin' hot, babe. You sure your head's good after all that champagne you had yesterday?" He slipped his cut over his tight black T-shirt.

"Yep. If I take two aspirins before I go to sleep after drinking a lot, I never get a headache in the morning. I wish I would've known that trick while I was at college."

He tweaked her nose and then kissed it. "You're kooky. We gotta get going."

"I'm so glad our wedding went smoothly. I was a nervous wreck about it until I had some drinks in me. I know Viper wouldn't try anything at the club today. I wonder why he didn't do something yesterday."

"I figured he wouldn't do anything, but I still wanted the security just in case. The last thing he'd want is all that public exposure. Fuck, he's playing a goddamned game with me. Fuckin' asshole."

"Do you think he knows we know?"

"Fuck yeah. Anyway, let's not ruin our day." Hawk led her to the parking lot.

"Aren't we taking the limo?"

He laughed. "I thought you knew me, babe. No way I'm showing up at our biker wedding in a damn limo. The guys would never let me live that one down. I brought my Harley."

"Really? When?"

"Early yesterday morning I rode it over here then had a prospect take me back to my place."

"Of course. I lost my head for a minute there. You and your bike are attached at the hip." She smiled. Hawk helped her onto the back of his Harley. She slinked her arms around his waist and placed her head on his shoulder. In a matter of seconds they were off.

When they'd arrived at the clubhouse, the parking lot was filled with iron and chrome machines, the light from the sun's rays blinding her momentarily. He helped her off the bike and they walked into the club. The great room was packed and the minute the men saw Hawk, a cacophony of deafening whistles, cheers, and hoots rushed around them. Cara clung tighter to Hawk's arm as he strolled through the crowd, bumping fists and clasping shoulders of the brothers who greeted him.

They finally went outside and Cara saw smoke coming out of the ground. "What's going on there?" she asked, pointing.

"Some of the brothers have been slow-roasting a whole pig for the celebration. They smoke it slow for twenty-four hours. It tastes fuckin' awesome."

Cara spotted a wedding arch with sunflowers, mums, and carnations in the colors of fall away from the long buffet table that had been set up near a bar. "What am I supposed to do? Do we just stand under the arch?"

"No, babe. They will line up on both sides to form an aisle. Since we're already hitched—" He bent down and brushed her lips. "—we'll walk down it together. As we pass, each brother you will rev his engine. The sound is fuckin' awesome. My bike will be up front and after the preacher renews our vows, I'll ride you out of the ceremony on the back of my bike while all the brothers honk and rev their engines. It's something to see. The club opens the back gates so there'll be room for all the bikes." Hawk's eyes shone with excitement, and Cara pulled his face to hers and gave him a full-on kiss. "Fuck, babe," he mumbled as he grabbed her ass and pressed her close.

"You gonna do this or just give us a show?" Banger laughed and gave Hawk a bear hug. They spoke for a few minutes about the logistics of getting all the bikes lined up as Cara went over to say hi to some of the old ladies. Addie, Kylie, Cherri, Kimber, and Baylee all looked like they'd dragged themselves out of bed for the biker ceremony. They were at her traditional wedding the night before, and she'd noticed how much they drank and danced. She smiled knowingly at them.

"How in the fuck do you look so good after last night? I'm dying here," Cherri said as she sipped a glass of water.

"Aspirin is my secret."

"I wish you would've shared it with me. Fuck, my head is pounding. Axe kept telling me to slow down, reminding me about today, but I was having such a good time. Your wedding was beautiful." Baylee hugged Cara.

"It was like a fairytale wedding," added Kylie.

"I'm glad it went without any problems. I don't think that many people paid attention to the security team. I think they thought they were supposed to be there. They figured they were all invited by Hawk." Cara laughed.

"When I get married, I want you to be my wedding planner." Kylie shoved her hand in her jeans' pocket.

"No biker wedding for the president's daughter? How're you going to get around that?" Kimber took a sip of her beer.

"I want to do what Cara's doing—two weddings. One will be classic and dreamlike, and the other will have the leather and chrome. I love that you did it this way," Kylie replied.

"I have to admit I'm dragging my ass, but I wouldn't deny this special day to Hawk. The brotherhood is his family."

"I heard they have a Harley Davidson biker wedding chapel in Las Vegas. That would be so fucking awesome to get married there with a handful of friends. What do you guys think?" Cherri poured some water in her glass.

"Has Jax asked you?" Addie and Cara asked.

"No. We're not there yet, but when we get to it, I'd love to go to Vegas. That's my idea of a dream wedding." She slipped an ice cube in her mouth.

"You'd still have to have a kickass party for the rest of the brotherhood when you got back. That's the way this club works. They're closer than blood relatives." Cara glanced over at Hawk, who motioned her over. "I'm being summoned. I think the event is ready to begin." She sashayed over to him.

He pulled her close and kissed her. "We're ready to start."

The whole ceremony was so different from the one they'd had the night before, but Cara felt just as giddy as she had then. The bikes were the loudest sound she'd ever heard, and when she stood under the arch with Hawk and the biker preacher officiating, she knew that her life would always consist of living in two worlds, and she embraced it wholeheartedly. When the preacher asked if Hawk wanted to say anything to Cara, he took her hands in his and gazed at her intently.

"I knew you were the one for me the first time I saw you, and each day since has made me more sure that you're the only one I want in my life forever. I love the way you press up behind me on my Harley. I wanna share the ride only with you through countless sunsets and sunrises. You're the one I wanna wake up to and fall asleep with. I promise to love you, to remain honest and faithful to you. I'll always be there for you, babe. Life can be a rough, twisty road, but we can hold on tight together and deal with anything that comes our way. I love you, babe. Please take my heart and ride with me."

Tears flooded Cara's eyes as she smiled at the man she adored. "I love you more than anything, and I promise to always love and cherish you. I love that you've given me the privilege of being the only one who has seen your sweet, soft side. I will always be your partner in life, and I look forward to a lifetime of riding with you. You're my sweet honey forever." Her voice cracked and she leaned in to him. He cupped her chin, tilted her head, and kissed her tenderly.

The preacher smiled broadly, and all the cheers were soon drowned out by the roar of fifty Harleys. Hawk led her to his bike and helped her on. He switched it on and they drove out of the yard and down the aisle of motorcycles until they reached a clearing by the edge of the Colorado River. He killed his engine and swung off his bike. She got off and he drew her close. "Fuck, what you said back there tore me all up, babe."

"I loved what you said. I'm so happy you're my husband." She kissed his chest.

"And I'm fuckin' proud you're my wife." He kissed her deeply and they held each other, listening to their breaths in tandem with the rush of the river behind them. After a long while, he whispered, "We better get to the party." They walked hand-in-hand toward the yard.

That night they would feast, tell silly jokes, dance, and enjoy the moment of celebrating their happiness and love with their friends. They'd drink too much and fuck too hard, and they wouldn't have it any other way.

The following afternoon they'd leave for their honeymoon, but that night was their time with friends. Hawk had his brotherhood, and Cara had become good friends with several of the old ladies. She never could have imagined how beautiful her two worlds would have entwined in her heart.

And she wouldn't trade one moment of it.

CHAPTER SEVENTEEN

Three months later

SINCE THEY'D COME back from their honeymoon and settled in their new house, Hawk had grown more wary about when Viper would strike. And he *would* strike, Hawk was certain of that. The scum was still at large, and the tension of not knowing ate away at the vice president. When he entered the Insurgents' parking lot, he smiled when he spotted Steel's customized Harley with chrome skulls and brightly painted flames on the body of the bike. He and Steel had been buddies ever since Hawk joined up with the Insurgents. Steel had been with the club for a few years, but had to return to Alina, in the south of the state, when his mother became ill. He missed the brotherhood, so he started his own club after talking to Banger about it. Banger had decided to make the Night Rebels an affiliate of the Insurgents, and the brothers couldn't be happier.

Hawk cursed the frigid air as he got off his bike. Riding in freezing temperatures could turn a biker's balls blue. If not for the love of the ride, his ass would've been in his SUV on the heated leather seats. A burst of warm air greeted him when he walked into the club. He saw Steel leaning against the bar in conversation with Rags and Throttle.

"Hey," Hawk greeted the trio. He clasped Steel on the shoulder. "When did you get into Pinewood Springs?"

"Early this morning." Steel grabbed Hawk and gave him a bear hug. "I heard you got married. Congrats, man."

"Yeah, I finally took the plunge. How were the roads coming up?"

"Fucking brutal. I had to pull over several times. I ended up shacking up with a chick I met at a road stop. She kept me damn warm." He winked at the guys and they all laughed. "The ride took days longer 'cause of the weather, but there's nothing like riding around the backroads. Everything is so white and silent. It's like you're the only one left in the world. It's mind-blowing."

"I hear you," Hawk said as he picked up the beer the prospect placed in front of him. "What brings you to our neck of the woods?"

"My aunt's real sick and my ma couldn't make the trip, so I came out to see her. I don't know if she's gonna make it. She wants to go back to the reservation to die, and her son—my cousin—is being a goddamn prick about it. I came to set him straight. She lives about thirty miles from here, so I made the trip over here to see all your ugly mugs and to talk to you and Banger about some heavy shit that's been going on in my county."

"You still got trouble with those fuckin' Skull Crushers? I thought when we beat their asses last summer they'd settle the fuck down." Throttle slammed his fist on the bar.

Hawk raised his eyebrows. "You still got something with the fuckers?"

Steel threw down a shot of tequila. "Nah. I'm pretty sure they're not involved. We got smack in the county, and it's snaking its way into the reservation." Steel was part Apache and had grown up on the reservation near Alina in the Four Corners area of the state.

"You got H? How the fuck did that happen?" Hawk asked.

"That's what I'm trying to find out. Have you noticed any of it in your county?"

"No. We monitor that shit real carefully. The only problem we had was with meth and we ran the Skull fuckers outta here. You gotta get a handle on it, dude. It can spread like wildfire."

"No shit. And the sheriff is looking at us to do something about it. We need him and his crew to stay the fuck outta our business, so I gotta figure this out."

Hawk nodded. "Talk to Banger. He may have heard something over the network. I was out of the country for a bit, and I've been preoccupied with moving into the new house. You'll have to come by and see it." Hawk put his empty beer bottle on the bar and shook his head at the prospect when he came over to give him another one. "You hear anything about Viper down where you are?"

"The badges still haven't caught him? Fuck. Do they have their heads up their asses?"

"Seems that way," Throttle said, and Rags laughed.

"I'm positive he was in Alina staying with the fucking Skull Crushers. A couple of my brothers spotted a guy who didn't fit in with those fuckers, hanging out with them at their strip bar and the pool hall. He kept a low profile, but he was tall, skinny, and had long, stringy hair."

Hawk felt a throb in his gut. "That's the bastard. When was he in Alina?"

Steel ran his hand through his jet-black hair. "Let's see… must have been a little more than a month ago. No sign of him since then."

"'Cause his ass is in Iowa," Rags said.

"We think he's hangin' with the Demon Riders. They got some real issues with us, so it makes sense." Hawk pinched the bridge of his nose. "I know the fucker is gonna strike. Why the fuck can't we get something on him?"

"That's tough, him being after your old lady. I'm assuming you got her covered?"

"Yeah, but she's not used to this fuckin' shit. She's acting like she's cool but I see the fear in her eyes, and I wanna stomp the motherfucker to death for putting my woman through this. He's a goddamn pussy. He's hiding in the shadows and coming at me through my wife. Why the fuck doesn't he come at me directly? Face-to-face, man-to-man. Fuck his pussy ass. I'm gonna tear the asshole apart once I get my hands on him."

"'Cause the fucker knows you'll kick his ass. He doesn't stand a chance with you. We'll get him, Hawk. He's biding his time, but so are we. I got a ton of feelers out. We'll nail his balls to the wall," Throttle said. Hawk tilted his chin as he kicked over a barstool, an intense, violent anger coursing through him. *You're fuckin' dead, Viper.*

"I'll keep my ears open too. He can't stay hidden forever." Steel motioned for another drink. The prospect placed a shot of tequila in front of him.

"How long are you staying?" Hawk asked.

"If the weather is good, I'm gonna take off tomorrow morning. I gotta get back."

Hawk clasped Steel's shoulder again. "If you need any help cleaning up the smack problem, let me know. We're always here to help."

"Thanks, brother. I know that."

"I'm gonna head home." Hawk took out his gloves.

"You're not gonna stay for the party?" Rags asked.

"I don't wanna leave Cara alone. We'll probably come by on Saturday night."

"Steel, you gotta try out Della. She's our newest club girl, and she can suck a cock like a fuckin' vacuum. And she loves it deep in her throat." Rags grinned.

"Yeah? I definitely have to try her out. My club girls are great, but no one can deep throat the way I like it." Steel scanned the room. "Which one is she?"

"The one by the TV with her ass practically out. She's got on the purple shorts." Rags pointed to the back of the room.

As if on cue, the pretty brunette glanced at the group of men and smiled, then padded over. She ran her finger up Hawk's arm. "You talking about me?"

Hawk shook his head. "Not me. I'm outta here." He jerked his head to Steel. "Our out-of-town brother needs some attention. Treat him real good."

Della glanced at Steel and smiled wide. "You're good-looking. I don't see men with black hair and green eyes very often. You need some company?"

Steel caught Hawk's gaze and they both laughed. "Yeah, but come back in an hour. I got a pool game I'm gonna win."

"Like fuck you are," Throttle said.

"I'm outta here." Hawk turned around and walked toward the door, chuckling as he heard Steel and Throttle negotiating the terms of the game.

The icy air slapped him and his cheeks reddened from the shock of it. *Fuck, it's cold.* He wiped off the seat of his Harley, revved the motor, and took off into the frosty darkness.

When he came into the house from the garage, the smell of rosemary and garlic tantalized his nostrils. He kicked off his boots in the mud room and went into the kitchen, expecting to see Cara by the stove. Instead he saw a couple of pots cooking on the burner as the delicious smell of roasted pork seeped through the oven door. All at once his stomach growled, and he realized that he hadn't eaten since early that morning. The shop had been busy even though the weather had turned frigid the past week.

He walked over to the stove and lifted one of the pots, revealing boiling potatoes. The other had some sort of sauce cooking on a low boil. There was a colander of fresh greens in the sink, and he smiled when he saw a package of mushrooms on the counter. He loved mushrooms, especially sautéed in butter, garlic, and dill—just the way his woman made them. His stomach gnawed, and he picked up a cucumber slice off the cutting board and popped it in his mouth. He was damn hungry.

He went to the staircase and noticed the dining room table was set. *Did I forget that we're having people over?* He rushed up the stairs and went into the bedroom. Cara wasn't there. He stripped out of his clothes and jumped into the shower.

Changed and showered, he walked back down the stairs and into the family room, his heart filling up when he saw Cara in the kitchen facing the stove. He shuffled quietly over to her and curled his arm around her waist. He laughed when she cried out. "You scared the shit out of me," she chided, her hand covering his.

He nuzzled her neck, whispering, "I wanted to surprise you."

"Well, you did that."

"We having people over?"

"No. Why?"

"You have the dining room table set."

"I decided to have dinner in there tonight. People never use their dining rooms unless they have company over. I thought my sweet kickass husband deserved a wonderful meal in a room without a television."

He smacked her butt and then bit her earlobe as she moaned softly. "I'm the one who's supposed to be spoiling you, not the other way around."

"You deserve to be spoiled sometimes. You make me so happy."

"You fuckin' do the same to me, babe." He slipped his hand into her yoga pants and brushed her crotch. "We got time for an appetizer?" he breathed raggedly.

She groaned and leaned her head against his chest. "Not really unless you want overdone pork, burned glaze, and limp mushrooms."

"Sounds like a good trade-off." The scent and feel of her fueled his fire. He slipped his finger between her slick pussy lips. "Just the way I love it. Dripping." She swung her arms behind him and squeezed his ass, then slapped it. *Damn!* It took him by surprise. "What the fuck, babe?"

"Don't like your ass smacked?"

"Not really." He leaned down and kissed her on the nose. "It feels fuckin' weird."

She laughed and then twisted out of his arms. "I have to finish this dinner. It'll be ready in five minutes." She shoved him lightly away. "Pour water into the glasses on the table, then come back and help me bring in the food."

"Pretty bossy tonight, aren't you?" She stuck her tongue out at him, and he cupped his hand and slapped her sweet rounded ass cheek. He loved the way her firm but soft butt wiggled against his hand when he gave it a good smack. It fucking turned him on each time.

He pulled out a large bottle of water from the refrigerator and took it into the dining room. The china they'd received for their wedding was on the table. Before he finished pouring the water, Cara came in with a bowl of boiled potatoes and set it on the table. "Can you bring in the roast pork, honey? It's on the platter."

When all the food was dished out, they talked about their day, shared laughter, and stared lovingly into each other's eyes. At the end of the meal, Hawk grasped her hand, bringing it to his lips and kissing it. "That was a fuckin' awesome dinner, babe. Thank you."

"Did it make you happy?"

"Fuck yeah. *You* make me happy."

She rose to her feet and went to him. "Scoot your chair back a bit. I want to sit on your lap." He pushed back and she wiggled onto his lap, his shaft starting to wake up. She put one arm around his neck and kissed him firmly on his lips. "I love you so much."

"Me too, babe."

"I bet I could make you happier than you are right now."

"No fuckin' way." He brushed his lips across her cheek.

"Wanna bet?"

He chuckled. *My wildcat wants to play a game.* "All right. Sure. Name your bet."

"If I'm right, then you have to teach me how to ride a Harley and buy one for me."

"Whoa. What the fuck? I know you mentioned it a year ago, but I thought you were only teasing and trying to piss me off. I don't want my wife on her own bike."

"Why not?"

He shrugged. "I don't know. It's not the way it's done. It doesn't feel natural."

"Says who? Kimber has a cute Harley and you don't seem to have a problem with that."

"Kimber's not my woman. And the very fact you referred to a Harley as 'cute' speaks volumes, babe. You're not a biker, just my biker chick."

"Throttle is a bigger chauvinist than you, and he's cool with Kimber and her bike. Anyway, she said she'd teach me if you decided to stay in your cave."

He shook his head. "Don't you like riding on my bike with me?"

"Of course I do, and I'd never give that up. This is just something I want to learn, that's all. Chances are I'd probably be scared to death to go out on the streets with cars. Anyway, do you want to bet that?"

He snorted. "Sure, why not? I know nothing's gonna beat tonight. So fire away, babe." *She can be so damn stubborn, but she's fuckin' cute when she's that way. Her riding a Harley. Ha!*

She cupped the side of his cheek and kissed him on the lips, pushing her tongue through his seam. They kissed passionately before she pulled back, looked deeply in his eyes, and said softly, "You're going to be a daddy."

Everything shut down. *What the fuck did she say?* He sat there blinking for a few seconds, his gaze on her smiling face, her words not quite sinking in.

"Did you hear me?" A tinge of worry echoed in her voice. "We're going to be parents. I'm pregnant."

He hugged her tightly and peppered her face and neck in kisses. "Fuck, babe, that's awesome. You got our baby in you? Fuck." He kissed her again. "You're so beautiful. How long have you known?"

"I just found out today. I knew something was off, but I wasn't really sure. I'm six weeks."

"Fuck, babe. Damn, I love you."

Cara laughed and hugged him as a mixture of love, tenderness, disbelief, and joy spread through him.

"You happier than you were earlier?" She ran her finger along his jawline and down his throat.

"Fuck yeah." He kissed her again, that time harder, more possessively.

"When are we going to start my motorcycle lessons?" she said against his mouth.

He pulled away and guffawed. His woman touched him deeply.

"Not until the baby is born. You gotta take care of yourself."

"But you will teach me? I won the bet."

Fuck. I could eat her up. He smiled. "Yeah, babe. You won the bet… big time."

Later while they sat on the couch, her snuggled close to him, he still couldn't believe that he was going to be a father. He rubbed Cara's stomach as they watched a movie. *I fuckin' swear I'm gonna be the dad I always wished I had. I'll never hurt you, little one. I'll always have your back no matter what.* He kissed the side of Cara's head. "You feel okay? Can I get you anything?"

"I'm good. I'm not sick, honey. I'm pregnant. Oh damn, I like the way that sounds."

"Me too." He dipped his head and tugged up her T-shirt, then kissed her belly. "You've done good, woman."

She tangled her hand in his hair. "We both did," she said softly.

He sat up and kissed her again. "What about fucking? Can we do it?"

She laughed. "The doctor said we can do it up until the eighth month."

"So we can make love and fuck? I don't wanna do anything to hurt you and the baby."

"You won't." She put the palm of her hand over his crotch and kneaded it.

"Fuck, you're killing me," he muttered under his breath.

"Why don't we go upstairs and make love?"

Without answering, he stood up and stretched out his hand. She placed hers in his and he pulled her to her feet, then picked her up and carried her to their bedroom. He'd secured the house right after he'd come in, and that night he was going to shut off the apprehension that had been haunting him since he'd learned about Viper's escape.

He was going to make love to his woman, his wife, the mother of his child, and no matter what happened in his life, he'd always remember this perfect moment.

He watched Cara as she lay naked on their bed, then took off his clothes and came to her, hovering over her, and kissing her lovingly. He pulled back and took her in, loving the way the muted light from the lamp made her skin glow and her eyes sparkle.

That night, they would be frozen in the moment, suspended from the harshness of reality, existing only in each other's gaze. And he would make slow, passionate love to her.

CHAPTER EIGHTEEN

S PRING SLOWLY CREPT in, banishing the frigidness of winter. Tulips and daffodils sprung up, adding punches of color to front lawns still brown from the winter's snow. Wildflowers sprinkled the mountains and valleys, and the new growth of evergreens and pines scented the air. The wind had lost its icy bite, and its warmth blew branches and wrapped around pedestrians. Cara's tousled tendrils whipped about her face and she brushed them away while balancing an armload of files. Before she entered her office building, she tilted her head toward the sky, loving the sunlight's warm kiss.

"Hi, Asher. Any calls?" Cara asked as she entered her office.

"Only Hawk, like twenty times." Asher smiled.

"I'm sure he's freaking out because he couldn't get a hold of me on my cell phone. I was in court and put it on silent. The damn battery ran out. Poor Hawk."

"First-time dads are the worst. My brother drove my sister-in-law crazy, as well as me and my parents."

Cara cocked her head. "I can definitely see you freaking out if the tables were turned."

"I'd like to think I'd be as calm and cool as the expectant mothers seem to be." He chuckled. "But you're right. I'd be worse than my brother." The two of them shared a laugh. "Oh, your four o'clock cancelled, and you have three more people who set up consultations. Two are for tomorrow afternoon and one is for Thursday afternoon at four thirty. I wasn't sure if that was too late for you."

Cara frowned. "Are they heavy-duty cases? I've been trying to slow down and just handle the children guardian cases."

"All three are misdemeanors, first-time offenses. I put the information on your desk. I can call and cancel them if you want."

She shook her head. "No. As long as there aren't any felonies, it'll be fine."

As she walked into her office, the phone rang. She heard Asher say, "She just walked in, Hawk. I'll put you through." He smiled at Cara as she went into her office.

She leaned over her desk and picked up the phone while she settled into her office chair. "Hi, honey. I just got back from court."

"I've been so fuckin' worried. I didn't hear from you. I called you on your cell, but I didn't even get a damn text from you. What the fuck, babe?"

She swung her chair around so she could look out at the Rocky Mountains. The only remnant of winter was the brilliant snowy peaks of the mountains that ringed the town. "I'm sorry, honey, but my phone died. I'm going to recharge it now. I was in a hearing all afternoon."

"You gotta make sure your phone is always charged. Fuck, I didn't know what the hell was going on."

"Didn't Asher tell you I was in court? I mean, even if my battery hadn't died, I couldn't have contacted you during the hearing," she said softly.

"I know. I just worry, you know, baby?"

"I know, but I'm fine. I'm feeling great. And Sinner and Pike are still everywhere I go. I'm surprised Banger has let them do this for six months."

"Yeah, well... we know the motherfucker is waiting until we take them off you."

She sighed. "They can't watch me forever. I wish the cops would find Viper. I want to get back to the way it was before."

He blew out a long breath. "I know, babe. He's gotta come out at some point. He's not gonna wanna stay hidden for the rest of his life."

"Maybe he's already blown out of here. Maybe he's given up on this whole revenge thing and gone to Mexico."

"Nah, he's still around. An outlaw *never* gives up."

A knot formed in the pit of her stomach; she knew Hawk was right. Viper wouldn't be out of her life until he was caught. She felt like an invisible hand was smothering her, and no matter how hard she tried to break free, she couldn't. All of a sudden, a strong sense of foreboding that something brutal was going to happen overcame her. She pushed it down, hoping it was just a feeling and nothing more. "Did you still want to come to my doctor's appointment with me tomorrow afternoon?"

"Yeah. You okay? You sound funny all of a sudden."

She swallowed hard, trying to quell the quivers climbing up her spine. "Yeah, I'm okay. I guess the whole Viper thing just spooks me. Most of the time I don't think about it, but when I do, it just kind of takes hold."

"I'm gonna kill that motherfucker for putting you through this." Anger radiated over the telephone. "We got a shit ton of feelers out. The reason nothing's coming back is because he's holed up somewhere."

"I know. I feel safe with you and the prospects watching me. And I've got the whole club behind me. I'm just being silly."

"No you're not. I can't tell you too much, but just know we're working on getting him. How's the baby?"

She laughed. "The baby's fine."

"I can't wait for tomorrow, even though I don't know what the fuck you do in the doctor's office."

She giggled. "I'm getting a sonogram. It's going to be so exciting."

"Yeah." She heard the smile in his voice. "You feel like El Tecolote for dinner?"

"I'll meet you there at six."

She spent the rest of the afternoon working on cases, talking to clients and witnesses, and rubbing her small baby bump. She loved the way it looked, and Hawk was crazed about it, always kissing it and circling his hand over it. It was endearing, and each time it made her heart melt.

Later that night, after dinner, Cara watched Hawk as he stripped down to his boxers. They'd had a wonderful dinner of enchiladas, tamales, and chile rellenos, and the bliss of a full stomach and a comfortable bed made her feel warm and cozy. Watching Hawk's muscles ripple as he took off his clothes was a huge bonus.

"Do you miss not riding your bike when we go out?" She stretched her legs out as she lounged against the headboard.

"Yeah, but it's not forever. I'll miss you being behind me at the bike rallies."

"I miss holding you tight as the wind rushes around me."

He winked at her. "Spoken like a true old lady."

She watched as he hung up his clothes and put his boots in his walk-in closet. She had actually filled her huge walk-in closet already, so she had to take half of his. She sighed. *Shopping… one of my guilty pleasures.*

"I'm gonna grab a beer. You want something?"

"A bottled water, please."

He smiled, then came over and kissed her. "Sure thing, babe." He ran his hand over her belly and ambled out of the room.

She jumped up and rushed to the bathroom, brushing out her hair and swiping a bit of gloss over her lips. She'd been horny for him ever since he walked into the restaurant earlier that night. She slipped on a sheer red teddy that had lace over the bodice and was spilt down the front, showing off her belly when she moved. Spritzing her vanilla cream body spray over her, she hurried back to their bed, slipping under the cool sheets.

"Here you go," Hawk said as he came into the room and put her water on the nightstand. He plopped on the bed next to her and took a long gulp of his beer. "You wanna watch some TV?"

"Not really." She inched closer to him. With her fingernail, she traced the outline of his fierce hawk tattoo, its eyes piercing into her. "How's your beer?"

"Good." He picked up the remote from the nightstand and turned on the TV. "I'm gonna catch the scores. Then I'll turn it off, okay?"

She shrugged, replacing her fingernail with her tongue and trailing her fingers down his chest, past his stomach, circumventing his dick and settling on his inner thighs. She lightly pinched his flesh, moving her digits up near his balls, but never touching them. She smiled when he sucked in his breath. His hand entwined in her hair and he pulled it lightly. She kicked off the covers and rose up on her knees, locking her gaze with his desire-filled one. He reached out and grasped the sheer fabric of her teddy. "Is this new?" he asked in a thick voice.

"Uh-huh. Do you like it?" She cupped her hands over her breasts and pushed them together. He nodded, his eyes transfixed on her tits. "That's good. I wanted to show it to you." She moved away. "Go ahead and watch your program."

She heard the remote click and the sportscaster's voice faded away. "Get the fuck over here," he growled as he grasped her arm and tugged her backward. She swung around and scooted her butt by his feet, slowly licking, kissing, and pinching her way up his powerful legs before grazing her chin over his hardness. She lavished wet kisses over his abs while running her fingernails over his arms. "Fuck, baby," he muttered as he grabbed her shoulders.

She gently pushed his hands off her. "No touching yet. Just feel what I'm doing, honey." She placed his arms on the mattress and continued licking him, loving how he moaned and moved under her tongue as she flicked his nipples. "I like the way your body feels," she breathed against his taut skin.

"Babe, you're fuckin' killing me."

She sniggered but put his hands back down on the mattress. "You're better at giving orders than you are at taking them, aren't you?" she teased as she threw him a sexy smile. While she inched her way up his body, her eyes held his, and the fire burning in them pushed her arousal to the max. As she skimmed her hot tongue over his throat, she rubbed her breasts against him.

"I gotta touch your tits, baby."

She shook her head and held his hands down. When she finally reached his face, he lifted his head off the pillow, his mouth hungrily capturing hers. Their tongues tangled together in a heated dance of seduction. "Oh, baby," he whispered, and she swallowed his words. Throwing off her hands, he broke free and glided his fingers under her teddy, cupping her ass and squeezing it hard. He sat up and rolled her under him as he ravaged her mouth, his hands journeying over every inch of her body. "You're even more beautiful now that you got our kid growing inside you. Fuck, babe. I think you're so damn sexy. Your tits are getting bigger and I fuckin' love that." He nuzzled his face between her breasts as he tweaked her red nipples.

She arched her back, pushing her breasts closer to him. "Every time I think about how wonderful it is for me to be carrying our child, I want to smother you with kisses and hold you tight. I never want to let go." Her fingers raked through his hair.

He lifted his head up. "I don't want us to ever fuckin' let go of each other." He bent down and gently kissed her on the lips as he continued tweaking her nipples.

"I want you to treat me nasty tonight." She pulled his face closer. "Think you can handle that?" She chuckled.

A devilish smile curled on his lips. "Tell me what you want me to do." He licked her bottom lip and then pulled it between his teeth, sucking it.

She moaned softly as she squeezed his biceps with her hands. He pulled away, his hot gaze burning into her. "I love the way your body feels, so ripped and firm," she said. "I fucking love your biceps. I could squeeze and drool over them all day."

"Oh yeah?" He ran his tongue down her neck and over her shoulder. "I fuckin' love how soft you are, and how good you smell and taste. Tell me what you want."

"I want you to play with my boobs until I can't stand it. Then I want you to touch and kiss me all over."

"Go on." He trailed his mouth back to hers and took it in a deep, wet, claiming kiss. He pulled back and she locked gazes with him. Desire heated his eyes, the look sending a bolt of fire between her legs. "What do you want me to do after I kiss you all over?" he murmured against her skin as his lips wandered down her neck and over to the pulse in the hollow of her throat.

"Touch me. Play with me. Make me come."

"Fuck, babe." He stroked her side and then moved over the curve of her hips, pinching their soft flesh between his fingers. His lips spread feathery kisses on the swell of her breasts, and he circled his tongue around her nipples, his hot breath making the skin around them pucker. When he flicked the tip of his tongue over them, she groaned and clenched her legs together. He chuckled and spread them apart with his hand. "None of that, babe. Keep your pretty legs open and wide." He resumed teasing her hardened beads.

She opened her legs and watched as he devoured her breasts with his mouth, teeth, and tongue. "It feels so good, honey." He shifted his weight, and she felt the jut of his hard cock against her hip as he ran his hands over her inner thighs. Each time he pinched the soft flesh, she held her breath, hoping he'd touch her aching mound. But he only grazed it very lightly. He kept stroking her everywhere but where her body craved the most. Then his tongue left her tits and slowly inched its way over her ribcage to her stomach. His hand stroked the skin of her belly as he peppered kisses all over it.

"I can't stop touching you. You're growing big with our baby. It's fuckin' hot, babe."

Her heart soared, and she grabbed a fistful of his hair and tugged it. "I love watching you kiss my stomach. It's like you're kissing our baby."

He raised his eyes up and her breath hitched when she saw the mix of love, tenderness, and desire in them. "I am, babe. You and the little one own my heart." He swirled his tongue in her belly button, then explored other areas of her body. His wandering tongue set her senses on fire. Electric anticipation grew deep within her as she watched it draw a path toward her pulsing mound. He looked up, lust shining in his heated gaze, and a smile twitched at the corner of his mouth.

He skimmed across her swollen lips, barely touching them, and landed on her inner thighs, biting and kissing them. Her hands grew clammy and she scrubbed one over her face. "Touch me," she said.

"Not yet."

"Hawk, I want you to touch me. I can't stand it anymore. I've been wanting you since we met for dinner."

"You should've told me, then. I could've made you less horny, babe." He resumed feasting on her thighs, her hips, and the soft skin above her clit, but he didn't put one lick or one touch on her throbbing sex.

"Please?" she breathed. She snaked her hand down and tried to touch her sex.

"No fuckin' way, babe. That's mine. All mine." He moved her hand away and held it tightly in his grasp. "Love the way you want me so bad."

"I do. Don't you want some?"

"Oh yeah, but I can wait. You've got to learn a little patience. It'll feel more awesome if you wait."

She twisted her hand out of his clutches. "I don't want to wait. Please, honey? Please touch me."

He pulled up, his blue eyes—dark with desire—staring down on her mound. The way he stayed silent, checking out her most private parts, made every fiber in her body burn. He licked his lips and glanced at her through hooded lids. "What do you want me to do, babe?"

"Play with me. I need you. I'm dying here."

He shook his head and went back to massaging her thighs and tracing figure eight designs over them. She snorted impatiently. His chuckles were deep. *He's enjoying this, and I'm ready to explode. Not funny!* As she closed her eyes, fuming, she felt Hawk pushing her legs apart even farther, opening up her glistening pink pussy. She opened her eyes and saw his gaze fixed on her quivering sex.

"Fuck," he breathed as admiration shone in his eyes. "You have the most beautiful pussy." He ran his fingers up from her ankles to her inner thighs. Goose bumps covered her skin and she shivered under his touch as a small moan escaped her lips. Settling lower between her legs, he dipped his tongue between her folds, hitting her sweet spot. Moans of pleasure escaped her as each long stroke of his tongue sent another shiver of pleasure through her body. She grabbed the back of his head and pushed his face into her pussy.

His low chuckle pulsed against her skin, searing it. "Fuck, babe. You're greedy." He slipped a finger through her wet slit, and a jolt of white-hot pleasure arced through her body. She writhed beneath him as she pulled at his hair. His touch, his words, his scent teased her, pushed her arousal through the roof, and she craved to be filled and devoured by him.

"You like the way it feels, baby?" Hawk was fingerfucking her while his tongue expertly lapped up her juices, bringing her closer to her release.

"It feels awesome. I want you inside me. I need it." She tried clenching her legs together, but his shoulders kept them grounded.

He removed his dripping finger from her pussy and ran it over her puckered opening. The nerves around her rosy entrance exploded, and she ground down the best she could on his finger. "It feels so good. You know what I like, honey," she panted.

"You want me to fuck your hot little ass?"

"Yeah. I love that."

"I'm gonna fuck your pussy first, then finish in your ass. Does that turn you on?"

She nodded, the desire and anticipation making her face flush. When he entered her she cried out. His size always filled her up on contact and her walls quickly clung around him, encasing his dick. He started off slow and gentle, but she kept yelling, "Harder," so he picked up his speed. She knew he was holding back because of the baby, even though she assured him the doctor said it was okay for them to have their usual sex during the second trimester, and she loved him for it. As he pumped into her, her hips met his thrusts and they rocked together, their bodies sliding against each other, their hearts beating erratically. She never loved him more than she did at that moment. Then she went over the edge with a high-pitched scream. "Hawk. Oh God. Hawk." And she shattered into a million tiny pieces, just dust floating everywhere in the universe, and it was good. *So damn good.*

He kissed her as she crossed over into ecstasy. She opened her eyes and met his smoldering ones, a large smile on his face. "I fuckin' love watching you come. It's so hot and beautiful." She wrapped her arms around his neck, and they kissed and held each other until the frenzied pitch inside her had subsided to a warm, pleasant hum.

He kissed her breasts and played with her nipples before gently helping her up. She went up on her knees, her ass facing him. He stroked her back and brushed his fingertips down her spine, and the hairs on her arms rose as goose bumps carpeted her body. He rubbed her rounded globes and she felt him kiss each one tenderly, then more feverishly until he was biting and licking her ass cheeks all over.

"Did you like my cock in your pussy?" he rasped as he slapped her ass.

She yelped, then said, "Yes. I loved it. Your dick was so deep inside me."

"It's gonna go even deeper in your sweet little hole. You want it, babe?"

"Uh-huh."

Another smack. "Good girl."

As he spanked her over and over, kissing and rubbing her inbetween, her sex dampened. By the time she felt the coolness of the lubricant he spread over her ass, she knew her pussy was glistening from need. When she felt the tip of his dick at her puckered entrance, she held her breath as she always did. It always seemed as though her body didn't have room for air and his dick at the same time. She relaxed, waiting for him to ease into her and fill her up. She loved the way it felt, like a fine line between pain and pleasure.

Hawk grunted as he pushed in farther, his hand stroking her back until he was deep inside. "Fuck, that feels good," he said raggedly. Pleasure radiated through her whole body. He slowly thrust in and out, his finger finding her sweet spot again. She closed her eyes and let the sensations of fullness and sweetness overtake her as he placed two fingers inside her. While he rode her ass with his dick, her pussy with his fingers, and stroked her hardened bud with his thumb, her deep groans met his hot breaths, which soon became panting grunts.

As the tension grew in her, she could feel Hawk's balls tight against her and she knew he was close. He leaned down and bit the back of her neck, then growled in her ear, "You only belong to me. You're mine. I love you so much." Then he snapped away and a groan of pure pleasure came through his lips. "Fuck, Cara. Fuck!" His warm seed filled her, marking her from the inside.

Then the wave of euphoria hit her for a second time. As it crashed over her, she rode it, flying high and out of her body, love, tenderness, and raw pleasure cocooning her. Her arms and legs gave out and she crumpled on her side, her small pants blending with his deep ones, filling their room. She felt his arms tug her to him and she curled close, her body fitting perfectly against his. He brushed the hair away from her damp face and cupped her chin, pushing her head back until their gazes locked.

"That was fuckin' incredible. You own my heart and body. I love you, babe." He kissed her softly on her lips.

"I can't even tell you how much you mean to me," she whispered, her eyelids growing heavy. She loved him with a fire that could never be extinguished.

He reached over and turned off the switch, the room suddenly cast in darkness.

They fell asleep locked in each other's arms in total exhaustion.

CHAPTER NINETEEN

STRIPS OF LIGHT leaked in from the corners of the shutters. Propped on his elbow, Hawk watched Cara sleep, loving the way her face glowed in the early morning sunlight. He lightly ran his hand over her belly, an intensity of emotion jolting him as he pictured their baby growing inside. A small snort escaped from Cara's parted lips, and he laughed quietly to himself. As the time went by in her pregnancy, she'd begun to snore, and he thought it was fucking adorable. He leaned down and kissed her on her cheek, then brushed away the hair strands that clung to her face. *She's so beautiful when she sleeps. Peacefulness surrounds her, and I wanna keep it that way.*

Suddenly, his face went grim. Viper was lying in the brush, waiting to pounce on his prey, like a wild beast. Hawk's frown was filled with cold fury. *I need to annihilate him so Cara and I can rest easy again. I know she's scared, and it kills me every time I see it in her eyes. Oh, baby, I wanna hold you close and never let you outta my sight.*

"You up?" her sleepy voice broke through his thoughts.

He looked down on her, smiling as she fluttered her eyes open. "Yeah. Did you have a good sleep?"

"The best. You wore me out last night." She giggled and pressed her ass against him. "I get so tired."

He wrapped his arm above her stomach. "You're working for two, babe."

She smiled and nodded. "I wish I could stay in bed all day today, but I can't. Maybe next week I'll take a day off and just do nothing but sleep and watch TV."

"You need to do it. You should cut back on your cases." He ran his fingers through her hair, brushing his lips on it. He loved how silky it was and how it smelled like the wind on a fresh spring day.

"I'm starting to. I'm not taking any more felonies, just taking a few extra clients. I picked up one the other day. Once the baby comes, I'm just going to do appellate work. I can do it all at home from the computer. My mom can spot me if I have to go to court."

"Or if I'm hungry and come home during lunch." He raised his eyebrows and winked when she craned her neck and looked at him.

A wide grin broke out over her face. "You've got it all planned out, don't you?"

He squeezed her close. "Fuck yeah, babe. We gotta have some time for us too."

"I'm pretty sure you'll be on top of that." She lifted his hand and kissed it. "I've got to get my butt in the shower. My doctor's appointment is in an hour." He moved her hair and kissed the back of her neck, then rolled away and rose to his feet. She padded to the bathroom and closed the door.

An hour later, Hawk sat on a chair in the reception area of the doctor's office. Cara's hand was warm in his. "Mrs. Benally?" Hawk looked over at the young woman dressed in pink pants and a pink smock with various Disney characters all over it. Cara stood up. Hawk leapt to his feet and followed Cara and the Disney lady through a door. The woman led them to a sterile room, motioning them to sit down. As Cara and the woman chatted, Hawk stared at a poster showing the different stages of pregnancy and the growth of the baby.

The woman left and closed the door softly. "Is she the nurse?" he asked Cara.

"Yes. The doctor should be in soon. I'm super excited. If the baby's in a good position, they can tell us what the sex is. What do you want?"

He took her hand in his. "I don't know. I just want the baby to be healthy."

"Me too."

"And it's not like we can't keep trying until we get one of each." She just shook her head, a twinkle in her eye.

The door opened and a tall, slim man of forty came in. "Hi, Cara. How are you doing?" His glance shot over to Hawk. "Is this your husband?"

"Yo." Hawk jerked his chin up.

The doctor smiled and put out his hand. "Nice to meet you. I'm Dr. Penborne." He turned back to Cara. "So you're a little past seventeen weeks, and the ultrasound will be able to tell us how well your baby is developing. I don't anticipate any problems at all. We have a tech in the office, so I'll just show you to the room. Please feel free to ask any questions and to see the screen as she conducts the test. You can ask her the gender if you want to know it." He opened the patient room door and scanned both their faces. "Do you want to ask me anything?"

They both shook their heads before following him to another room. The tech was waiting for them and she had Cara lie on a table, then squeezed a bunch of gel on her abdomen. She dimmed the lights and grabbed the wand, moving it over Cara's stomach in slow circles. The machine beeped and bright green lights flashed as she kept moving the wand over Cara's belly.

Hawk watched as grainy shadows jerked on the screen. He sucked in his breath when he spotted a small figure with a much larger head than the rest of its body. He could see arms, legs, tiny hands and feet. A rush of blood pounded between his ears. "Fuck," he muttered under his breath.

The tech glanced at him sideways and smiled. "That's your baby. Do you want to know the gender?" Hawk nodded and then looked at Cara, who nodded as well. "It's pretty clear. You're having a boy."

A son. Fuck. He blinked furiously and looked away, coughing and then swallowing the lump forming in his throat. Cara reached out for his hand and he gripped hers. He wiped his eyes and looked at her, losing himself in that moment of love and joy. As they locked gazes, the bond between them grew stronger, and he knew he'd do anything in the world for her and his son. *I'd give up my life for them.* He kissed her hand before leaning over to wipe the tears escaping from the corners of her eyes.

"Your baby is doing great. Everything is exactly where it needs to be, but of course the doctor will see the pictures and have the last word," the sonographer said to the new parents. "He'll be in soon." She turned the screen to them and pointed to a spot on the screen. "See? Here are his tiny ears. They're fully formed. He'll start to hear. Don't be surprised if you feel him when a loud noise like a doorbell or a siren startles him. You can start talking to him." She smiled.

Warmth radiated through Hawk's body and he beamed. "Fuck... like wow." He stared at the screen watching the tiny baby, not quite believing he was going to have a son. When the doctor came in, he did a second pass over Cara's stomach, then had the parents listen to their son's heartbeats. When Hawk heard the fast beats, he stood up, bent down, and kissed Cara deeply. "Thank you, babe," he whispered. Cara stroked his cheek while sniffling. He wiped her tears with his thumbs.

"Your baby is healthy and progressing beautifully. You are at seventeen weeks. Unless something comes up, we don't need to do another ultrasound. You will be feeling your baby more and more. At this stage and later, babies are very active—punching, kicking, turning around in the uterus. He's going to be having a ball."

Cara laughed, then blew her nose. "I've been feeling some fluttering. Very light, like a butterfly's wings. Is that our son?"

With a broad smile, Dr. Penborne nodded. "The fluttering will turn into all-out jabs. Just watch for them."

The doctor chatted for a few more minutes, then left the couple alone. Cara went into the bathroom and Hawk waited in the hallway, the enormity of what he'd experienced still buzzing in him. When she came out, he draped his arm around her shoulder. "Do you want to get something to eat?"

Her eyes brightened. "Hell yeah. I'm starving."

"Burgers?"

"No. Pasta... like a huge bowl of it. Let's go to Little Peppina's."

He laughed and kissed the side of her head. "I love you," he said softly. Then they walked out of the office and headed to the car, both beaming and holding each other.

"IT WAS JUST fuckin' awesome," Hawk said to Banger as he recounted the images he saw at the ultrasound the previous day. "I still can't believe I'm having a son. Fuck, I can't believe I'm even married. How the hell did I get so lucky?"

"You met the right woman. When you meet the right person, everything falls into place. It's fuckin' weird that it does that, but it does."

"Yeah. Damn, it's just so fuckin' surreal." Hawk placed his foot up on the chair as he watched his brothers shuffle into the room for church. He was anxious to see if anyone found anything out about Viper. Now that he'd seen pictures of his boy, he was rabid about smoking out Viper and getting rid of him once and for all.

The club discussed their income flow and resources, as well as their newest project in the farside of west Pinewood Springs—a second strip mall. The first was doing fantastically, so they voted to build another; the goal was to keep increasing the club's income.

There was some discussion on the problem of heroin creeping into the southwestern part of the state. Hawk cleared his throat. "Steel's got a mess going on. He said that smack's hit the reservation, and chances are pretty damn high it's on the streets of Alina as well."

"Are the fuckin' Skull Crushers behind it?" Chas asked.

Banger and Hawk shook their heads. "Doesn't look like it. Besides, they know the score now that we've had to teach 'em a couple lessons. I don't think they're that stupid to fuck around like this in a county with a strong Insurgents presence. They know Night Rebels are our affiliates. Don't think they're that dumb, but these wannabe outlaw punks always surprise me, so I could be wrong," Banger said.

"I don't trust those fuckers at all," Hoss said.

Hawk held up his hands as the brothers started to talk loudly. "Let's keep the griping about those asswipes to a minimum. I'm with Banger on this—it's not those fuckers. It's not the Deadly Demons either. The grapevine is quiet on this, so I don't think it's an outlaw club. It's not the damn cartels either. This is a citizen who is acting for himself. I told Steel if he needed help, he should contact us. I'll monitor this. If it gets outta control down there, it'll find its way into our county, and we're not gonna stand for that shit."

The brothers agreed and promised to be there to help Steel and his brothers if they needed them. Rock whistled loudly, the din of voices growing silent. "I got some info on that piece of shit who calls himself *Viper*." He said the name like it was something repulsive. "The Demon Riders are helpin' him out. He's not just staying at the mother chapter. He's been bouncing around like a world traveler, only his journey is contained to Iowa and Illinois. He never stays in any one place too long. The fucker's slippery, that's for damn sure."

Hawk's senses sharpened. "What ties does he have here?"

"My sources are sayin' that he's got a couple of citizens being his eyes in our town. They think they're the ones who're letting him know when it's okay to come back here to do shit to you and your woman. And that is his intention. Your old lady is the means to get to you. He wants to nail your ass to the ground, brother."

"What a fuckin' pussy. He has to go after my woman? Prison made him more of a weak fuck than he was before he went in. His ass is probably some dude's bitch." Sniggers circled around the room. "I bet the fat fuck I saw at my house before the wedding is one of his stooges. The asshole was definitely an amateur. I gotta flush him and his partner out. I'm sure fuckass is paying them a bunch of money. He's so damn desperate that he had to use dumb fucks who don't know what the hell they're doing."

"No way would a Skull Crusher put his toe into our territory," Jerry said.

"Damn straight," Hawk replied.

"How much did you have to pay for the info?" Banger asked.

"A few AK-47s and some prime pussy." Rock grinned.

Banger nodded. "Not bad. Keep pushing to find out who these citizen fucks are. Could be some assholes he met in the pen."

They wrapped up the meeting and the brothers dispersed to the great room to relax with a few beers and warm bodies. Hawk and Throttle grabbed a table, and before they could plop down, two beers were placed in front of them. "At least we got shit confirmed. We'll find them, bro." Throttle clasped Hawk's forearm.

He jutted out his chin and nodded, then took a deep drink of beer. *I'm gonna find these fucks who're helping the asshole. I know they're in town, and when I find them, they're gonna tell me everything I wanna know before I slit their goddamn throats.*

He raised his arm and motioned for another beer.

CHAPTER TWENTY

O N THURSDAY AFTERNOON, Cara glanced at her clock and sighed when she saw it was four fifteen. She was exhausted, and all she wanted to do was go home and lie down on their big bed. *I should've canceled my four thirty appointment. I'm so tired. I definitely have to stop taking these late afternoon consultations.* She rubbed her temples. *Right on cue—my afternoon headache. And I'm starving. Again.*

She pulled open her drawer and took out an apple and a small bag of mixed nuts, then reached behind her and grabbed a bottled water from a small cooler she brought to work with her. She munched on her snack as she stared at the clock, counting the minutes until her appointment came. *The sooner I finish, the faster I can get home. I think I'll take tomorrow off. I'm so damn tired.*

Asher poked his head in. "Your four thirty is a little early. You want me to send her in?"

She gathered her apple peelings and tossed them in the trash. Swiping some gloss over her lipstick, she nodded. "Yes. Thanks, Asher." Cara took another gulp of water, then searched for her legal pad. She looked up when she heard a soft knock on her door.

Standing in the doorway was a very busty, bleached-blonde woman. She looked as though she could've been prettier back in the day, but at that moment her face was worn, like it'd endured too much drinking and drugs. She had hard features and a tough look like she would beat the shit out of anyone who crossed her—man or woman. She wore skintight black leather pants and a body-hugging T-shirt that was a size too small for her. Her ample cleavage spilled out over the top of her shirt.

"Come in," Cara said as she stood up. She extended her hand. "I'm Cara Minelli." The woman took her hand and shook it, then sank down on one of the chairs in front of her desk. "How can I help you?"

"I come about my man. He's been fucking shafted."

"First of all, what is your name?" Cara picked up her pen.

"Glory May."

"Is May your last name?"

"Ya."

Cara scribbled down the name. "So you're here to see if I can help your man. What's your relationship with him? Are you married?"

"We's shackin' up." She opened her purse and took out a stick of gum. She pushed it into her mouth and chewed.

"Has he been arrested?"

"In the past." She crossed and uncrossed her legs in tandem with folding and unfolding her hands.

Her fidgeting is driving me crazy. Why didn't I just cancel? Cara's head pounded. "So how do you want me to help you?"

"Like I said, my man was shafted and I want you to prove he's innocent."

Cara's eyes widened. "I'm sorry, but I can't help you out at this stage. I'm a lawyer, not a PI." She flipped through her Rolodex until she found Dean Wesley's phone number; he was her favorite private investigator, and he'd helped on a ton of her cases. "I can give you a very good investigator. I'll write his name and address out for you.

As Cara wrote out his name on a piece of paper, the woman stood up and moved in front of her desk. "I don't want no PI, bitch." Glory shoved the Rolodex off the desk, then grabbed the paper Cara was writing on and tore it up in several pieces. "You're gonna tell the court my man is innocent."

Cara stared in disbelief at the woman whose lips were twisted in anger. *Something's not right here.* Being a criminal defense attorney, Cara had her share of crazies, but something about this scenario told her this was more than a crazy woman who thought her man was innocent. She gazed at her pointedly. "I'm sorry, but I'm going to have to ask you to leave." She went to push the button to Asher's desk, but the woman grabbed her wrist, scratching her.

"Don't you even fuckin' think of doing anything stupid, bitch. It's your fault my man was sent to prison. You think you're something. A hotshot lawyer. I say fuck you!" Spittle formed at the corners of her mouth.

Cara inhaled deeply. "I don't even know who you're talking about. If you'd give me a name, I can pull his file and try to explain why he received a prison sentence."

"Fuck you!"

Suddenly Cara's blood runs cold. The woman was coming unhinged. "If you don't leave now, I'm going to call the police. If you calm down, then you can tell me the name of your boyfriend."

"Do you need any help?" Asher's asked. Cara breathed a sigh of relief.

She nodded. "Ms. May needs to be escorted out. Thanks, Asher."

"I'm not leaving, bitch." Glory crossed her arms and glared at Cara.

Cara stood up, her eyes pleading with Asher. He started to come in, but then his eyes widened, his face stiffened, his lips pressed together, and the muscles on his neck visibly strained. "Cara…." Then he fell on the carpet.

"Asher! What's wrong?" She rushed toward him, then stopped dead in her tracks. A knife stuck out of his back, a red stain soaking up his shirt. "Oh my God! Asher!" The image of him on the floor bleeding didn't seem real. She couldn't comprehend how he had a knife in his back. He'd been fine a few seconds before. Her mind was a whirl of jumbled thoughts, images, and emotions.

She started toward him again, screaming, but Glory blocked her way. Before Cara could say anything, the woman snarled, "Shut the fuck up, bitch!" then slapped her hard across her face.

Cara stumbled backward and reached out for the desk. *I can't fall down. The baby. What the hell is going on here? Asher. Oh, Asher.* Tears stung her eyes as she looked at Asher's body crumpled on the floor. She had to get him help. She heard the clang of chains and snapped her head up, hoping it was one of the prospects. Viper's cruel eyes impaled her. The sound of her heartbeats thrashed in her ears. She stepped backward somehow, thinking her desk was her refuge. Her lips and chin trembled, and the room began to spin.

"Long time no see, *sweetheart*. Did you miss me?" His thin lips curled up. In three quick strides he was next to her. She screamed, but his bony hand clasped around her mouth like a vise. He ran his gaze over her body, his eyes brightening as they lingered on her bump. "Fuckin' perfect. Your man knocked you up. Congratulations." He punched her in the face. "I've got some fun stuff planned for you." He yanked her around her desk. "Get the fuck outta the way," he said to Glory.

She jumped to the side. "I'm sorry, baby."

He threw her a dirty look. "Don't fuckin' piss me off or I'll beat your ass good."

"I won't, baby. I'm always tryin' to do good things for you."

Cara lost it. "Please, I'll do anything you want. Please don't hurt my baby." Her wild look scanned his hardened face. *My baby! I can't let him hurt my baby. I know Sinner and Pike called Hawk. I have to stall until he gets here. He'll put everything right again. Hawk!*

"I like it when you beg. You're not the stubborn, proud cunt you used to be." He frisked her and took her cell phone out of her jacket pocket. "No way I'm making that mistake again, bitch. I'll let Hawk know where you are when I'm ready. I've waited a long time to kill your fuckin' man, but first I want him to know what it's like to lose everything. Having a brat inside you is a fuckin' bonus."

Cara's heart dropped to her stomach. *I can't let him take me away from here. Where's Hawk?* "I'm going to be sick. I have to use the bathroom." *I have to stall. Hurry, honey. We need you.* She stared at him, her chin raised in defiance.

"Too fuckin' bad. If you puke, cunt, you're gonna eat it up. I'm in charge here, not you." He dragged her behind him and made her put on her coat. "If you yell out when we get outside, I'll gut you like the dirty pig you are. Got it? And don't count on the prospects helping out. They're fuckin' history."

He killed Sinner and Pike? Her pulse raced as black spots danced in front of her eyes. She glanced back over her shoulder. *Asher. I can't believe this.* The tears for her fallen friend ran down her cheeks. She and Asher had worked together for more than six years. He wasn't just her assistant; he was her friend. Her heart tore as the madman yanked her out of the office. He laughed as he opened the big glass doors, Cara securely by his side. Glory popped her gum and followed the duo out into the cool evening air.

Viper shoved her in the backseat and bound her ankles and wrists tightly, then flopped Cara onto her back. She flailed about like a hooked fish, and he leaned over and grabbed a fist of her hair, pulling it hard. He kissed her hard and then bit her bottom lip, drawing blood. "That's a preview for our night of fun." He slammed the door and slid into the passenger's seat. "Move it," he said harshly to Glory.

As they drove away from the lights of the town, Cara felt something she hadn't felt in a very long time—hopeless. She closed her eyes tightly and whispered good things to her baby. She didn't want him to be scared before he was even born.

The SUV slipped away from the town.

CHAPTER TWENTY-ONE

HAWK WALKED OUT of the liquor store, a bottle of Jack in one hand and a twelve-pack in the other. As he made his way to his Harley, he noticed a guy unlocking the door on his Jeep. Instantly, Hawk stiffened, his senses on high alert. *I know that Jeep. It's the fat fuck.* He quickened his pace and changed direction. As the man opened the driver's door, he looked up, recognition and fear lacing his eyes. He jumped into the Jeep as Hawk threw down his purchases and made a mad dash toward it. He was almost able to jump on the bumper, but it was out of his reach by a hair.

"Fuck!" Hawk yelled.

The pudgy man laughed and stuck his arm out the window, his middle finger held high.

"Fuckin' asshole!" Hawk ran after the Jeep, noting the license number. He whirled around, ran to his Harley, and leaped on.

He switched on the engine and the cams screamed as he revved the motor and dashed out of the lot, a few people flailing their arms and cursing at him. He took out his phone.

"Hey, buddy," Throttle said.

"I need you to run these plates like fuckin' now—9782WTJ. I need a name and address. Call me back." Hawk slowed his pace and waited. Every second seemed like an hour until his phone rang. "Tell me you got it."

"Yep. Fuck's address is 5610 Wind River Court. You know where that is?"

"Yeah. I owe you."

"You need any help?"

"Not with the asshole. I can handle the fucker with my eyes closed, but I'll need a way to transport him to the hole. Bring your truck and meet me at the address. I'm headed there now." He shoved his phone in his pocket and sped over to the address, taking shortcuts that cars couldn't. He killed his motor a couple blocks away and parked it on a side street. Running through back alleys, he spotted the house, smiling when he saw a large evergreen next to the garage, perfect for hiding.

He'd just positioned himself behind the tree and was putting his gloves on when he saw the Jeep turn the corner and come down the street, swinging into the driveway. The man kept looking in his rearview mirror, and when his garage door opened, Hawk saw relief spread over his moon face. *He looks fuckin' smug. The fuck's gloating that he lost the outlaw. Fuck that, dough boy. Your nightmare's just beginning.* The man pulled into the driveway and Hawk crouched close to the ground, walking stealthily. He flattened himself against the brick wall when he heard the man close his car door. He snuck a peek and saw the man's back was to the garage door opening, and Hawk used the opportunity to quietly go into the garage. The man leaned into his car and pressed something that was on his visor. The garage door began to close. Then Hawk pounced on his prey. The man cried out but soon gasped and sputtered as Hawk held him in a choke hold. "Why the fuck are you running from me, asshole?"

The man's eyes bugged out as his face turned red. Hawk let up a bit on the pressure around the man's neck. The chubby fellow coughed and gasped as he tried to take big gulps of air into his lungs. "I don't know what you're talking about. You came after me in the parking lot. I thought you were going to rob me." All the words tumbled out without him taking a single breath.

"Wrong fuckin' answer." Hawk punched him hard in the kidneys. The man yelled out and sweat poured down his face. "Wanna tell me the truth?" Before he could answer, Hawk's phone beeped. With one hand around his prisoner's neck, he took out his phone. He moved back a few steps, dragging the man with him as he reached into the Jeep, found the remote control, and hit it. The garage door opened and Throttle's pickup came into view in the driveway. He drove it into the garage as far as he could get in, then leaped out of the truck.

"This is the fuck who's been a thorn on your side?"

"Told you he'd be easy. Do you have some rope?" The man twisted and wriggled in Hawk's arm. He punched him again. Harder. "Will you fuckin' stop all that moving? If you keep it up, I'm gonna knock you out." The threat seemed to have done the trick because the portly guy didn't make another sound.

After he was trussed, gagged, and a bag was placed over his head, the two bikers threw him on the backseat of the truck. The man groaned. "Thanks, dude." Hawk clasped Throttle's shoulder. I'll see you at the hole." Throttle nodded and took off.

Hawk rode to the clubhouse, his insides burning with rage. He parked his bike and headed straight to the hole, a concrete room built under the barn on the property that the club used for interrogating people. The brothers lovingly called it the "room of persuasion." It was where people who messed with them met painful deaths. Various tools of persuasion were laid out on long steel tables, and chainsaws and drills hung on hooks mounted on the thick walls.

When Hawk opened the steel doors, he saw the man he was going to kill bound to a chair. Hawk snatched the bag off his head, and the guy's beady little eyes blinked repeatedly as he looked around the room. Throttle leaned against one of the steel tables holding a knife with a very thin blade in his hand. Rock stood against the steel door, his arms crossed, his biceps bulging. Jerry had taken one of the chainsaws down from the wall and rubbed his hand over it as he stared at the bound man.

Hawk bent down and hissed in the man's ear, "We can play out this scene one of two ways. The long, slow, painful way where my man here"—Hawk tilted his chin toward Throttle—"flays you with his knife, or you can answer my questions without bullshitting, and you'll be gifted a quick death."

The man's eyes widened. "If I tell you everything, will you let me live? I never really wanted to be a part of any of this. I fucking needed the money so bad to pay off the damn loan sharks. They threatened to break all my fucking bones." He whimpered.

"When we get finished with you, you're gonna wish you took the fuckin' loan sharks up on their offer." Rock chuckled, and the men in the room sniggered with him.

"Again, you can choose option one or option two. There's no fuckin' option three." Hawk stood back and gazed at his bound prisoner. The man was shaking like a leaf, sweat soaking his shirt and dripping off his face. "You fuckin' made a mistake to take up a partnership with Viper and to come after an Insurgent. Bad move, motherfucker."

"I didn't want to do it. Tommie and Pierson talked me into it. They told me it was a cake job. All we had to do was keep our eyes on some chick who had a fucking great rack." His head bounced back from the force of Hawk's fist on his face. Blood poured from his split lip.

"Don't fuckin' talk about my old lady with disrespect. Who the hell are Tommie and Pierson?"

"Some guys I know at the pool hall. I don't know their last names or anything. They got me involved with this Viper guy. I'm really not the heavy in this. I even tried to warn your woman when I threw the rat at her. I was trying to scare her so she'd know Viper was after her."

Hawk let the nervous man talk, but he knew the man was painting himself in the best possible light. He was bullshitting, and Hawk didn't believe his innocent bystander story for one second. He clenched his fists.

Fuck, this is gonna be a long night.

CHAPTER TWENTY-TWO

CARA SAT ON the cold, concrete floor, leaning against a wall. She was in the basement of a house on the outskirts of Pinewood Springs. The foam padding along the walls and seams told her the room was probably soundproof as well as windowless. She tried for the umpteenth time to loosen her bindings, but all she'd accomplished was breaking open her skin from the constant chafing against the rope. From the distance, she heard a door open. She cringed and her stomach lurched with each footstep on the creaky wooden stairs.

"How are you doing, *sweetheart?*" Viper kneeled next to her and pushed the hair from her face. He was acting tender, and that scared her more than his normal cruel self. She winced as he rubbed her cheek. "Does it hurt?"

She blinked at the memory of Viper's fingers digging into her cheek, causing it to discolor from the bruises and broken capillaries. Now they were back on her skin, and she knew he wanted to hurt and break her. She didn't scream. She didn't fight. She stayed silent. She knew if she fought him he would hurt her worse than he was going to, and she couldn't risk losing the baby. Even if she never got out of this dank, disgusting hellhole, she still wouldn't do anything to put her son in jeopardy. *But you will get out of here. You have to. For the baby.*

When she was first shoved into the room, the claustrophobic stink had caught her off guard—urine, month-old body odor. She shivered but then remembered Viper was still stroking her cheek. He stared at her intently, and she couldn't tell what he was thinking. Then, as if he'd swallowed the potion Dr. Jekyll had prepared, he turned into a beast. His fingers dug into her skin again, his sharp thumbnail drawing blood as it impaled the side of her mouth. "That's how I like you. Silent. Taken. Broken."

She yelped when he twisted her tender nipples, her hand instinctively touching her belly. She tried to concentrate on her deep breathing, picturing herself running through the meadow with Hawk beside her, carrying their small son who had a shock of black hair.

"You like this, don't you, cunt? Look at the way you're smiling. Is pain the way you get off?" Viper's hard voice crushed her thoughts. He slapped her repeatedly; the taste of metal had now become familiar to her. "Glory! Get your ass down here. Now!"

Glory's heels clacked on the wooden stairs and Cara saw hatred in her brown eyes when she entered the room. She went over to Viper and swung her arm around his neck, kissing him deeply. "What do you want, baby? Why don't you leave the bitch and come upstairs with me? I'm making you your favorite dinner—smothered pork chops."

At the mention of food, Cara's stomach growled. *And to think that I was planning a quiet night with Hawk tonight. And poor Asher. How can I ever forgive myself for putting him in the center of danger? Asher... I can't believe you're gone. Sinner and Pike too. They were all so young.* She shook her head as if to dislodge the memories that threatened to shatter her heart in front of a madman and his female sidekick.

"Get the fuck off me." He pushed Glory away from him, then pointed at Cara. "When you look like her, then you can be all over me."

Glory glared at Cara, and if she could, Cara would've turned herself inside out. *The bastard is pitting her against me.* Glory went over to Cara and pulled her hair viciously. Cara cried out and Viper cracked up.

"What's she got that's so special?" Glory kicked Cara's leg and turned to Viper.

"Let's find out. Do you wanna strip her clothes off nice and slow or give her a whipping?" He licked his lips, staring fixedly at Cara. She swallowed hard, her insides a mess.

Glory smiled and grabbed the flogger from Viper's hand before strutting over to Cara and looming over her. "Get up, cunt." The evil look in her eyes made Cara curl up. Glory grabbed her by the hair and pulled her up. Cara gasped in pain, hating the dark-rooted witch with a passion. Viper clapped and laughed heartedly like he was watching a show.

Viper's woman pushed Cara against the wall. "Will you cut this damn rope off her?" she said to Viper. He came over and complied, and Cara shook out her arms, wincing as the blood started circulating through them again.

"I'm gonna love watching my woman whip the shit outta you," he snarled in her ear, then bit down hard on her earlobe. Cara's legs felt weak and she feared she would collapse. The bleached-haired witch roughly grabbed Cara's arms and secured her wrists in cuffs. She then reached around the front of Cara's pants and unzipped them, tugging them down her legs before ripping off her white lace panties and rubbing her ass cheeks.

Viper whistled behind her. "You got a fuckin' nice ass, *sweetheart*. Only thing missing is some nice marks and bruises, but my slut here's got you covered, don't you?"

"Anything for you, babe. I'll make this cunt pay for what she did to you." Glory dug her nails into Cara's globes, then slapped them real hard over and over. Cara held her breath, secretly praying that the madwoman didn't strike her stomach. She knew if she told her not to, the bitch would do it to please Viper. *The woman's pathetic.*

Without warning, Cara heard the flogger whoosh through the air and strike her buttocks. The sting echoed through her body. She leaned her forehead against the concrete wall, gritted her teeth, and concentrated on not breaking down. The strikes kept coming fast, along with Glory and Viper's running commentaries. She blocked them out and forced herself to inhale and exhale deeply. The blows were raining down on her body, from her shoulder blades down to her thighs and back up again, over and over as the woman panted heavily and Viper laughed.

Soon her clothes were torn and her whole back was on fire. She gritted her teeth harder and shut her eyes tightly. She refused to move;

she at least had control over her dignity. Finally, Glory stopped. "I'm tired and bored. Let's go up to eat," she whined. Cara heard her footsteps walk away.

A weight fell against her beaten back and she bit the inside of her cheek to keep from crying out. "Don't worry, *sweetheart*. I'm not gonna forget about you. When I'm done eating and drinking, I'll come back down and play with you some more. I'll show you how I have to fuck since your motherfuckin' old man cramped my style. I think you'll like it." He uncuffed her and she fell in heap onto the floor, the coolness welcome against her burning back. "Now give me a kiss." His mouth covered over hers, darting his serpentine tongue deep inside. She didn't resist. She had no more energy. He pinched her cheek hard and then left, his chuckles bouncing off the walls.

She lay on her side, the tears streaming down her face as she massaged her stomach. "I love you so much. We're going to be fine. Your daddy's coming to get us. Don't worry about anything."

Please come, Hawk. We need you.

HAWK GLANCED AT his phone as it vibrated against the steel table. His brows furrowed when he saw Vince Minelli's number blinking on the screen. He wiped his bloodied hands and answered the phone, pushing open the doors and walking outside into the crisp, night air.

"Vince. What's up?"

"I'm just calling to make sure Cara is all right."

Hawk's heart squeezed. "What do you mean?"

"I've been trying to get a hold of her for the last two hours. She's not answering her phone. I called her landline at work and the machine picked up. I even went over to the house to make sure she hadn't fallen, but she's not there. Then I went back to her office, and that's when I noticed her car in the lot across the street. What the hell's going on? Have you heard from her?"

Fear gripped his heart. *Fuck. This is bad. Cara's in trouble. Where the hell are the prospects?* "Did you call Asher?"

"I've been trying him as well, but there's no answer."

Adrenaline rushed through his body as his nostrils flared. "Don't worry. I'll take care of it. I'll have Cara call you later."

"Take care of what? Is my little girl in trouble?"

"No. I'm gonna make sure she's good. Don't worry. I gotta go." He clicked off the phone, marched back to the concrete room, and slammed the doors open. Picking up the chainsaw, he went to the fat man, who was bloodied and bruised. "Where the fuck is Viper? You got one minute to tell me or I'll dismember you alive. Your time starts now!" Hawk saw the surprised looks on his brother's faces. He turned to Rock. "Try calling Sinner and Pike. Some bad shit has happened, and this fucker knows where Cara is. I'm not gonna fuck around with him anymore!"

Hawk placed the chainsaw between his legs and pulled on the starter rope a couple times. The saw vibrated in his hands and he placed the whirring blade next to the portly man. He turned his head and stared at it, horror etching his face as tears ran down his cheeks. He mouthed the words, "Please. No."

Hawk handed the saw to Jerry, then bent down and yelled in the man's ear, "You gonna tell me where Viper is? Your minute is up." The man nodded and Hawk motioned to Jerry to turn off the saw.

Rock came back in the room. "We got a hold of Sinner. He's hurt bad. Bones, Wheelie, and Hoss are going to bring him back. I already called Doc to get his ass over here. Pike's gone."

A white-hot rage consumed Hawk. Pike was only twenty years old; he was someone's son, brother, grandson, uncle, and nephew. "I'm gonna make sure that motherfucker pays for everything he's done. And if he's hurt my woman and son, I'll fuckin' find out who his family is and kill every last one of them!"

The men looked at Hawk. "Your son?" Throttle asked.

Hawk nodded, his eyes glistening. "Yeah. Cara's over four months pregnant. We were gonna tell everyone at the family barbecue this weekend."

Throttle clamped his hand on Hawk's forearm. "Fuck, that's tough. Let's go get your family and kill some Viper ass."

Hawk looked at Rock and Jerry. "You know what to do with this piece of shit. After him, get the other two who were in on this and do what needs to be done." The two brothers nodded.

"We gotta take my SUV. No way can we take the bikes," Hawk said. Throttle had run back into the club and gathered Axe, Jax, Chicory, Puck, Johnnie, Rags, and Chas. As he slipped a couple knives in his boots, his phone rang. He didn't recognize the number, but his gut tightened and a darkness crept over him.

"Who the fuck is this?"

A deep chuckle. "Your woman's keeper. We're having a real good time."

His facial muscles twitched as the boiling lava inside him churned, hungry for destruction. "You're dead, you motherfucker."

A dry cackle. "I was about to say the same thing to you."

Burning rage and hatred smoldered in his narrowed eyes as he imagined the various ways of exacting revenge. "You gotta hide behind a woman? Let's end this shit between us, man-to-man."

"But your woman is so fun to play with. Anyway, I had to finish what I'd started a couple years ago. Ask your slut how she's loving our time together."

"Hawk?" Cara's voice hitched.

A stab of tenderness sliced through his hatred. "Baby? Fuck. Are you hurt?"

"No."

He heard the tears in her voice. "Oh, Cara.... Are there a lot of bikers with the fucker?"

"No."

"Is the baby okay?"

"I think so."

"I'm coming to get you."

"I lo—"

"Your chat is over," Viper's hard-edged voice said. "I'll let you know the time and place for us to meet. I'm growing tired of this fuckin' game. I'm gonna fuck your whore real good. I'm gonna use a long, thick stick. I can't wait to ram it in her cunt and ass. Fuckin' sweet. It's—"

"I'm gonna love beating you to death, you fuckin' sonofabitch!" Hawk slammed his fist on the table.

The phone went dead.

A guttural roar ripped from his throat as his ears pounded. "I'm gonna fuckin' punch his ass, then slit his goddamn neck!" His muscles strained against his skin. "Let's go. Now!" He stormed out of the club and sprinted to his SUV. When he swung open the car door, he felt a hand on his shoulder. He spun around and met Banger's icy blue eyes.

"The brothers filled me in. I wanna go with you to help kill the vermin."

"Thanks, brother, but you're needed here. Sinner's in a real bad way, and the doc is on his way. I got my crew." Hawk whistled and motioned for the men to come over.

"You got enough brothers? Take some more. The Demon Riders may be swarming the place."

"Cara said there weren't a bunch of bikers."

"But she probably doesn't know who's on the outside."

Hawk nodded. "I don't think fuckass would risk attracting the attention of the fuckin' badges by having a bunch of bikers in the county. A shitload of bikers can't go unnoticed, but you have a point. I'll bring a few extra men. I gotta go. Cara needs me."

Banger pulled him into a quick hug, and then they bumped fists. "You need backup, just let me know."

"Thanks."

"Do me a favor."

Hawk reached under the driver's seat and took out his 9mm Glock, tucking it in his jeans' waistband. "What?"

"Bring me back Viper's balls."

He smiled blandly. "I'll also bring back the sonofabitch's limp cock." He tilted his chin at Banger, then slid into the driver's seat. Throttle and Jax jumped in next to him while Chas, Rags, Puck, and Johnnie crowded in the back. The six other brothers piled into Chicory's SUV. The two vehicles peeled out of the lot and sped toward their destination.

As Hawk drove, his hands clutched the steering wheel. A pitch-black feeling consumed him. It was twisted and distorted and burned like fire, lacing his veins and creeping up his spine. He was intoxicated with the desire to destroy and exterminate, the emotion leaving a bitter taste in his mouth. He pushed down hard on the accelerator, anxious to wreak havoc in the most basic and brutal way.

He swallowed the lump in his throat.

Hang on, babe. I'm on my way.

CHAPTER TWENTY-THREE

As THEY DROVE, Hawk had the other SUV on speakerphone, mapping out a course of action for when they arrived at Viper's lair. Hawk knew the element of surprise was on his side. They parked their cars off the road in a dense patch of trees and crept toward the house in a large span. Hawk concentrated on the task before him, pushing aside the sound of Cara's quivering voice and the images he'd seen on the sonogram screen. He filled his veins with ice, detaching from all emotions including hate and rage. He'd learned the importance of dispassion when he fought in Afghanistan. As a member of the Marine Corps Reconnaissance, nerves of steel and ultimate objectivity were the attributes that kept the ground forces informed and better equipped to do battle. There was no room for error.

The Insurgents spread out and searched for any possible lookouts as they slowly approached the nondescript ranch-style house set back from the road. Hawk immediately noticed all the basement windows were boarded up and knew in his gut that his beloved was being held captive down there. He motioned for Chas, Hoss, Rags, Jax, and Axe to check out the back side of the house.

"I'm gonna go in," he told Throttle in a low voice. "Spot me."

Hawk, on his stomach, snaked his way toward the front of the house; the overgrowth and darkness of night helped to keep him concealed. When he came nearer, he saw two men in cuts smoking weed, the glow of the tips of their joints like tiny beacons. He looked beyond them and spotted the outlines of Axe and Rags. *Are these two the only fucks standing watch?* He couldn't believe how cocky Viper was. The one thing Hawk had learned throughout his life was to never underestimate a person or situation. *Fuckass just lost the goddamn war.*

He lay hidden until the two men turned to face the house, then pounced. As he did so, Axe and Rags followed suit. The three Insurgents took the guards totally by surprise. Soon, Hoss and Chas came over to help subdue the two men. On closer inspection, Hawk recognized one of the men from the Demon Riders—Chewy, Kimber's ex—who'd started all the ruckus at the expo the previous summer. As the men punched the two Demon Riders into oblivion, Throttle came up behind Hawk.

"I can't fuckin' believe these fuckers are the only ones keeping watch," he said.

Hawk shrugged. "The fuckass is incredibly stupid." Rustling from the trees behind them made them spin around, drawing out their guns. They put them down when Chicory approached. "What's up?" Hawk asked.

"We picked up two fucks who were lurking around. They aren't bikers. They may be the two assholes you're looking for."

After he described them, Hawk pressed his lips together. "They fit the description of the guys the fat fuck gave up. What'd you do with them?"

"Secured on the ground. After we're done with shit here, we'll take 'em to the hole." Chicory spat on the ground.

"It seems that we've penetrated Viper's security." Hawk smiled wryly, then turned to Axe. "Check to see if either of these assholes has a key. I gotta get in there. A lot can happen in a matter of seconds." A tinge of fear pricked at Hawk's tough shield, but he dispelled it.

"Got it." Axe handed a keychain with a single key on it to Hawk. "There's a bigger ring with a bunch of keys, but my guess is the single one is for this shithole."

Hawk nodded. "Throttle and Rags will come with me. You guys stand watch. Don't fuckin' underestimate anything." He trudged up the broken sidewalk, his two brothers close behind him. On the porch, the men walked toe to heel, which muted their footsteps. He slowly tried the doorknob. It was locked. He slipped the key in the door and turned it. It opened. *Fuck, this is too easy. Either this is a goddamn trap, or prison has rendered fuckass brain dead.*

The house was small with very little furniture. A light glowed in one of the back rooms that Hawk guessed was the kitchen. Other than that one light, the rest of the rooms were dark. He motioned to Throttle and Rags to check them out. The two men drew their guns and slowly stalked to the back of the house. Hawk, gun in hand, went through the two rooms in the front of the house. They all met back in what appeared to be the living room. "Nothing," Hawk whispered, and the two men nodded in agreement.

"She has to be in the basement. We gotta fuckin' get this right because I know he'll try to kill my old lady if his balls are against the wall." Hawk pushed the image of Cara's battered and lifeless body out of his mind. *Focus, man. You're here on a mission. Execute your goal—kill the target and save the captive.* He took a couple deep breaths. "Okay. Let's move."

Hawk opened the basement door quietly. From the top of the stairs, they could hear the low murmur of voices. One sounded like a woman. *It doesn't sound like Cara.* He looked at the stairs. Wood. *Fuck!* Hawk closed the door. "I'll bet the stairs creak like hell. We gotta take our boots off, and then we'll head down. Place your feet as close to the wall as you can. Let's go."

The men glided their knives out of their boots before they took them off. Tucking their hardware into their pockets and waistbands, they faced the basement door. Hawk opened it slowly and placed his foot on the first step, ball of the foot down, close to the wall. He spread his weight as much as possible and placed his foot on the next stair. Step by step, the three Insurgents descended into the bowels of Viper's funhouse.

They hugged the walls in the empty basement, inching toward the room with the light and voices. As they came nearer, Hawk heard Viper's voice. He sucked in his breath, making himself concentrate on the mission.

"I'm ready to make another phone call to your man, *sweetheart.* It doesn't seem fair for me to be having all the fun." He laughed. "I can't wait to show him how hard I can fuck your cunt with this large baton."

Hawk recognized Cara's gasp and he stiffened, his pulse racing. Throttle gripped his arm. "Easy," he said in a barely audible voice. The Insurgents stayed against the wall for a couple minutes to make sure no one but a woman was in there with Viper and Cara. Satisfied that it was only the three of them, Hawk gave the signal to rush the room.

In seconds, Hawk, Throttle, and Rags flooded into the room, their guns drawn. Viper lounged against a table while Cara stood naked, facing the wall, her arms and legs cuffed spread-eagle. A bleached-blonde woman was next to her, a paddle in her hand. Red lashes, oozing welts, and black and blue bruises streaked Cara's back, buttocks, and thighs.

White-hot fury melted the cool detachment Hawk had been exercising, and he roared from deep within him as he leaped on top of Viper. He pummeled blow after blow onto Viper, trying to smash him into the ground. He didn't just want him dead; he wanted him busted, wiped out, nothing left to bury.

Stunned, Viper tried to defend himself by punching back, but he was no match for Hawk's fury—a fury driven by love. It was a rage that could neither be contained nor stopped. The attack on Viper was fierce and deadly. Long after his life had ended, Hawk kept pounding him until Throttle put his arm around him and said, "It's over, dude. Enough."

Hawk bowed his head, his chest heaving. Suddenly, the reality of where he was flooded through him. He spun around and saw Cara wide-eyed on the floor, her arms wrapped around her knees. He dashed over and held her close, peppering her face, neck, shoulders, and arms with his kisses. "Oh, baby. I'm so fuckin' sorry I couldn't have prevented this. I love you." He stroked her hair as she stared straight ahead, shivering. Spotting a blanket nearby, he dashed over and grabbed it, then draped it over her. "Can you talk to me, baby? Are you okay?"

"I knew you'd come. I kept telling the baby that his daddy would help us." Her teeth chattered.

"How's the little guy?" he asked softly, slipping his hand between her arms to rub her belly.

"I don't know. I feel pain in my abdomen. I need to get to a hospital," she chattered.

Throttle came up behind him as the bleached-blonde screamed and wailed. He gripped Hawk's shoulder. "Get your woman to the hospital. I've got this."

Hawk looked over his shoulder and locked eyes with the woman. Black streaks stained her face. "Slit the cunt's throat," he said icily. He lifted Cara in his arms and rushed out the door.

Upstairs, most of the Insurgents were there, with a few of them standing watch outside in the front. Rags came up to Hawk. "Take care of your woman. I'll handle things around here. We'll make sure there aren't any witnesses. We'll let the fuckin' badges think whatever the fuck they want. Knowing them, they'll claim credit for finding the fuckass. Go on."

Warmth flooded through Hawk as he watched his brothers taking care of business. No matter what happened in the world, he and each of the club members knew the brotherhood always had their back. Through thick and thin they stood united until the end of time. It touched him to the core.

He jerked his chin at Rags and the others and stepped outside.

CHAPTER TWENTY-FOUR

A TELEVISION SET was perched on a shelf facing the hospital bed. The picture was on—a news show—but the sound had been muted. Cara slid her eyes sideways to Hawk, who sat close to her, holding her hand. She wasn't sure if the watery light coming in through the mini blinds indicated dusk or dawn. She had no idea how long she'd slept. All she remembered was Hawk's strong arms lifting her and taking her away from the madman and his assistant. She looked at the IV, wondering which liquid was pushing through her veins.

"You up, baby?" Hawk's deep voice startled her.

"Yeah," she croaked. Her lips and mouth were so dry. It felt like she had cotton balls stuffed in the back of her throat.

"Want some water?" Hawk reached behind him and produced a glass with water and a straw in it. "Here, let me raise your head a bit."

She closed her eyes and felt her head and upper body move up, letting Hawk place the straw between her chapped lips before she drank deeply. "What's going on with me?" Her gaze scanned his face for any hints of worry.

"You were pretty much exhausted and dehydrated." Hawk put the glass back on the table, then leaned over and kissed her on each cheek. "The doctor's putting fluid in you to hydrate you."

"And the baby?" She touched her stomach.

He smiled widely. "The baby's fine. He's a fighter. He'll make a good Insurgent when he grows up."

She grimaced. "Don't say that. Worrying about you in the club is about all I can take." His head dipped down over her and they locked gazes. With her fingertips, she brushed some stray hairs away from his forehead. "I was so scared for the baby." Tears misted her eyes. His lips sought hers but she turned away and they fell on her cheek.

"Why'd you turn away from me?"

"My lips are so chapped. It's gross."

He scrunched his eyebrows slightly. "Really, babe?" Then he placed his hands around her face and covered her mouth with his, kissing her deeply. "I love you," he murmured.

Someone clearing his throat drew their attention. A medium-built man in a white coat and stethoscope around his neck walked over to the right side of the bed. "I'm Dr. Tortello. How are you feeling?" He took the stethoscope from around his neck.

"I feel much better now that I've slept. What time is it?"

"Five o'clock in the evening. You slept very soundly, which is exactly what you needed." He smiled and placed the tips in his ears and the chest piece over her torso. He moved the cool metal piece around for a bit, then pulled out his earpieces. "You're doing well." He took out a handheld Doppler monitor, covered it with gel, and moved it around her belly until their baby's heartbeats were detected. "Sounds strong and healthy."

Cara tightened her grip on Hawk's hand, and he leaned down and kissed her softly. "I'm so glad. I was so worried."

"If you would've been directly struck in your belly, you'd have had a problem. I checked for bleeding and leaking fluid, and you didn't have any. Also, since the pain is in your back and upper stomach near the ribs, it's just hurting you and not the baby. You were lucky."

"I know," she whispered.

"When does my wife get to come home?"

The doctor looked up from his chart. "I want to keep her in for one more night. I'll check her sodium and potassium levels, and if everything looks good, she can go home tomorrow afternoon." He put his pen in his pocket. "If you don't have any more questions, I'll leave you to it."

After he left, Hawk ran his fingers through her messy hair. "I can't wait to have you back home, woman." She smiled. "The fuckin' badges are gonna be here to ask you shit about what happened to you. The hospital had to call them because of your back." His eyes narrowed. "My blood boils every time I think about what that fuckass and his dirty slut did to you."

Cara patted his hand. "It doesn't matter anymore. It's over and we're together again… and we're going to have a baby boy! Life is good, honey. Let's put the darkness of the last two days away and let light in. Don't let it eat at you. If you do, then the mean asshole won."

Hawk nodded in agreement. "You're right, baby. Anyway, the badges are gonna want to know what the fuck happened to you. We need to come up—"

"I'll tell them I was attacked, blindfolded, beaten, and left for dead. That when my dad called because he was worried about me, you traced where I was through my phone. Then you came and found me, and took me to the hospital. It sounds plausible, doesn't it? I can say the blonde woman who came for the four thirty appointment was a ruse, and she and a guy were there to rob and hurt me for fun."

He shook his head. "You're a kickass old lady, woman. You know the fuckin' score."

"Yes, I do." A tear slipped down her cheek and she wiped it away. "Remembering that horrible woman made me think of Asher. I can't believe he's gone." A small sob escaped her throat and her shoulders slumped.

"Fuck, baby. I forgot to tell you that Asher's gonna be okay."

Her head jerked up. "Okay? Then he's not… dead?"

"Nah. He's injured pretty bad, and you'll be without an assistant for a while, but he pulled through. After the fuckers took you, Asher was able to call 911 before he passed out. He's in ICU, but he's doing good."

Her face was wet and her eyes shone. "Thank God. What wonderful news. I'm so happy. This *is* a miracle." Her voice broke.

"I said he's gonna be fine. No need to cry." Hawk wiped the tears off her face and held her tight. "Damn, babe. Life is just one fuckin' freefall." He looked over his shoulder when a knock sounded on the half-opened door. Two men in suits walked in and stood at the foot of her bed, flashing their law enforcement badges. "Showtime," he whispered in her ear.

She stared blankly at the detectives, then smiled when she recognized one of them, Earl McCue. "Hi, Earl. Why don't you both take a seat." She took a deep breath and waited for the onslaught of questions, grateful for Hawk's firm hand on hers. She'd put on the best performance of her life, knowing full well neither of the men would believe a word she said.

It was a game in the outlaw world.

A game of survival, and she'd learned the rules well.

CHAPTER TWENTY-FIVE

I T WAS AN early evening in August. The air was pleasant and the chirping crickets sang out from the branches of maple and elm trees. Pink and orange wisps rubbed out the perfect blue sky from earlier in the day, their rose-gold glow reflecting off the cragged mountain peaks. Cara squirmed in the cushy wicker chair, her swollen feet resting on a soft ottoman. At eight months, she was so ready to give birth; it felt like she had been pregnant for a lifetime. She readjusted the pads in her bra and, once again, tried to slide her butt farther back in the chair to relieve her lower back pains.

The months that followed her abduction by Viper had flown by in a whirlwind of baby showers, doctor visits, and birthing classes. She'd been shocked when Hawk had agreed to be her coach. She'd made it her mission to get him to do it, but his instant agreement took the wind out of her sails, in a good way. He was so involved with the pregnancy that it made her heart soar and brought tears down her face several times, especially in the past month or two as her hormones bounced all over the place.

Asher, one hundred percent healed, had been doing a fantastic job of keeping things in order at the office. He'd just finished taking his law school admissions test, and Cara hoped he'd done real well. She had mixed feelings in that she hated to lose him, but she knew he'd make a stellar attorney. She was happy for him and told him that he'd always have a job at her practice.

The horror that Viper and his crazy girlfriend put her through threatened to shut her down, as it had with her past encounter with him two years before. She'd gone back to her therapist and worked through the chains of fear and nervousness that bogged her down. She didn't want the shadows to lurk in her mind, only positive and loving thoughts for her baby.

"What're you thinking about?" Hawk asked as he raised his beer to his lips.

"How I can't wait to get rid of my horrible heartburn. What about you?"

He chuckled. "I'm thinking about how beautiful you look." He leaned over and tugged up her top, sprinkling kisses on her large belly as he rubbed his hands all around it. "I fuckin' love seeing our son growing in you. You're so sexy, babe."

She snorted and took a sip of lemonade. "I don't *feel* sexy. My back is killing me, I can hardly breathe, and my feet are like small watermelons."

He grabbed her hand and kissed it. "You're the sexiest I've ever seen you, babe."

She giggled. "Thanks for saying that."

"I mean it. I find you damn sassy and sexy—a lethal combination." He winked.

She playfully swatted his arm, watching him intently. "Since you're in such a good mood, I want to share something with you." She took another drink of lemonade, the sweet liquid waking up her mouth. She looked at him and he cocked his head. "Ever since I found out I was pregnant, I've been doing some research. I think it's important for children to know where they come from." She licked her lips.

A small frown began to materialize on his face. "Go on."

She took another sip of her drink. "I'm just going to tell it to you straight—I found your mother."

His face darkened like clouds during a thunderstorm. "You what? Did I ask you to do that?"

"No, but hear me out. I thought if—"

"You shouldn't have thought anything about this. I didn't ask you to do this."

"I know. I just thought it was important for our son and future kids to know their paternal grandmother. They'll know my side real well, but your family will be a mystery to them."

"No, it won't. My family is the Insurgents. What the fuck were you thinking?"

Crap. I didn't think he'd be this *mad.* "I just thought it would be nice for them to know her if they wanted to."

"I don't give a fuck if they know her or not. I don't want her anywhere near my son."

"I understand your anger, I really do, but you're not really sure why your mother left. Maybe it was survival."

He gave her a long, hard stare. "I know exactly why she left. She was a selfish fuckin' whore who put her happiness and her love for a man over her own son. She left me with a monster, and she fuckin' knew how he was. Hell, she was escaping from him. She told me she would take me, and she left me all alone with him. And he fuckin' punished me every chance he got for her leaving him. I don't give a fuck about her, and I don't want her in my life or our child's."

"I'm sorry. I just thought I could help you put all the anger and resentment you feel toward her to rest. Forgiveness can be quite freeing," she said softly.

"God forgives, but I don't. I made peace with my childhood a long time ago."

"She lives in St. Petersburg, Florida."

Hawk narrowed his eyes, his lips a straight line. "Cara, leave it alone. Back the fuck off on this one. I'm not interested to know anything about her. She was a shitty mom, and she doesn't deserve the privilege of knowing her grandchild. This conversation is over." He sat back in his chair and finished his beer.

The tension and anger rolling off him was palpable. She was so hoping he could learn to forgive his mother so he could let go of the anger about his past. She knew it was still inside him, somedays stronger than others. She'd hoped to bridge the way to releasing anger and embracing forgiveness, but it hadn't worked out. *I want to tell you that you have a half-sister and brother in Florida, but you want to keep the door closed.* And she respected that.

She pushed herself up from the chair and waddled over to him. Taking out his hair tie, she raked her fingers through his silky hair, drew it up in a sleek ponytail, and tied it again. "I'm sorry I upset you. I didn't mean anything bad from it."

He tugged her onto his lap and kissed her neck, jaw, and cheeks. "It's okay, babe. It's just that you need to respect the fact that, to me, my past died the day I walked through the Insurgents' clubhouse doors. From that day on, my family has always been the brotherhood. You and the baby are now part of my family. I don't need or want anything else in my life."

Her heart warmed as she gazed into his love-filled blue eyes. "I screwed up. I keep thinking that biological parents and siblings are what matters when it sometimes has nothing to do with being a family. I love you so much that I thought I was helping you to understand. Now I realize that you've been the one who has helped me to understand the meaning of family, no matter how unconventional." She kissed him passionately.

They held each other well after the sun set, her head pillowed against his chest, his hands on her belly. Then her stomach growled and he laughed. "You hungry, babe? Let's go inside and I'll grill you a thick steak. You can just lie on the couch while I take care of everything."

"You're spoiling me again," she joked.

He kissed her hard and deep. "I plan on spoiling you for a lifetime, so you better fuckin' get used to it."

They went inside and he made her the most delicious steak and baked potato dinner that she'd had since the previous week when he'd grilled for them. After dinner, he cleaned the dishes, then took her hand and led her to their bedroom. He slowly undressed her, his tender gaze roaming over her nakedness from head to toe and then back up again—slowly. "Fuckin' beautiful," he said in a low voice. Crimson colored her cheeks as he drew her to him and embraced her.

He walked her to the bed and eased her on her side before coming up behind her and cradling her in his arms. He put her leg over his and slid his hand down to her warm sex. Each time his finger stroked her clit, a bolt of desire shot through her until she moaned and ground against his hand. Then he entered her and her breath caught in her throat.

"Your pussy feels real good, babe." His voice was tender and raspy and it drove her wild. He placed little kisses all over her shoulder and neck, and her body smiled all over.

As he moved in and out of her, she craned her neck and his mouth covered hers, and they rocked together in a gentle and erotic dance. His gentle yet arousing movements stole her breath and reminded her why she fell in love with him.

His pants turned into grunts and his thrusts quickened as he stroked her wet clit. Her body soon exploded in a funnel of euphoria, and it was glorious. His deep growl echoed in her ear as he came right behind her. "I love you always, babe," he rasped, his breath hot against her neck.

"I'll love you forever," she whispered back. She slipped a pillow between her legs and tucked Hawk's hand under her chin.

And they fell asleep in each other's arms, sated, happy, and in love.

CHAPTER TWENTY-SIX

HAWK RODE THE lawn mower over their vast yard. The sunlight streamed through the trees, and the air had a subtle hint of fall. Some of the aspens were already showing a small tinge of gold around the edges of their round leaves. At the edge of the woods, he maneuvered the machine and rode it in a straight line to his back patio. He saw Cara on the deck, waving her arms at him. He rode up to the edge of the brick and turned off the motor.

"Did you want something?" he asked as he wiped his brow.

"It's time to go to the hospital. My water broke and my contractions are consistently coming every five minutes. I called the doctor and he wants me to go to the hospital."

Hawk had already leaped off the lawn mower and had his arm around Cara. His face was taut. "Let's go. You can tell me the details in the car. I'll get your suitcase." He ushered his wife into the house, pausing long enough to get her suitcase from the front closet before he led her to the garage. "You feeling okay? How's the pain?"

"I'm okay," Cara grunted as she bit her lower lip. Hawk settled her in the car, flung her overnight bag in the backseat, and took off toward Pinewood Springs Hospital. When they arrived, Cara was whisked off to a room while Hawk parked the car. As he crossed the parking lot on the way back to the hospital, an amalgam of emotion hit him: elation, nervousness, empathy for Cara. He hoped her labor wasn't too long or painful. He entered the elevator, not sure what to expect when he got to her room. The doors closed and he rode up to the fifth floor, lost in his thoughts.

Five hours later, he stood by her, helping her shift her position to get comfortable. He placed a cool washcloth over her forehead while he wiped the sweat from her face with another one. "Are you sure you don't want something for the pain, babe?" His insides were clenched. *I fuckin' hate to see her suffer like this.*

"I'm good," she panted. "It's actually getting better. You've been really good at distracting me when the contractions start. It helps…. Oh crap, here they come." She grabbed onto Hawk's hand and he encouraged her to focus on a breathing pattern. "Damn, honey. I can feel the baby coming. Get the goddamn doctor! Fuck!"

Hawk stared for a few seconds and then ran out in the hall, grabbing a nurse as she walked by. "Get the doctor. My wife said the baby's coming."

The nurse ran into the room and went over to Cara's spread legs. "She's right. I'll be right back." She dashed out of the room.

"Where's the damn doctor? The baby is coming out!"

Hawk shook his head. "Fuck. What am I supposed to do?"

"Go over and stay there to get the baby. I feel it coming."

"Can't you hold it in until the doctor comes?"

"Are you fucking serious? What the hell do you think? It's coming!"

Hawk stood transfixed as he saw a spot of jet-black hair at her opening. "Fuck! He's coming out!"

"That's what I've been saying," she panted as her face turned red from pushing.

"What the fuck do I do? They didn't teach this shit in the birthing classes."

"Maybe they should," Dr. Penborne said.

Relief washed over Hawk. "I'm fuckin' glad to see you, Doc."

He smiled. "Go to your wife. Your son is doing things his way."

Cara said, "Like his father" at the same time as Hawk replied, "Like his mother." They both chuckled, and then Cara let out a loud scream. Hawk ran to her side and had her squeeze his hand as he soothed her with calming words, telling her to focus on her breathing pattern. Then he heard the cry and he jerked his eyes up to the most wonderful sight he'd ever seen in his life—his newborn son. A shock of ebony hair covered the baby's small head, and he peered through brand new eyes as his tiny legs kicked in a jagged motion.

"Fuck," he muttered as he turned his glossy eyes to Cara. "We have a son," he said in a voice that was almost broken. She reached for his hand and held it, tears spilling down her face. For a suspended moment they were locked together through a bond so strong that it took their breaths away. Then she turned from him and looked at her baby as the nurse set him on her warm abdomen, drying him off and covering him with a blanket before she placed a cap over his head.

"He's beautiful," Cara gushed.

Hawk swallowed hard. He'd never seen anything so awesome in his life as the birth of his son. The tiny baby who rested on his wife's belly was his boy. The little one had his blood flowing through him, and it was mind-blowing. *This is what can take a man down. I can't fuckin' believe he's* ours.

With two fingers, he stroked the baby's hair, marveling at how soft it was. He slipped his small finger under the blanket and caressed his son's tiny hand, grinning when his baby's fingers grasped it. He bent over and kissed Cara deeply, his heart bursting, his life complete. "I love you," he said against her mouth.

"I love you too. We have a son!"

"Shall we try breastfeeding?" the nurse asked. "The doctor recommends having your son in direct contact with you until after the first feeding."

Hawk grabbed a chair and pulled it close to Cara's bed. He planned to spend the night with Cara and their boy, but he'd leave and let her parents have some private time with her and their grandson. He wanted to call Banger, Throttle, and Jax and tell him that he had a healthy baby boy.

"Have you come up with a name yet?" the nurse asked as she helped to position the baby on Cara's breast.

Cara nodded. "Braxton Vincent Benally."

"It has a good ring to it." The nurse smiled.

Fuck yeah. And I'm gonna make sure you have the best life possible, little man. I promise to always be there for you, no matter what. I'll fuckin' try to be the best dad to you. I just want you to know that.

I'm a dad.

Fuckin' awesome.

TANGERINE AND GOLD licked the blue, cloudless sky. A nip in the air hinted that winter wasn't too far away. Falling leaves tumbled to the carpeted ground as semi-bare branches scraped against the country club's windows. Looming above the town, the jagged peaks of the mountains had a dusting of white. Hawk held his six-week-old son in his arms while the guests took their places at the table. That morning he and Cara baptized their son, and the godparents—Banger and Sherrie—looked somber as the priest vocalized their responsibilities in the baby's life. Cara's parents, aunts, uncles, and several cousins were there. The baptism meant a lot to Cara and her family, so Hawk went along with it, glad to be part of a ritual in her citizen's world.

As they ate lunch at the country club, Hawk couldn't stop looking at his wife who simply glowed. *She's even more gorgeous now that we have Braxton. I can't get enough of her. I can't wait to fuck her.* The doctor had told Cara that it was best to wait at least a couple months before she had sex, and Hawk had been counting down the days. He loved holding her, kissing her, and cuddling with her, but he wanted between her legs in the worst way. Even though she was so tired most days, the hungry looks she gave him told him she was missing him too.

"Do you want anything, honey?" she asked as she speared a cube of pineapple with her fork.

He swept the hair away from her ear and whispered, "You."

She grasped his thigh under the table and ran her fingers up close to his bulge. "I want you too."

"We got two more fuckin' weeks to go."

She laughed. "Are you keeping track?"

"Fuck yeah. I can't wait to be inside you, babe."

At that moment, Braxton woke up with a loud cry. Cara started to get up when Hawk said, "I'll get him." He leaned over and picked up his son and the boy stopped crying. He stroked Braxton's forehead with his finger, and the baby closed his eyes. And Hawk held his son until he secured him in a car seat in the back of the SUV.

When they came home, Cara picked up Braxton. "I'm going to feed him. I'm glad today's over. I'm exhausted."

He pulled her close, his arms wrapped around her and the baby. "After you're done, let's watch a movie. You need to relax, babe."

She smiled and walked into the sun room.

An hour later, Hawk stroked Cara's hair as she lay in his lap, their baby pressed close to her on the couch. A movie about invaders from space flickered on the big-screen television. From the way Cara was breathing, he knew she'd fallen asleep. He looked down at his wife and son, both so sweet and peaceful-looking, and his heart swelled with love and pride. *I have everything I could ever want.*

I'm one fuckin' lucky sonofabitch.

He smiled wide as he watched the earthlings battle it out with the alien spaceships.

CHAPTER TWENTY-SEVEN

Christmas Eve

CARA PULLED OUT the stuffed mushrooms from the oven and placed them on the counter to set. She glanced over and saw Hawk opening another bottle of wine as he threw his head back, laughing at something Throttle had said. She ran her eyes over her man's tall, ripped physique and her stomach fluttered as it usually did when she thought of how much she loved and desired him. *I wonder if I'll be this horny when I'm in my eighties.* She walked over to him and scratched him lightly on the back of his neck. He looked over his shoulder, his eyes sparkling when he saw her. She brushed a kiss on his cheek, then squeezed his ass cheek quickly before she went back to the mushrooms on the counter.

"Do you need any help?" Clotille asked as Cara arranged the appetizers on a platter.

"I'm good, but when things settle down a bit more, you're going to have to teach me how to make some of your awesome Cajun dishes," Cara replied.

"Only if you teach me how to make your spaghetti sauce. Rock's crazy for it." Clotille smiled and popped a mushroom in her mouth. "Delicious."

"Life still good between you guys?" Cara swiveled to the oven to take out a batch of quiches.

"Fantastic. I've never been this happy in my life. And I'm officially Rock's old lady. He gave me a cut with his property patch earlier today." Clotille took a sip of her white wine.

Cara gave her a big hug. "That's awesome! We were all wondering when he'd ask you to be his old lady. I'm so happy for you. Loving these men is great, isn't it? I can't even imagine what would make me happier than I am right now." Cara took the spatula and scooped up several quiches, placing them on a sliver tray.

"Another baby would do it," Hawk said behind her, his face nuzzling her neck.

She giggled. "That tickles. I can't just pop babies out, even though I know you'd love for me to do that." She looked at Clotille. "We're planning on waiting a year or two before the next one."

"I can't wait to start trying after everyone leaves. I'm gonna give it to you real good, the way I know you love." His hot breath against her skin sent tingles up her spine. She shifted her weight, dampness coating her panties. "I know your little dance means you're getting fuckin' wet." He pulled her earlobe between his lips and bit down. She suppressed a yelp.

"I love the way you stuffed the brie cheese with walnuts and apricots. It's sinfully addicting," Addie said as she came over to the kitchen island. She took a water cracker, cut a slab of brie, and took a bite. "Yum."

Hawk cupped one of Cara's ass cheeks and squeezed it before pinching it. "Just a taste, babe." He winked and swaggered over to Chas, Axe, Bear, and Jerry.

"I love Christmas parties. It's my absolute favorite holiday." Kylie's blue eyes sparkled as she poured a scoop of brandied eggnog into a crystal cup.

"How does it feel to only have one semester left of school?" Baylee asked as she joined the group of women in the kitchen.

"So great! I can't wait to move back here and get a house with Jerry. All this commuting has been a pain in the ass."

"I don't know how you did it. When I had to go to Denver to work on that huge building project my firm got, it drove me nuts not being with Axe except for the weekends. And the drive back and forth totally exhausted me. When I came back here, I slept for two whole days. Axe was raring to go and all I wanted to do was sleep." Baylee chuckled.

"Just when are these men *not* raring to go?" Belle asked as she poured more wine into her glass. The women burst out laughing, and the men threw them a suspicious look. "They know we're talking about them," Belle said in a hushed tone. The women laughed louder.

Jack and Andrew ran up to Addie and Clotille. "Can Jack spend the night at our house, Mom? Please?" Andrew snagged a sugar cookie and took a bite, his dark eyes looking anxiously at his mother's.

"I'm sure his parents want him to be home with them on Christmas Eve," Clotille said as she threw a glance at Addie. "We're going to spend Christmas with them tomorrow, so there'll be plenty of time to spend with each other." Cara smiled when she saw Andrew's and Jack's faces fall.

"Please, Mom?" Andrew pleaded, then Jack took up his pleas with Addie. Soon, Chas and Rock walked over.

"What's going on here?" Chas asked as he put his arm around Addie. She told him and Chas shook his head. "You guys are gonna see each other tomorrow. Tonight it's family time." Jack opened his mouth to protest but closed it when his dad gave him a hard stare.

"Okay, Dad," he said glumly.

"But we're not doing anything special. Why can't we hang out?" Andrew pressed his lips together. Cara laughed inwardly. *He's got Rock's fire in him, that's for sure.*

"Because your mom and I said no. That's the fuckin' end of it." Rock snagged his arm around Clotille's waist and tugged her to him. Andrew's dark eyes flashed but he didn't argue. *Oh boy, Andrew's going to give them quite a run when he hits high school. And I'm positive Rock won't let him get away with it. Crap! I forgot about the mini hotdogs.* Cara rushed to the refrigerator and took out a pack of them. She'd bought them for the children because she remembered how much they loved them when she'd brought them to a family picnic. She took out a jar of barbecue sauce she'd received from the chef at Big Rocky's and poured it in a pot on the stove to warm it up.

"Braxton is hungry," Hawk said.

She turned around and smiled when she saw her baby, dressed in a Christmas onesie with a big snowman on the front of it. She took him from Hawk and cuddled him, kissing his soft cheeks and forehead before she opened the refrigerator and pulled out a bottle of her breast milk. As she cradled him in her arms, Harley toddled in-between her and Hawk. Banger came over and lifted him up, nuzzling his face in the boy's chest. Hope clung onto her mother's pants—she was a shy child—and Paisley combed the long hair of her Rapunzel doll while Cherri sat next to her on the couch.

The party was a huge success, and they decided it should be an annual event with each couple taking turns to host it. As the evening wore on, the people thinned out until Throttle and Kimber were the last to leave. Cara stood at the door waving to the couple as they made their way to their car, snow covering their heads and coats like a blanket. Cara shut the door and rubbed her hands over her arms. "It's so cold outside. I'm glad we don't have to go out in it. The snow is really coming down." She kicked off her heels. "I'm going to change into something comfy."

When she came back downstairs, the scent of pine swirled around her. She went into the family room and saw Hawk huddled in front of the fireplace, stoking the fire. Braxton was fast asleep on a down blanket on the floor. The Christmas tree's lights twinkled and danced in the semi-darkness of the room. She went over and kneaded Hawk's shoulders. "It's been a long day. I'm so glad we're going over to Aunt Teresa's for Christmas dinner."

Without a word, he pushed up and drew her to him, wrapping his fist in her hair and tugging her head back. He looked intently in her eyes, and a rush of heat blazed through her. He dipped his head down slowly and his hand brushed the hair from her cheeks. He was a couple inches away from her face, and she could feel his warm breath fanning over it. His gaze never left hers, and it kept pulling her in like a magnet. One of his arms held her tight around the waist and the other hand caressed her hair. She got lost in his scent; it filled her senses and fueled her arousal. With the tip of his tongue, he traced her lips, sending shivers of desire racing through her. Then he covered his mouth over hers and kissed her deeply, sensuously, and passionately; it seemed like eternity stood still during that one solitary kiss. After what seemed like hours, he pulled back and smiled, his thumb stroking her cheek.

She exhaled. "Wow… what was that for?"

"For coming into my life." His gaze spoke of love, tenderness, and desire.

She threw her arms around him and hugged him tightly. "Let's put him to bed, and then I'll show you how much you mean to me." She nipped at his neck and his throaty moan hit her wet mound. She picked up Braxton, who opened his eyes and twisted momentarily, then fell back asleep.

After putting their son in his crib, they went to their bedroom. Hawk stoked the fire, and the lively flames crackled as they burned the wood in the fireplace while the flickering glow illuminated the room. Outside, the snow still fell, wet snowflakes drifting windlessly under the cloud-filled sky.

Cara shed her robe and lay out on the bed, wearing only red bikini panties. He shrugged off his clothes and came over to the bed, his dick stiff and glistening as his gaze roamed over her body. The feral, predatory look in his eyes skated from the tips of her breasts, down her stomach, and straight to the wetness between her legs. He grabbed her arms and pulled them over her head until her fingers grazed the headboard. "Keep them there," he rasped. He reached out and touched her aching breasts, and she moaned. "It's gonna be a long night, babe," he whispered as he ran his mouth down her throat.

Chills and hot bolts streaked through her body simultaneously as she sighed and spread her legs for him. Their shared anticipation was thick in the air. She arched her back as his tongue painted her body.

"You'll always be my sexy wildcat," he said against her pebbling skin.

She tilted her head into the pillow and closed her eyes, wanting to feel every touch he made on her pulsing body. She wanted to feel the intensity of purely *him*. She bit the inside of her cheek as her body responded to her husband.

Yes, it's going to be a deliciously long night.

The End

Make sure you sign up for my newsletter so you can keep up with my new releases, special sales, free short stories, and other treats only available to newsletter readers. When you sign up, you will receive a FREE hot and steamy novella. Sign up at:

http://eepurl.com/bACCL1

Visit me on Facebook
facebook.com/Chiah-Wilder-1625397261063989

Check out my other books at my Author Page
amazon.com/author/chiahwilder

Notes from Chiah

I have so many people to thank who have made my writing endeavors a reality. It is the support, hard work, laughs, and love of reading that have made my dreams come true.

Thank you to my amazing Personal Assistant Amanda Faulkner who keeps me sane with all the social media, ideas, and know how in running the non-writing part smoothly. You are always ready to jump in and fix everything when I'm pulling my hair out. You are so cheerful, and when I hear your bubbling voice, it instantly uplifts me. So happy YOU are on my team!

Thank you to my editor, Kristin, for all your insightful edits, excitement with the Insurgents MC series, and encouragement during the writing and editing process. I truly value your editorial eyes and suggestions as well as the time you've spent with the series. You're the best!

Thank you to my wonderful beta readers, Kolleen, Paula, Jessica, and Barb—my final-eyes reader. Your enthusiasm for the Insurgents Motorcycle Club series has pushed me to strive and set the bar higher with each book. Your dedication is amazing!

Thank you ARC readers you have helped make all my books so much stronger. I appreciate the effort and time you put in to reading, reviewing, and getting the word out about the books.

Thank you to my proofreader, Daryl, whose last set of eyes before the last once over I do, is invaluable. I appreciate the time, attention to detail, and suggestions you always give to each book.

Thank you to the bloggers for your support in reading my book, sharing it, reviewing it, and getting my name out there. I so appreciate all your efforts. You're truly invaluable!

Thank you to Carrie from Cheeky Covers. You put up with numerous revisions, especially the ambience I wanted to create between Cara's classy wedding and background to Hawk's gritty one. We went back and forth on so many revisions, that I swear I heard you yell "Yay!" when I told you, "Yes, that's the cover!" Your patience is amazing. You totally rock. I love your artistic vision.

Thank you to Ena and Amanda with Enticing Journeys Promotions who have helped garner attention for and visibility to the Insurgents MC series. Couldn't do it without you! Also a big thank you to Book Club Gone Wrong Blog who is hosting and promoting *An Insurgent's Wedding*. Totally indebted to you.

Thank you to the readers who've supported the Insurgents MC series through nine books. You have made the hours of typing on the computer and the frustrations that come with the territory of writing books so worth it. You make it possible for writers to write because without you reading the books, we wouldn't exist. Thank you, thank you!

An Insurgent's Wedding: Insurgents Motorcycle Club (Book 9)

Dear Readers,

Thank you for reading my book. I hope you enjoyed the ninth and final book in the Insurgents MC Romance series. I have been so blessed to have such loyalty from you, and each time you picked up one of my books, you made me so happy to be a writer. We've come a long way with these bad boys and their women, but the series has come full circle: it began with Cara and Hawk exploring their love and ends with them sealing it.

My new series will be about the Night Rebels MC. The first book will be about its President—Steel. You may remember him in some of the Insurgents MC books (Books 3, 7, and 8.) Night Rebels MC is an affiliate club of the Insurgents MC, so some of the old gang may make an appearance or two. The Night Rebel bikers hail from southern Colorado which is hotter than Pinewood Springs which suits these hot-blooded rough guys just fine. I'm excited to write about the trials, tribulations, and romance of this hard and gritty MC.

Romance makes life so much more colorful, and a rough, sexy bad boy makes life a whole lot more interesting.

If you enjoyed the *An Insurgent's Wedding*, please consider leaving a review on Amazon. I read all of them and appreciate the time taken out of busy schedules to do that.

I love hearing from my fans, so if you have any comments or questions, please email me at chiahwilder@gmail.com or visit my facebook page.

To hear of **new releases, special sales, free short stories**, and **ARC opportunities**, please sign up for my **Newsletter** at http://eepurl.com/bACCL1.

A big thank you to my readers whose love of stories and words enables authors to continue weaving stories. Without the love of words, books wouldn't exist.

Happy Reading,

Chiah

STEEL

Book 1 in the Night Rebels MC Series

Coming in February 2017

A new series about hardcore bikers.

A fierce and feared warrior. His name is Steel, and he's President of the Night Rebels MC. Part Navajo, part Irish, Steel is a respected leader of his brotherhood. With his tatted muscular body, ebony hair, and green eyes, he is a magnet to women. Never turning away a sexy body, he indulges in casual sex, but nothing more.

For him, defending his brotherhood and protecting his teenage daughter are foremost. Falling in love and being in a long term relationship don't even make it on his list. He gave his heart to a woman when he was young and weak, but now he's strong and has no room in his heart for love.

Then he meets his daughter's social worker. His attraction to her is intense. Desire flares through him, and he's drawn to her in a way that angers him. He doesn't have time for a woman, but he can't get the feisty, spirited caseworker out of his mind.

He wants to run his callused fingers through her hair.
He wants to crush his mouth to hers
He wants to devour her.

But she resists him. No woman has ever resisted him.

When he looks into her eyes, he sees the depths of sorrow and a spark of passion. She's touched him. He's never wanted a woman as much as he wants her.

And he always gets what he wants…no matter what.

From the moment Breanna Quine laid eyes on the rugged biker, her body betrayed her. And when she spotted the outlaw's MC patch on his leather jacket, her blood turned to ice.

Hating bikers since her father gave up his family for the brotherhood, Breanna swore to never be around them again. Then the captivating Night Rebels President's blazing, green-eyed gaze catches hers, and she is drawn to him like a moth is to fire.

But she can't let herself fall for him, no matter how much her body buzzes whenever she is near him. As hard as she tries to fight her attraction to the dark, dangerous man, her resistance is weakening. Then when she sees his tenderness toward his daughter, it melts her heart. She has to keep reminding herself that he's not only a biker, but he's the worst kind—an outlaw.

Steel has his hands full trying to figure out who is supplying drugs to the teens of Alina, Colorado. Time is running out for him as danger comes knocking at his door threatening to destroy his family and the woman whom he has vowed to make his own.

Can two independent people put their past behind them in order to come together? Will they fight for love against the shadows and the danger that lurks all around them, threatening to destroy them forever?

This is the first book in the Night Rebels MC Romance series. This is Steel's story. This book contains violence, sexual assault (not graphic), strong language, and steamy/graphic sexual scenes. It describes the life and actions of an outlaw motorcycle club. If any of these issues offend you, please do not read the book. HEA. No cliffhangers! The book is intended for readers over the age of 18.